# SCREWED

www.facebook.com/leekauthor

www.twitter.com/leekauthor

# SCREWED

BY

CRAIG LOWNDES

First Published – 18.12.2017
This edition published 18.12.2017

ISBN 9781973406259

Copyright ©Craig Lowndes 18.12.2017

This book is a work of fiction and, except in the case of historical fact any resemblance to actual persons, living or dead, is purely coincidental

All rights reserved. No part of this publication may be reproduced, stored in or introduced into a retrieval system, or transmitted, in any form, or by any means (electrical, mechanical, photocopying, recording or otherwise) without the prior written permission of the publisher. Any person who does any unauthorised act in relation to this publication may be liable to criminal prosecution and civil claims for damages

A catalogue copy of this book is available from the British Library.

Cover Design: spiffingbookcovers.com
Printed and bound in the UK

www.facebook.com/leekauthor

"Better to do something imperfectly than to do nothing flawlessly."

~ Robert Schuller

SCREWED

# PROLOGUE

Prison Officer Gillmore splashed water on to his face and took a long look at his reflection in the mirror. His eyes were bloodshot, and his nose looked red and sore. His newly acquired nickname of Razor seemed a million miles from how he felt. With a sigh, he clipped on his black, prison issue tie and left the locker room.

Razor retrieved the bunch of keys from his belt and unlocked the barred gate that led to wing 1A. He passed through the gate, locked it behind him and then momentarily savoured the silence. He knew it would be short-lived. Once he began unlocking the cell doors, the noise would increase to headache-inducing level. Razor trudged up the metal staircase to start opening the cells on the top landing. As he approached cell number 308, a familiar knot began to form in the pit of his stomach. He paused then inserted his key into the lock. He pulled open the heavy metal door and tossed the cigarette packet containing the contraband on to the single metal bed. The occupant of the cell briefly lifted his head from the magazine he was reading and shot Razor a look of distaste but said nothing. Feeling his blood beginning to boil he slammed the cell door in frustration, yet again he'd risked his job and his freedom. He was walking on quicksand, sinking deeper and deeper with each passing day. Razor couldn't see a way out of his predicament; he was a captive in his own life. He realised that people were starting to notice his mood swings and a general change of character, or was it just paranoia? Maybe he should just quit his job as a prison officer, or soon he may find himself on the other side of the door.

SCREWED

# CHAPTER ONE

Prison officer had never been Razor's chosen profession; initially, he had joined the police force at age eighteen after just scraping through his A levels in English and history. He'd served eight years in the force before suffering a knee injury while arresting two drunks on a Friday night in Doncaster. The powers that be had offered Razor, or PC Ian Gillmore as he was then known, or Gilly to his mates, a couple of options. One was to move from active duty and take a desk job, or his other option was to leave the force with a golden handshake. Razor figured that if he could land a security job, the pay wouldn't be much worse, so why not have the bonus of the payout on top? Razor took three weeks' sick leave to 'consider his options'; however, he spent that time looking for new employment. After a couple of unsuccessful interviews, Razor came across a recruitment advert for prison officers at HMP Doncaster. The hours sounded OK, and the pay was only four grand less than what he was currently earning. Razor attended the interview, and after a brief tour of a couple of the wings within the prison, he was told the job was his. Razor enjoyed twelve quiet and laid-back months at Doncaster. The lack of activity was largely down to the fact he often worked the night shift.

# SCREWED

There was relatively little to do, apart from looking through the hatch in the cell doors every couple of hours to check that no prisoner had harmed himself or his cellmate. The other good thing about working nights was that he was spending practically no money, thus his payout from the police was still intact. He figured that by the time he reached thirty, he would be able to purchase a small terraced house for cash instead of renting substandard, overpriced accommodation.

Things changed for Razor in early August when he received a text message from an old mate who was getting married in September and was planning a stag do in Leeds at the end of the month.

'Count me in,' Razor instantly replied.

A text came back from Tony, 'the stag', promising to call him in the week with the details. Razor had been good mates with Tony while he was on the force but since starting work, at the prison, they had lost touch. In fact, Razor estimated that during the past year he had only seen Tony two, maybe three, times tops. Compared to the weekly Friday night piss-ups they used to enjoy and never miss, this was pretty poor. He knew Tony was seeing someone but was yet to meet his soon-to-be wife. Razor was

## SCREWED

especially looking forward to a blowout in Leeds as since starting work at Doncaster his social life had virtually ceased to exist. On top of this, most of his colleagues were OK on a professional level, but not exactly his first choice for a night down the pub. However, he did have a slight crush on a female officer named Lucy and, as a result, had spent many a night shift fantasising about her. He knew, however, that in reality, nothing would ever come of it as Lucy was engaged to a manager of a local gym, who turned out to be rather jealous and possessive, and who didn't like her going anywhere without her on his arm. It surprised Razor that Lucy would allow herself to be treated this way, considering what a hard case she appeared while on the wing.

A few days later, just as Razor had finished a Sunday shift, his phone buzzed. He was in the locker room, changing into his civvies, and, glancing at the ID, saw it was Tony, so he took the call.

'Tone, been a while. How's it going?'

'Great mate. All good with you?'

'Perfect. Listen Tone, I'm just coming out of work. Do you fancy a couple of swift halves?'

'You read my mind mate. I've just clocked off too. How about Wetherspoon's in twenty?'

'Sound. I'll see you in there.'

# SCREWED

## CHAPTER TWO

Eli Bexley, or Techno as he was more commonly known to those around him, including his parents, was what most people would describe as a geek. At nineteen years old, he stood at an impressive six-feet-six-inches tall and had done since he was about thirteen. Despite his height, Techno was thin as a rake, which appeared to make him taller still. He wore thick-rimmed glasses and metal braces on his teeth, which had been a permanent feature for the past ten years or so. Techno had never really been popular at high school and preferred to have his nose in a book, rather than be playing football or chasing girls like his peers. Techno had been born into second-generation Jamaican family. To his father's annoyance, Eli had lost all traces of the Jamaican accent. His father put this down to the private education that Techno had received from four years old up until his thirteenth birthday when, due to a couple of bad investments, Techno's father could no longer afford the fees commanded for a private education. Eli was then sent to Sheffield High School to complete his studies. His mother had been devastated; she knew her son had a gift for learning and was sure he was destined for Oxford or Cambridge. Then, who knew, a career in law or politics? Now,

## SCREWED

thanks to his father's rash business decisions, their son had been forced to finish his education at Sheffield High. The average class size was somewhere north of forty and only four in ten pupils left with a GCSE at C grade or above. In Eli's first year at the school, Ofsted had threatened its closure, and the police had raided it twice looking for drugs. What chance did her son have there?

The truth was that since starting his private education, Eli had worked hard to lose his Jamaican accent. He had felt different to many of the other kids, not because he was the only black kid in his class of twenty, or one of only five black faces in the whole school, but he spoke differently too. Even the other black kids sounded white middle class, and Eli had decided that he too wanted to talk this way. By the age of eight, all traces of the old Jamaican accent had vanished. He couldn't have been happier. He loved the school and found the lessons a walk in the park. His teachers soon realised that there was something special about Eli. He had a natural gift for learning and understanding, and could work out the most complicated of sums without a calculator or pen and paper. His IQ was off the chart. Eli also had another talent, electronics. From the time he could walk, Eli would be trying to dismantle and rebuild everything electronic. To

## SCREWED

his mother and father's despair, by five years old Eli had disassembled the video, hi-fi and the vacuum cleaner, by the age of eight, though, he was able to dismantle and then put them back together.

Bonzo was the total opposite of Techno. He had no interest in education and spent most of his school years causing havoc on the estate where he lived. Bonzo wasn't particularly tall, but he wasn't bad looking and had a bad boy charm that attracted a certain type of female. As his grandmother would have put it, not the kind of girl you'd bring home to meet your parents. Techno and Bonzo were an unlikely friendship, but they became acquainted when Techno first came to Sheffield High. Techno, after taking an initial induction exam, was put into the top sets for all of his subjects, while Bonzo was in the bottom sets for all of his.

It was the arrival of a new English teacher at Sheffield High that threw Techno and Bonzo together. The new teacher, Mr Bolton, was a new breed of teacher, fresh out of university and under the illusion they could make a difference to inner-city schools. Mr Bolton had the idea of a pupil mentor system. The idea was simple; pupils from the top sets of his English groups would be paired with students from the bottom sets for an hour each week. The students from the higher classes

## SCREWED

would then give one-to-one mentoring. Mr Bolton had read an article in the *Daily Mail* on how mentoring had been successful in prisons and considered that it might also work in schools.

Techno and Bonzo had Mr Bolton's mentoring scheme to thank for forcing them together. It didn't take the two teenagers long to realise that together they made an excellent team. Techno was the brains and Bonzo had an aptitude for reading the street and the people on it. By sixteen years old Techno and Bonzo had a thriving drug business dealing cannabis, Ecstasy and amphetamines.

# SCREWED

# CHAPTER THREE

Razor walked into Doncaster city centre Wetherspoon's just after 6.20 p.m. to find the place wasn't quite as busy as it was the last time he'd frequented it. He guessed that most of the lunchtime drinkers had headed home and it was still too early for the evening crowd. He headed to the bar and ordered a pint of lager from the disinterested, poorly dressed student-type. That was one of his dislikes with the Wetherspoon's brand, the lack of personality. In these faceless chains, there was little chance of any conversation with the staff. It appeared that they were there solely to serve drinks and not interact in any way. He usually preferred to go to a local pub where the landlord and barmaid would know not only your name, but what you liked to drink.

Razor paid for his pint and took a long, satisfying gulp, and then turning his back on the bar, he leaned back and let his eyes wander around the pub. After all, spending ten hours a day with ninety-four all-male prisoners, it was nice to rest his eyes on the odd female or two. He checked his watch; it was 6.30 p.m. Razor's eyes moved towards the door to see if Tony was making an entrance yet. Just near the exit, there was a table with two women sat at it. His gaze froze and settled on one of the occupants. Jesus, she was

## SCREWED

gorgeous. Her blond hair rested just above her shoulders framing a heart-shaped face with high cheekbones. Her oval eyes were the deepest blue and seemed to dance as she spoke to her friend. Razor's eyes then shifted to her feet. He didn't quite know why he did this, but he always checked them out for good shoes and painted toes, way before looking at the areas where men typically looked. Razor noticed that she had perfect toes with immaculately painted red nails peeping out from open-toed, Christian Louboutin shoes. He'd never admit it to his mates, but he'd instantly recognised the trademark red soles of the expensive designer shoes. It would cost him two weeks' wages should he ever wish to purchase a pair, for any deserving female. His gaze moved up approvingly from her feet and on to her legs. They were long and shapely, and clad in tight black, shiny leggings. Not the type of leggings worn by women on *The Jeremy Kyle Show*, nothing like the cheap, baggy ones that made the wearer's bottom look like a bag of busted Brussel sprouts. The ones that this woman wore were in a whole different league, undoubtedly expensive and classy. Exactly the way he would describe this beauty. His eyes took in her cashmere jumper that was simple but extremely well fitted, hugging nicely around her ample breast and finishing just above her curvaceous hips. She must have felt

# SCREWED

Razor's gaze because as his eyes returned to her face, her eyes momentarily met his. She gave him a smile that was indescribable and made him go weak at the knees, and then her gaze left him and settled back to her friend sitting across the table. Razor didn't notice Tony enter the pub and walk right up beside him.

'Alright, Gilly? Sorry, I'm a bit late, mate.'

Razor hadn't heard a word of what Tony said.

'Gilly!'

Razor jumped and then finally noticed Tony stood at his side.

'Sorry Tone, miles away.'

Tony looked over to where Razor's gaze had been seconds before.

'Bloody hell, I wouldn't say no to that.'

Razor turned to face his old mate.

'You're a married man. Oh, congratulations by the way,' replied Razor, as he clasped Tony's hand to give it a hearty shake.

'Not quite married yet, mate and looking at her, I'm having second thoughts,' grinned Tony.

'Greedy fuck. Spare us singletons a thought, will you? Anyway, what are you drinking?'

'Lager mate.'

Razor ordered a beer for Tony and a refill for himself. Then taking their drinks, they went to find an empty table. Razor made sure that he got the chair that gave a clear view of the blond.

Razor and Tony chatted about work, former colleagues and women, or the lack of in Razor's case. Tony then filled Razor in on his wife-to-be and, more importantly, the plans for the stag do. They were going to meet in Doncaster Wetherspoon's early Saturday morning for a fry-up and a pint, and then take a taxi up to Leeds. On arrival, it was going to be a paintballing session then on to the hotel around three. They were going to eat in the hotel then hit the pubs and clubs in Leeds city centre, and then end up in a strip club or casino. It sounded good to Razor as he couldn't remember the last time he'd had a good piss-up.

Tony was saying something about the up-and-coming wedding, but Razor had stopped listening. The blond had left her chair and was heading across the room towards the ladies. Razor watched her every step along with every other guy in the pub.

'Guess you haven't had any for a while then, Gilly?'

'Yeah, er no. She's stunning.'

'Out of your league.'

'Bollocks.'

'Pint says you ain't got the balls to ask her out.'

'A girl like that is bound to have a fella.'

'See, you've not got the balls,' laughed Tony.

At that moment the blond walked out of the ladies and across to the bar. Razor jumped out of his seat, walked to the counter and stood next to her. The student was serving another customer at the opposite end of the bar. Razor was looking down the bar towards the bartender putting the blond directly in his line of vision; she turned her head and smiled at him revealing perfect white teeth. Razor became distracted as he noticed a tiny white fleck just below her left nostril.

'Hi, er, you have something...' Razor left the sentence hanging as he pointed to his nose.

Razor had never used drugs, but that didn't mean he had a problem with people who did, provided they could afford to pay for them.

'Oh... right. Thanks,' she replied, opening her Chanel handbag and taking out a small compact mirror and dabbing her nose with a crisp, white handkerchief. 'That could have been embarrassing. I'm Deborah by the way,' she said, holding out her hand.

'Ian, but my friends call me Gilly,' he replied, taking her hand and giving it a gentle shake.

# SCREWED

Wow, her hand felt good. Petite, slender, perfectly manicured with nails that matched her toes. Just then the bartender appeared in front of them.

'Hey, can I get you a drink?' asked Razor.

'I'd love to, but I'm with my friend over there, and she's just split up from her boyfriend.'

'It's OK I get it,' said Razor with sagging shoulders.

She ordered her drinks and Razor ordered his and Tony's. Razor's drinks appeared first. Feeling embarrassed, he grabbed them up and began to move away from the bar utterly dejected.

'Nice meeting you, Gilly. I'll see you around sometime.'

As Razor spun around, he caught her giving him a huge smile and a cheeky wink.

## CHAPTER FOUR

Bonzo always knew that, like his father, he would at some point end up in prison. He had always accepted it was a case of not if, but when. Such a thought had never entered the sharp mind of Techno; never in his worst nightmares could he ever imagine spending so much as a day in a prison cell. Therefore he was ultracautious in the drugs business; he was firmly in the background. He would set up the equipment needed to provide the drugs then control it all from a safe distance via his laptop. He could control everything; heat, lighting, watering cycles, the little cannabis farm was fully automated. Techno even had a system that accelerated the growing time by twenty per cent and therefore the profits too. Techno also took care of money. All the records were carefully encrypted and stored in virtual clouds over three continents. Bonzo, on the other hand, was at the sharp end of their little enterprise. He harvested the drugs, delivered the drugs and collected the money. It was Bonzo's hands-on approach that had landed him a three-year sentence in HMP Doncaster. It was more bad luck than carelessness that earned Bonzo a stretch. Bonzo never transported drugs in his typical car, a BMW M3 that had set him back £60K. A young, black man in a new BMW was a wet dream for the coppers

## SCREWED

that cruised the estate where Bonzo still lived. Instead, he had a white Transit van, not just a plain white van though – Techno had decided the perfect cover for delivering large quantities of drugs would be a white van – but with the added extra of a sign. 'Speedy Plumbing & Heating – 24-HR Call-Out' screamed the signs on the back, sides and bonnet of the van. A plumber's van could be seen anywhere, day or night, without arousing any unwanted attention. Techno chose the name Speedy as a bit of a piss-take, as more often than not the van would be transporting speed.

PCs Bartholomew and Taylor had just come into the night shift. They were both rookies and therefore pulled the shitty shifts. The night shift started at 9.00 p.m. and went through the evening until 7.00 a.m. Their job was to drive around the Drake Marsh estate and make a police presence felt. It was a mind-numbing shift, and most of the officers assigned to it merely found a quiet place to park and took a few hours' sleep.

'Tell you what, Barty. We'll have a quick brew and a quick circle around the estate then I'll have first kip,' suggested PC Taylor.

PC Bartholomew, or Barty as he was known to everyone at the station, had been on the job six months. He'd joined the force around at the

## SCREWED

same time as Taylor. As they were the new boys, they got allocated the night patrols. Barty, unlike Taylor, wanted to make a name and get promoted through the ranks, he was hungry for action. Taylor, on the other hand, just wanted to cruise through his shifts with as little work as possible.

'OK a quick brew, but then a good drive around. I can't be arsed to be just sat in this car listening to you snore.' Barty said this with a little more aggression than he intended.

'Time of month is it?'

Barty didn't respond.

'OK then, quick brew and forget the sleeping. OK?'

Barty merely nodded and poured two cups of tea from the thermos flask they had in the car.

Barty finished his drink, Taylor was still sipping his. Barty glanced down at the dash to check the time, 9.12 p.m., it could be a long night. As Barty's gaze returned to the road, he noticed a white Transit van, with Speedy Plumbing & Heating stencilled on the back doors, pull out of a side street. Nothing unusual in that except that a back light was out. Barty started the engine.

'What you doing? I haven't finished my tea.'

'Tail light out on that van.'

## SCREWED

'Bloody hell Barty, it's no big deal. Let it be.'

Barty had already put the patrol car into gear before Taylor had finished his sentence.

'Bollocks,' Taylor said, wiping the hot liquid off his trousers then throwing the remainder out of the window.

Bonzo clocked the cop car behind him.

'Stay calm,' he muttered to himself.

The van had tax and insurance, the tyres were good, and he was driving 10 mph above the speed limit – Techno had explained to him that driving on or below the limit looked suspicious – he had nothing to worry about except the canvas bag in the back of the van that contained nine ounces of cannabis. Normally the bag would be inside a toolbox, but tonight he'd been rushing as he was on a promise with the tart from the chip shop, so he'd just thrown the bag into the back of the van not giving it a second thought. After all, he was on his way to the last drop of the night, and it was only half an hour away from the last customer who'd taken a whole kilo. The other problem was while his drugs stash had decreased, the cash he was carrying was now more than ten grand. Bonzo decided he was panicking over nothing. He saw a right turn up ahead, checking his mirror, he signalled and made the turn. He checked his mirror again, shit the cop car was still there.

'You going to waste our time on this? It's a bloody light bulb out. We still have to write it up,' complained Taylor.

Barty ignored him and hit the blues and twos. Bonzo's heart sunk. He couldn't think of a valid reason why he'd get pulled over. He knew it wasn't the drug squad, they wouldn't be coming in a patrol car, and they'd want to catch him when the van was full. He was worrying too much. Just a routine stop, show his documents, and then on his way. He hit the indicator, pulled to a stop and killed the engine.

PC Bartholomew walked to the driver's window with Taylor sauntering behind. Bonzo rolled down the window.

'Evenin' Officer.'

PC Barty then went through the usual routine of checking tax and insurance; all in order. Bonzo relaxed a little. PC Barty thought he'd show him the broken light, give him a warning, and then send him on his way. He asked Bonzo to get out of the van and accompany him to the back of the vehicle; it was then that his suspicions became aroused. Bonzo had stated that he just come from a job and he was heading to another call-out, which in itself was perfectly reasonable, however, Bonzo was sitting in the dark cab of the van when

# SCREWED

he had said this. When he got out of the cab and into the street illuminated by lights, PC Bartholomew could see what he was wearing. He wore a tailored, designer shirt, designer jeans and some expensive-looking shoes. All spotlessly clean. Not the typical attire for a plumber on a call-out. Taylor also noticed this too and gave Barty a wink. Bonzo hadn't yet realised his mistake. He followed the officer to the back of the van.

'The reason we stopped you tonight sir, is because of your defective rear light.'

Bonzo looked at the broken light. How could he be so stupid? Techno was constantly reminding him to check everything on the van on a daily basis.

'Don't give the Old Bill an excuse to pull you over.' Techno's words were ringing in his ears. Bonzo began explaining that he'd get the light fixed first thing in the morning. PC Bartholomew cut him off.

'The light sir, was the original reason we stopped you, now, however, I have reason to believe that you've not been telling us the truth.'

The statement caught Bonzo off balance; his mind was racing. PC Bartholomew continued:

'Just to recap sir; you say you've just come from a job.'

Bonzo nodded, not sure where this was going.

## SCREWED

'You're dressed rather smartly for work sir.'

Shit, shit, shit. Bonzo was trying to think of an excuse, he had a boiler suit that he was meant to wear, but he'd left it at home. He couldn't say his boiler suit was in the back of the van either, as the last thing he wanted was them snooping in there.

'I'm a clean worker,' was the best Bonzo could manage.

'Mind if we take a look inside the van sir.'

Bonzo knew he was beaten and unlocked the van. His subsequent arrest led to Bonzo being charged with intent to supply cannabis, his case was heard at Sheffield Crown Court and a three-year sentence followed.

Techno was not willing to step into Bonzo's shoes at the sharp end of the business. As he saw it, there was only one option and that was to put the drugs business on hold until Bonzo's release. Bonzo, however, had seen a new opportunity. After only a few days in prison, Bonzo soon realised just how many inmates smoked dope, it was a regular supply and demand situation. High demand, plus limited supply, meant high prices. Bonzo knew that to earn some decent money he'd need to get the gear in large quantities. During his first week in Doncatraz Bonzo was on wing 1A,

## SCREWED

a ground-floor wing. He had asked a few discreet questions about the supply of weed into the prison. There were a couple of ways weed, amongst other things, would get into the jail. The first was from the exercise yard that was outside the 1A wing. This particular yard was the only one located next to the perimeter wall. A prisoner would communicate with a friend on the outside, and then during exercise, a tennis ball would be thrown over the wall containing anything from drugs to mobile phones. The ball would be picked up by the prisoner in the exercise yard and the contraband was then on the inside. The guards soon cottoned on to the method, and prisoners were stopped from using that particular area. After the closure of the yard, the inmates had to get a little more inventive. Again a person on the outside would go to the wall that backed on to the now redundant yard, a tennis ball containing the contraband would still be thrown over, but this time the tennis ball would have fishing hooks taped to the outside. The ball was aimed to land near the wall of the wing. The prisoner would then hang a sheet from the window, and the fishing hooks would catch the sheet, allowing the prisoner to pull the ball into his cell. This time it took the guards around six months to catch on to this method. Within weeks, all the cells on the ground floor facing on to the yard had cages fixed over the windows. Bonzo decided it was the type of problem that Techno would revel in. He also knew that Techno would see the massive earning potential.

# SCREWED

# CHAPTER FIVE

The weekend of the stag do finally arrived. Razor had swapped his Friday night shift for a day shift that finished at two and he'd also booked the weekend off. Since he hadn't had a decent night out in recent memory, he decided to push the boat out and invest in some new gear. As Doncaster wasn't renowned for its excellent shopping, he decided to head over to the Meadowhall shopping centre in Sheffield, which had plenty of shops for all budgets. Before leaving for Sheffield, he called into one of the higher end barber's, that advertised itself as 'Doncaster's finest', for a haircut and a proper wet shave. Since his social life had slipped so had his appearance, his hair had got a little unruly, and he often went two or three days without a shave. The experience at the barber's set him back an hour of his time and fifty quid, but he felt it was well worth it.

Razor headed towards Sheffield feeling the best he'd felt in ages, he had money in his pocket and a great weekend lay ahead of him. During the drive, Deborah's words kept interfering with his thoughts. 'I'll see you around sometime'. In Razor's eyes that meant he was in with a chance of at least a drink with her. With that in mind, he planned to call into Wetherspoon's again on Sunday night on the off-chance she may be there, or maybe he might even bump into her in Leeds, but what were the chances of that?

Razor parked his six-year-old Astra in the car park at Meadowhall shopping centre and entered the huge building. He walked directly to one of the touchscreens in the lobby that would help locate the shops that he desired. There were four machines in a row beneath a large sign stating 'Information'. Razor looked at the first machine and thought how much it resembled those that the prisoners used to book visits, order their weekly food, or apply for jobs within the prison. He touched the screen, and the Meadowhall logo disappeared revealing the main menu. He selected designer menswear, and a host of designer names flashed up on the screen; Hugo Boss, Ralph Lauren and Armani to name but a few. Razor gave a few seconds' thought and hit Armani; his mind kept flicking back to the blond and if he'd see her again. He'd made up his mind if he was ever going to bump into her he was going look good, no matter what the cost.

    The screen directed him to a boutique-style shop on the second floor. He easily found the shop and walked in feeling excited. An immaculately dressed man in his early twenties greeted him immediately.

# SCREWED

'Good evening sir. May I help you with anything?' the assistant asked, looking Razor up and down with a glance of distaste. Razor wished he'd worn something other than his jogging bottoms and a hooded top.

Feeling a little embarrassed he replied, 'I'm just going to take a look around if that's OK.'

'By all means sir. My name's Carlo. Give me a shout if you need anything.'

Carlo then turned his attention to adjusting an expensive scarf on a mannequin.

Razor wandered around the shop taking in the various designer items. Every item was expensive, but Razor figured that as he hadn't bought any clothing for at least a year and this was quality, why not splash out, it wasn't as if he was short of money at the moment either. Razor moved from rail to rail, not knowing what he wanted to buy. From the age of seventeen, he had been one of those guys who wore a pair of jeans and an untucked shirt. The only variation in the shirts he wore would have been the colour or the occasional appearance of either checks or stripes. Now, almost eleven years later, he had to admit he still dressed the same way.

'Are you sure I cannot be of assistance, sir? Carlo asked, disturbing Razor from his thoughts.

# SCREWED

'Maybe you can,' replied Razor, looking down at his feet, his mood dampened considerably.

'Let me guess. Big night out or possibly a new love interest?'

'Wow, you're good; I'm in your hands. What do you suggest?'

Carlo gave him another look up and down, and then started to select various items from around the store. After what felt like an eternity, Carlo returned with a light grey suit complete with waistcoat, plain white shirt, two coloured shirts and a selection of ties. He led Razor to the back of the store to the changing rooms. Razor donned the suit, white shirt and a black tie, and stepped out to look at himself in the full-length mirror outside the cubicle. He had to admit that the suit fitted perfectly and made him feel fantastic.

'That one's the David Beckham cut,' Carlo informed him. 'This particular design is identical to the suit Sean Connery wore in the Bond film, *Goldfinger*, and I must say it's made for you,' continued Carlo.

With great enthusiasm, Carlo proceeded to go through different outfits with Razor, suit with tie, a suit without a tie, no jacket but waistcoat and trousers with different shirts. The combination of outfits went on and on.

# SCREWED

Razor was stunned at how good a few decent items of clothing could make him feel. He wanted it all but was starting to feel a little apprehensive about the price tag.

'Would sir like me to take these items to the till?'

'I don't know,' stammered Razor. 'I'd love to say yes, but what do you think it will all cost me?'

Carlo paused for a moment then replied, 'I'd say around two thousand should cover it.'

He desperately wanted his latest customer to make the full purchase, as management had offered a one-week, all-expenses-paid holiday for that month's top salesperson. Carlo knew he was currently number two, and this deal would elevate him to the number one spot.

'That's a little more than I wanted to spend, to be honest.'

Carlo's mind was racing; he so wanted this sale, and then the answer hit him.

'Tell you what sir. How about you take these lovely shoes, size eight I'm guessing. They are the bargain price of £500.'

Razor visibly paled.

'Please allow me to continue. If you take the shoes, I'll let you take the lot for £1,250 plus maybe a little tip for yours truly,' grinned Carlo.

Razor agreed. He genuinely couldn't believe it. Carlo was equally pleased; there was a

# SCREWED

fifty per cent sale starting on Monday to mark the end of the season. All Carlo had to do was sell Razor a voucher for £1,250 today and then put the transaction through the till on Monday. He explained to Razor that he would have to return on Monday to collect his receipt. Razor was more than happy to do this and left Carlo with a £50 tip.

Razor spent the rest of Friday evening trying on his new clothes and deciding what to wear for his Saturday night out in Leeds. He finally settled on the suit, no waistcoat and no tie, just the white shirt and his new Armani shoes. After appraising himself for the tenth time in the mirror, he decided it was time to pack. He carefully packed the suit into the complimentary suit carrier that boldly sported the Armani logo, he threw his toiletries into an additional bag, and he was now ready for action. Sitting down, feeling rather pleased, he enjoyed a couple of bottles of beer then opted for an early night as tomorrow was going to be a big one.

## CHAPTER SIX

Using the automated booking system on the wing's touchscreen machines, Bonzo organised a visit for Techno to come to the prison on Saturday afternoon. When Bonzo went into the visits' reception, he felt relief when he was informed that his visitor would be at table thirteen. Table number thirteen was near the middle of the room. Bonzo was pleased about this because he'd heard that the security department made recordings of corner tables four, eight, twelve and sixteen. Bonzo entered the visitors' area to see his close friend and business associate sitting at table number thirteen with a nervous look on his face. The table was made out of hard plastic and bolted to the floor, four plastic chairs surrounded each table. The chairs were also bolted to the floor and positioned a little too close to the tables. Out of the four chairs, one was grey, and the other three were red. The idea was for the prisoner to sit in the grey seat, while the visitors would sit in the red ones. The coloured chairs were designed to make it easier for the guards to distinguish between prisoners and visitors. Apparently, according to prison folklore, about ten years ago a prisoner had swapped places with his brother and simply got up at the end of the visit and walked out. The visitor was left in prison,

## SCREWED

sitting in the holding room between the visits area and the prison wing, for two hours until a guard realised the prisoner and his brother had swapped places. The prisoner disappeared along with the governor's job.

Bonzo broke into a broad grin when he spotted Techno, not only was he pleased to see his friend but he'd noticed that Techno was sitting in the grey prisoner's chair. Bonzo knew there was no chance of escape, as all visitors got fingerprinted when entering and leaving the prison, but he relished the thought of having some fun with his mate.

'Yo, Techno. Great to see ya bro.'

'Good to see you too, Bonzo. I trust you're settling into your new home.' As Techno said this he held out his fist. Bonzo paused slightly, then bumped fists.

'Fuck me. When did ya remember ya black bro?'

'I'd hate to embarrass you in front of your peers,' replied Techno with a grin. Techno had never been one for fist bumps and fancy hand manoeuvres, he always felt a simple handshake was far more civilised. Along with his well-spoken manner, this had caused some of his schoolmates to call him choc ice or coconut. The name-calling

## SCREWED

soon ended however, once his friendship with Bonzo developed.

The visitors' area had a small cafe where friends and family could purchase bacon sandwiches, burgers, cakes, tea and coffee. This food was considerably better than the food served on the wings. Prisoners were not allowed to go to the food-serving area or even leave their seats, however, visitors could purchase food for the prisoner to eat at the table.

'Do us a favour, bro and get us something to eat. I ain't had a decent feed since I got 'ere.'

'Of course. What would you like?'

'Double cheeseburger, gateau, Mars bar and a coffee wit' three sugars.'

'You'll end up getting fat.' Bonzo started to say something. 'I'm winding you up, Bonzo. I'm on my way.'

Techno stood up and was about to walk over to the cafe when the guard, standing by the entrance to the visits room, bawled, 'Table thirteen, sit down.'

Techno looked around to see if anyone else was standing, when he saw they weren't, he glanced down at the table to see a number thirteen painted on it in the corner. Staring at the number, then looking back at the guard, he quickly sat down.

# SCREWED

'They're a little abrupt in here, aren't they?'

Bonzo was doing his best not to laugh, but managed to say with a straight face, 'Yeah, it's 'cause they're used to speaking to cons all day. He'll let ya go when da queue gets shorter.'

Techno looked over at the cafe area and saw that only five or six people were waiting for food. He nodded. They exchanged a little small talk before getting down to business. Bonzo explained the problem of getting the drugs in and somehow turning those drugs into hard cash, instead of the usual prison currency of tobacco, biscuits and shower gel. Techno agreed to come back in the following week for another visit and the answer to their problem.

'Queue's gone now. How 'bout 'dat food?'

Techno stood again and this time got halfway across the room before the guard noticed him again. This time the guard was striding over and shouting.

'Thirteen, back to your seat now! Last warning.' Techno froze, lost for words. He just stood there as the guard got within eight inches of Techno's face, hissing, 'Are you fucking deaf or stupid? Prisoners stay seated.'

Techno found his tongue and managed to reply, 'But I'm not a prisoner, he is.' Pointing to Bonzo who had now lost the ability to control his laughter.

## SCREWED

The guard's jaw dropped a little lower than it should, as soon as he heard Techno's polished, privately educated accent.

'Oh, er, sorry sir. There's been a slight misunderstanding. I'm sure you understand.'

For a split second Techno thought about dressing the guard down, but figured it might be counterproductive in the long run, so replied, 'Of course Officer. A simple misunderstanding. No hard feelings, eh?'

Bonzo got his meal and five minutes before Bonzo's visit was due to end the guard walked past the table saying, 'Half an hour left, gentlemen.'

Bonzo winked at Techno.

# CHAPTER SEVEN

Razor entered Wetherspoon's just after 9.00 a.m. on Saturday morning. He subconsciously glanced over at the table by the door where Deborah had been sitting just two weeks before. What was he thinking? Did he honestly think she'd be sat there at the same table at 9.00 a.m. on a Saturday? Who was he kidding? Recognising many of the faces from when he was on the force, he headed toward the group stood at the bar.

'Bloody hell, Gilly. Didn't realise prison work paid that well,' commented one of the guys pointing at the Armani suit carrier.

'A new haircut too. You won the lottery, or something?' chimed in Tony, as a way of a greeting. 'What you drinking, mate? I still owe you a pint for daring to ask that bird out, even if she did blow you out,' he joked.

'I heard she was a right stunner. Way out of your league, Gilly,' one of others chipped in, slapping him on his back.

'She didn't blow me out, she was busy. OK?'
'Ooh, touchy.'

Realising he'd perhaps bitten a little too quickly, Razor said, 'I'll get 'em in, Tone. And I suppose all you gobshites want one too?'

Razor was all smiles again now. The group steadily grew to twenty, and all the guys spent the

## SCREWED

time reminiscing about work, drinking a couple of beers and consuming a greasy fry-up. At 10.30 a.m. two minibuses turned up and transported the raucous party off to a paintballing centre on the outskirts of Leeds. By midday, all twenty men were dressed in full combat gear and armed with paintball guns that resembled AK-47s. For the next two hours, they played at being soldiers. For the final twenty minutes, it was 'hunt the stag', whereby nineteen guys would have the chance to blast Tony with their remaining ammunition. Great fun was had by all and by 3 p.m. they were all back on the minibuses heading to the hotel in the city centre.

'Right guys, get checked in. You're all in twins. We'll meet down here at six, then grab a quick bite and on to show Leeds that us Donny boys know how to party,' shouted Tony.

The rest of the group gave a cheer, and there were a few lewd comments made about the female population of Leeds, causing the two hotel receptionists to exchange glances. They'd seen it all before, rowdy groups of men in their thirties and forties still thinking they were eighteen. In reality, a stag do was the only time these men were let out by their wives and girlfriends. Most of them wouldn't make it till last orders.

# SCREWED

At six on the dot, there were twenty men, showered, changed and stood in the hotel bar. Most had ordered food, but one or two of the hardcore members stated that 'eating was cheating' and were settling for a meal of the liquid variety. Razor stuck out amongst the group, as he was the only one wearing a suit. The quality stood out, and he was oozing confidence.

By 10 p.m. some of the group, who had drunk a little too much, staggered back to the hotel, four or five decided to go to the casino. Razor, Tony and a couple of his workmates had opted for a trendy wine bar that a hen party had mentioned earlier in the evening. Scott and Paul, who Razor had only met today, were good company, and the alcohol and banter were flowing.

'How about we finish these and check out a strip club?' suggested Scott.

'I'm up for that,' added Paul eagerly.

'What? You guys really want to pay money to see a bird's tits that you can't touch?' asked Razor.

He thought lap dancers were nothing but a tease and for guys who couldn't pull.

'Come on Gilly, me and Paul are married, and this silly sod is soon to be. We're not looking to cheat on our wives, but it is great to have a look at something different now and again.'

## SCREWED

'Come on, Gilly. If you saw the state of their women you'd know where they were coming from,' added Tony with a loud laugh.

'Alright you sad twats I'll come for a couple of drinks, then I'll be going to find a bird that I don't have to pay for.'

'They all cost you in the end,' snorted Paul.

No one was quite sure if he was joking or not. The four of them left the wine bar and jumped into a waiting taxi.

'Take us to a titty bar,' instructed Paul, as he took the front seat.

'Ten pounds up front,' barked the driver in an Eastern European accent.

Paul whipped out a ten-pound note and thrust it at the driver without a word. The driver put the car into gear, turned left, drove twenty yards, then pulled up beside the kerb.

'What's going on?' demanded Paul.

'Titty bar,' replied the driver, pointing to the building where they'd stopped.

All four looked left to see the big, pink neon sign proclaiming 'Perfect Tens – Lap Dancing Bar.'

'Foreign twat,' snarled Paul slamming the car door as hard as he could, causing the other three to erupt into hearty laughter.

# SCREWED

The four walked to the entrance of the strip club with Paul grumbling all the way, causing more laughs from the others. Two large, shaven-headed doormen, dressed in black suits complete with bow ties, resembling a pair of French waiters on steroids, flanked the door of the club.

'Good evening gentlemen,' said the first doorman, handing them each a small card. 'Up the stairs, pay at the desk and enjoy your night,' he instructed in a bored tone.

The second doorman merely nodded, as the four filed past and ascended the stairs into the club.

'Did he just say pay?' asked Razor to no one in particular.

'Yeah, if it were free you'd get all sorts of perverts hanging around,' commented Paul.

'What and we aren't?' shot back Razor.

'Come on you tight sod, dressed from head to toe in Armani; I think you can afford it,' added Tony.

The four reached the desk in the small reception area. Behind the desk was a quite average-looking woman who looked to be in her mid thirties.

'Fifteen pounds each please, gents.'

Before Razor could complain, Paul pulled out his wallet and paid for all of them on his credit card. As they waited for the transaction to complete, Razor glanced at the card in his hand, on it was a picture of two sexy women in very skimpy underwear, draped over a Porsche. The club owners no doubt, thought Razor. Turning the card over, he saw a list of the club dos and don'ts. Razor scanned the list; there were ten rules in total: do not touch the girls, do not proposition the girls, remain at least eighteen inches from the girls during dances. As the list went on, Razor wondered if he would have to sit an exam before he entered the club. He was pretty confident that there would be plenty more goons in black suits and bow ties to ensure the rules were abided by. The four entered the main club area. The club wasn't especially big, a girl of maybe nineteen or twenty, stood behind a bar in one corner, wearing nothing but black, lacy underwear complete with stockings, suspenders and six-inch heels. On the opposite wall to the bar was a small stage with a floor-to-ceiling silver pole in the centre. Around the rest of club, there were various leather settees and tables holding everything from beer bottles to ice buckets containing bottles of champagne. There were maybe twenty or twenty-five men, of all ages, sitting on the sofas or leaning against bar tables, watching the fifteen or so scantily clad women who paraded around seductively. In the centre of one of the walls was a doorway with a thick, red velvet curtain where two more doormen stood with folded arms. Razor noted that women were leading men by the hand through the velvet curtains. The whole place had very dim lighting, and the music was at a level where conversation was still possible. As the other three were engrossed in the sights on offer, Razor ordered four pints at the bar.

'Thirty-two pounds please,' purred the wannabe model behind the bar.

'Excuse me?' he said, convinced he'd misheard her.

'Thirty-two pounds please. Unless of course, you'd like to buy me one.'

He didn't reply and just slapped two twenties down on the bar and waited for his change. He couldn't believe he'd just paid eight pounds a pint for a beer that had never seen a bubble and was probably more water than beer. Razor turned around to hand the drinks out, to see only Scott left standing there.

'Where are the other two?' asked Razor.

'In there, having a private dance,' replied Scott, nodding towards the velvet curtains.

Just then he recognised three more of the group entering the club and making a beeline for the bar. They joined Scott and Razor, and ordered drinks. At that moment, Paul emerged from behind the curtain with a big grin on his face.

# SCREWED

Rejoining the group he said, 'Fuck me. Best fifty quid I've ever spent.'

'Where's the stag?' asked one of the guys, who'd just come in, laughing.

'He's still in there, throwing fifties around like confetti. He finished his dance with one girl then collared another one, who'd just come out of the VIP room, and disappeared with her,' replied Paul.

'Hey lads, how about we have a whip-round and get a couple of the birds to get Tony on stage and strip him?' suggested Scott.

Everyone thought that was a great idea and Scott went off to find out how much it would cost them. He nodded to one of the nearby girls who was just wearing a red, lacy bra that was fighting to hold her surgically enhanced breasts and a tiny G-string that left very little to the imagination. She sauntered over in her eight-inch platforms and whispered something into his ear. That was all it took for Scott to disappear behind the curtain with her. Minutes later, another girl approached the group. Initially she looked young, but on closer inspection, Razor could see that she was at least forty and was wearing too much make-up, but very little else.

'Anyone want a dance?' she said to no one in particular.

## SCREWED

One of the lads must have nodded or smiled, because without another word he was led off through the curtain. Scott returned to the bar after being gone for three or four minutes.

*Jesus these women must be making a fortune*, thought Razor.

'Right lads, if we throw in twenty a man, two birds will get Tone on the stage, strip him, whip him, tits in his face, the works,' informed Scott.

Everyone got out their twenties and handed them to Scott, who then went back to the lap dancer who had just danced for him. Everyone watched as Scott passed over the money. Tony finally appeared from behind the curtains looking like the cat who'd got the cream, grinning from ear to ear. He went straight to the bar and downed one of the waiting pints in one long gulp.

'God I love titty bars,' he slurred, wiping his mouth on his sleeve. He then leaned toward Razor and, with a huge smile on his face, whispered into his ear, 'You'll never guess who's been dancing for me with not a stitch on.'

Before Razor could reply, the music cranked up, and two lap dancers grabbed Tony and led him up on to the stage. All the men in the bar cheered and clapped as the two dancers stripped Tony down to his boxers. One of the dancers proceeded to put ice cubes into his boxer

## SCREWED

shorts, which were then removed, leaving very little to see as the ice had taken its effect. He was then bent over a chair and whipped with his belt. The dancer administering the beating appeared to enjoy this a little too much. The finale of the show involved both of the strippers covering their chests in large amounts of shaving foam and rubbing Tony's face into one load of foam, then the other. The whole thing lasted the length of two songs, but it was evident for all to see that Tony had enjoyed every second and didn't want it to end. The music returned to its previous level. While Tony fumbled with his clothes, some of the guys bought shots, and there were at least five lined up on the bar waiting for him. Razor wanted to ask Tony what he'd been talking about earlier, but Tony was in the middle of the group making a start on the shots. Razor downed his pint, turned back to the bar and waved his empty glass at the girl who'd served him earlier.

'Hi there. You want a dance?'

Razor looked to his left, to where the voice had come from, and there stood the girl who had taken Scott off for a dance earlier.

'No, I'm good thanks. I'm just having a drink,' he replied, as if to justify why he didn't wish to spend fifty quid on a three-minute dance.

'OK, would you like to buy me a drink then?' she retorted innocently, with a smile that suggested that she wasn't just after the contents of his wallet.

Razor considered it for a moment, then decided that buying the girl a drink would be better than spending fifty on a lap dance.

'OK. What can I get you?' he asked.

'She knows,' replied the dancer, nodding to the server.

Razor's pint appeared along with a glass of orange liquid, complete with straw and umbrella, that he could only assume was a fancy cocktail.

'Twenty-eight pounds please,' said the barmaid in a cold tone.

'Are you serious? Twenty quid for a cocktail?'

The barmaid glared at him, so Razor threw another two twenties on the bar.

'Come on then, let's see what's so special about this cocktail,' he said, snatching up the glass and sucking on the straw. 'Are you fucking kidding? Twenty fucking quid for orange juice!' With that he picked up his pint, downed it in one, then slapped Scott on the shoulder and said, 'I'm off back to the wine bar, mate. This place takes the piss.'

Before Scott could respond, Razor was halfway toward to exit. To get to the way out Razor had to walk past the red velvet curtains and as he did so, he couldn't help but glance through the gap, he froze mid step. There was another door beyond the room, with more curtains and a neon sign stating 'VIP Room'. The door was open and walking through it was Deborah from Wetherspoon's, it was evident this must have been who Tony was talking about earlier. Shit, she was a stripper, but she did look good. She was wearing more than the other girls in the club, a tight-fitting black minidress with lacy stocking tops peeping out from below the hemline. Another pair of Louboutins, covered in tiny silver pointed studs, covered her immaculate feet. Around her neck was a choker, complete with matching silver studs. She must have felt Razor's stare because she looked directly at him and a flicker of recognition appeared on her beautiful face. She smiled and walked toward him. Feeling his pulse begin to race, he smiled back.

'Hi there, Gilly. Fancy seeing you here.'

Jesus, she'd remembered his name.

'Hey, Deborah. I must admit, it's a bit of a shock bumping into you in a place like this.'

'Hope you're not disappointed in me,' she replied with a pout, while feigning innocence.

'Oh no, course not. I just didn't expect to see you tonight. You look great, by the way.'

'Aw thanks, Gilly. You look pretty good too. I love the new haircut.'

# SCREWED

Razor felt his cheeks flush as she gently touched his hair and couldn't find a reply.

'How about coming for a private dance, then you can see a little more of me,' Deborah continued.

Razor's face dropped a little. Was this why Deborah had come over, to try and extract fifty quid from him? He'd love nothing more than to see her naked, but he wasn't going to pay for the privilege.

'Sorry, but I'm not really into paying for such things,' he replied, feeling somewhat awkward.

'That's good to hear. How about a drink instead then?' she said, her face breaking into a genuine smile.

Was she still on the hustle like the last girl? Razor wasn't quite sure, so he replied, 'No offence Deborah, but another thing I'm not into is paying twenty quid for a glass of orange juice with a tacky straw and umbrella.' He quickly gave her a boyish smile, hoping that she'd understand that he wasn't a cheapskate and it was nothing personal.

She looked at him for what felt to Razor like an eternity, before saying, 'You're a wise man, Gilly. Tell you what, my shout and I only drink champagne. So how about we forget the OJ, OK?'

# SCREWED

Razor nodded, not quite knowing what to say, so Deborah took the lead and took him by the hand to a large settee in a darkened corner of the club. They sat down and sank into the comfortable leather. A waitress immediately appeared in front of them.

'A bottle of Bolly and two glasses please, Chantal.'

The champagne promptly arrived and was poured. Razor had never really drunk champagne, he usually only drank lager punctuated by the odd glass of wine at a wedding or special occasion, but wow, this was awesome, or maybe it was just the company that highlighted his enjoyment of the drink. He didn't dare speculate on what the bottle of Bollinger might have cost, but as it was her shout, he wasn't going to waste time guessing. After chatting away for about twenty minutes, Razor was feeling some serious attraction and was beginning to think it wasn't just one way. From the corner of his eye Razor saw movement, he turned his head to see Tony staggering towards them.

'Bollocks,' uttered Razor, a little louder than he was intending.

Deborah looked up, and Tony was upon them.

'Alright Tone? You having a good one?' asked Razor nervously.

# SCREWED

Tony ignored him; his eyes were firmly on Deborah.

'Come on, I want a dance,' slurred Tony.

'Sorry, I'm busy at the moment.'

'Busy? You'll get no fucking cash out of him,' Tony spat, swaying slightly.

'Look I'm sorry, I'm having a drink,' she said calmly but firmly.

By now one of the doormen, who was stood by the curtain, was looking over.

'I pay your fucking wages. Now come and dance,' snapped Tony, his voice rising considerably.

He grabbed at her arm but was so drunk he missed, lost his footing and fell into the table, knocking over the champagne and glasses. Razor moved quickly to pick him up, but the two doormen beat him to it and roughly dragged Tony to his feet.

'Time to leave,' said one of the doormen, in a tone that suggested you'd have to be stupid to argue.

'Fuck you and fuck your slag dancers,' Tony shouted, but all his bravado had evaporated.

'Come on, Tone. I'll get you back to the hotel,' said Razor, as the doormen began dragging him toward the exit. As he followed the bouncers and Tony, he turned back to Deborah, who was

# SCREWED

now on her feet, and said, 'Sorry about him. He's just had too much to drink. Stag do and all that.'

'It's OK, Gilly. Look, I knock off in an hour. Meet me in the Living Room. Just give this to one of the doormen and tell him you're a friend of mine,' she said, handing him a golden card with embossed lettering that Razor couldn't read in the dim light.

Razor quickly went over to the bar to let one of the guys know that he was going to get Tony back to the hotel. He hastily left the club to find Tony slumped outside, his head resting against the wall. Razor hailed a taxi and, as it pulled up, he put his arm around Tony's shoulders and helped him into the waiting car.

'Come on, mate. Home time.'

Tony merely grunted in reply. Razor managed to get Tony back to the hotel and into the room without further incident and left him passed out on the bed. Shortly before 1.00 a.m. Razor was back in a taxi, heading towards the Living Room lounge bar. Sitting in the back, he pulled out the gold card that Deborah had given to him and studied it. It was a VIP membership card for the Living Room that was an exclusive high-end, late-night bar.

As the taxi stopped outside the entrance, Razor noticed two queues outside the door, both very

# SCREWED

orderly. The one to the left of the door was extremely long and didn't appear to be moving, whereas to the right, behind a dark purple rope, was a very short, fast-moving queue. At the end of the purple rope was a golden sign, stating VIP entrance. Razor strode to the VIP entrance and flashed the card at the doorman, while telling him that he was a friend of Deborah's.

The burly man didn't even look at the card, instead he just looked at Razor and said, 'You're a lucky man then. The VIP room is at the far end of the bar. Enjoy your evening, sir.' The doorman then spoke into his radio as Razor entered the bar area. Razor smiled to himself, could the night get much better?

Razor strolled confidently towards the VIP area of the bar; some seriously attractive people filled the place. The music was pumping, and the dance floor was heaving. A solitary bouncer stood at the entrance to the VIP room. As Razor approached, the large double doors opened, and there stood a rather slight man in his late forties or early fifties. He wore an immaculate tuxedo complete with a pink dicky bow. He extended his hand and smiled warmly, as Razor approached.

'You must be the friend of the delightful Deborah?'

'Er, yeah,' replied Razor, feeling a little awkward as he shook hands with the man.

# SCREWED

'I'm Claudio, the manager. Any friend of Deborah's is certainly a friend of mine. Now come with me, my dear, and let's get you settled into your booth.'

Claudio spoke at a hundred miles an hour, was obviously gay and had a confident manner.

'I love the suit. Let me guess? Armani?'

To which Razor smiled and nodded. He was impressed with Claudio's knowledge of designer labels.

'I knew it; you carry it off perfectly,' continued Claudio. 'Now get yourself comfortable, and I'll arrange the drinks. I trust Bollinger is agreeable?'

Before he could reply, Claudio had disappeared. Razor began to take in his surroundings; the 'booth' was a horseshoe-shaped settee. The leather was black and extremely soft, and Razor enjoyed the feeling of sinking into the rich material. In the centre of the horseshoe was a low-level table made of black marble. The back of the settee sat against a wall on which hung a large picture, depicting two females in a very erotic pose. On each side of the booth hung thick purple curtains that could be pulled to if the occupants wanted some privacy. The open front of the sitting area faced the VIP room's dance floor. This one was smaller than the one in the main bar area, but equally as packed. Razor spent a couple

# SCREWED

of minutes watching two young women dancing and grinding against each other.

Claudio reappeared carrying an ice bucket, containing a bottle of Bollinger and two champagne flutes. He placed the bucket on the table, uncorked the champagne, filled one of the flutes and handed it to Razor.

He did all of this with great ceremony, before saying, 'I'll leave you to enjoy your champagne. If you need anything else, just shout.'

Razor thanked him, and he was gone, no doubt to pamper some other high-spending guest. Razor sipped the champagne, his second glass of the evening. He could certainly get used to this. He took another sip, closed his eyes and let his arm rest of the back of the settee. The bubbles danced on his tongue. He suddenly opened his eyes, sensing someone looking at him. Stood at the front of booth, wearing a figure-hugging short silver dress, was Deborah.

'What's a girl have to do to get a drink in here?' she teased.

Razor patted the cushion next to him and poured Deborah a glass of champagne, before refilling his flute. They touched glasses, and both took long drinks. Deborah then reached into her handbag and pulled out a silver vial that was roughly the size of an AA battery, she unscrewed the top and tapped out a small mound of white

## SCREWED

powder on to the back of her hand, she then snorted the lot up her left nostril. Razor's eyes locked on to every movement. Deborah expertly tapped out another small mound, but this time she offered the hand to Razor. He hesitated, not quite knowing what to do.

'I've never done anything like this,' he managed to say.

'Just close one nostril and sniff with the other. You'll be fine,' she assured him, flashing him a sexy smile.

Maybe it was the champagne that had lowered his inhibitions, but he decided to throw caution to the wind. After all, it was only a little sniff; it wasn't as if she was offering him a syringe full of heroin. He leaned forward, took hold of her hand and snorted deeply. His head immediately shot back, as the cocaine hit the receptors in his nose. He became instantly light-headed.

'Just relax now, Gilly and enjoy,' she purred into his ear.

The light-headedness was quickly replaced by a fuzzy buzz, he felt amazing, all of his senses suddenly heightened.

'Oh my God, I feel sharp as a razor. I'm a fucking razor,' he shouted.

## SCREWED

'Come on then, *Razor*, I wanna dance.' Deborah was pulling at her hand, which he was still holding.

She led him to the middle of the packed dance floor. Razor felt a million dollars as he strutted on to the floor, hand in hand with the sexiest woman in the place. He noticed other men staring enviously at him, wishing they could trade places. Deborah was moving effortlessly in time with the pumping music and began grinding against him. A wave of sexual energy swept over him, like nothing he'd ever felt before. Razor wanted to take her there and then, in the middle of the dance floor. He took her buttocks in both hands and pulled her closer, looking into her eyes, he kissed her hungrily.

'I want you now,' he whispered into her ear.

She slid a hand on to his crotch.

'Mm I can tell, but be patient. Let's get a refill.'

For the next two hours, they drank champagne, danced and snorted cocaine. At one point Deborah had to nip off to 'top up her supply'. Razor noted that she didn't have to leave the VIP room to do this.

The bar closed at 4.00 a.m., and Deborah suggested that they carry on the party back at her

# SCREWED

hotel room. Razor offered no objections. They managed to get just inside her hotel door before tearing off each other's clothes. More cocaine appeared, and Razor took great pleasure in snorting it off Deborah's large, firm breasts. The sex was amazing, like nothing he'd ever experienced before, he felt like a Roman god. They finally collapsed into a deep sleep around seven in the morning.

SCREWED

# CHAPTER EIGHT

A week later Techno was back for his second visit, this time sitting in the red visitor's chair. Techno was visibly excited but didn't tell Bonzo exactly how his plan would work, he just made Bonzo promise to follow his instructions to the letter the following night.

Bonzo couldn't wait to see what Techno had lined up. He counted down the hours until bang up at 5.00 p.m. then paced the cell for the remaining sixty minutes. At precisely 6.00 p.m. Bonzo turned off the light in his cell, counted to twenty, and then turned it back on. Exactly two minutes later he repeated the exercise, then two minutes later, turned off the light and left it off. Bonzo then waited and listened.

Techno drove his car up the narrow track that led to a small turning area. Off the turning area were two five-bar gates adjacent to each other. One of the gates had a wooden stile next to it. Techno retrieved a rucksack from the boot of his, now decrepit, Ford Focus and let out the dog that he'd borrowed for a couple of hours. Techno figured he'd look less suspicious walking a dog. If it all went to plan tonight, then maybe it would be worth investing in a dog.

## SCREWED

Techno slung the bag over his shoulder, put the dog on a lead and headed towards the stile. The dog hesitated, it either didn't want to or didn't know how to get over. Techno picked up the dog, glad he'd only borrowed a spaniel and not an Alsatian. He climbed over the stile and walked two hundred metres across the field, then began to climb the steep hill in front of him. The light was fading, but Techno was still able to see unaided. It took Techno just under fifteen minutes to reach the top of the hill. It was the second time Techno had made this little expedition in the past seven days and not only this trip. He'd been to the top of two hills, a multi-storey car park and a motorway footbridge, before finding this location. From where he stood he admired the view of HMP Doncaster and, more importantly, the outside wall of House Block One. Techno let the dog off the lead and began to unpack his bag. First of all, he pulled out a remote-control unit. It was about ten inches square, with a three-inch square TV screen in the middle and various controls to the left and right of the screen. On the side of the control box were a couple of extra buttons that Techno had installed himself. He set the control box on the ground next to the bag. Next, he pulled out the drone that looked like a cross between a flying saucer and a helicopter, and was roughly the size of a large dinner plate and about three inches thick, with a range of two hundred metres and a twelve-hour battery. The drone weighed about the same as a bag of sugar, around one kilo, and could easily carry half a kilo of payload, or enough weed to get half the prison high for weeks. The drone also had a tiny camera mounted on the front, and one on the bottom, that relayed images back to the control box. The camera was infrared and therefore was ideal for use in the dark. The other advantage was that the drone was virtually silent. Techno had purchased the drone via a site on the Dark Web for £1,900. He'd then spent a further £100 on modifications, an absolute steal in his opinion. He checked his watch, 5.30 p.m., plenty of time. Techno pushed the switch on the control box. The small LED indicator came to life with a red glow. He touched another button, and the small screen flickered into action. Next Techno picked up the drone and flicked the power switch to the on position. There was no LED on the drone, but a green LED lit up on the control box. Techno pushed a few buttons and the drone lifted off. He performed a few manoeuvres to check everything was working and he flicked between the two on-board cameras, all was perfect. He brought the drone to land next to the bag. Techno unpacked the last couple of items. Firstly, a metal box, roughly the same size as a box of large matches but a few inches longer. He knew this would fit

## SCREWED

snugly between the gaps in the grills that protected the cell windows. There was a small hook welded to each end of the metal box. To one hook, Techno attached six inches of string with a small magnet on the end. The hook at the opposite end of the box was connected to a winch on the underside of the drone, causing the box to hang vertically. Secondly, he placed two magnets inside the metal box. That was it. He was good to go. There would be no contraband going into the prison tonight, tonight's attempt was merely the dry run.

Techno checked his watch, 5.40 p.m. Twenty minutes to go and the last bit of daylight had all but disappeared. Techno spent the next fifteen minutes throwing a stick for the dog. He was relaxed but excited. He always got that excited buzz when he about to embark on a new scam. He hadn't said anything to Bonzo yet, but he knew his little drone could have a more profitable use than just smuggling in dope. He was getting tired of the drug business, the risks were too high compared to the profit, as Bonzo now knew first-hand.

At exactly five to six Techno launched the drone. It did not make a sound, and after ten feet, Techno could no longer see it. The drone flew silently towards the lighted windows of the prison. Techno could see everything on the TV monitor

## SCREWED

located on the control box, the view was black and green due to the drone's night-vision camera. At the moment all the windows were lit up. It took just four minutes for the drone, and its cargo, to reach the outside wall. Techno left the drone hovering about fifty feet from the windows. He had a perfect view of all of them, now just to wait for the signal and there it was, three windows from the end. On the ground floor, a light went off. He moved the drone closer and counted. Twenty, thirty, forty seconds. The light stayed off. Shit, wrong window. He manoeuvred the drone back to the fifty-feet point and watched again. There, ground floor , fifth window, light off. He left the drone in position. Eighteen, nineteen, twenty. Lights on, perfect. Two minutes later the light went off and stayed off. Techno manoeuvred the drone into position and deployed the winch.

Bonzo stayed in the dark cell staring out of the window. He was straining his ears. Then he heard it, a hushed whirring sound. Bonzo grabbed the plastic knife with his metal razor blade taped to the end. He held the metal end out of the window and through the top section of the grill that adjoined the outside of the window. Techno switched the view to the camera on the bottom of the drone; he could see the metal end of the razor sticking up from the top of the window cage. The

## SCREWED

string with the magnet on the end was swinging close by. A quick nudge on the control box and the drone shifted slightly to the left. The magnetic end came into contact with the razor. Techno let the winch down again. Bonzo felt the connection and heard the whirring sound once more; he pulled the plastic knife and razor through the window and into the cell. Attached to the razor, via a magnet, was a string. He then guided the metal box through the gap in the cage. That was it; the box was inside. Bonzo unclipped the crocodile clip from the top of the container and he gave the string a slight tug. Techno saw the image jerk and smiled to himself; the package was inside the prison. He hit a button on the control box; this would save the drone's route to memory for the next outing. He then hit the button marked home and the drone turned around. Five minutes later, Techno was packing the drone and control box into his bag. He shouted the dog back and headed for home.

Bonzo couldn't help laughing out loud. Jesus, Techno was a genius. He opened the metal box and took out the two magnets. He attached the magnets to the back of the box at either end. The cell windows were all metal so they enabled Bonzo to fix his black metal box to the outside of the window. Anything he kept in his little metal box would now be safe and undetectable. No guard, while doing a cell search, would think of checking the outside of the windows. Genius. For the next week, the drone flew back to the same window each night at 6.00 p.m. Every journey brought an ounce of cannabis into HMP Doncaster. Ideally, Techno would have preferred to bring in a larger quantity and only fly the drone once a week, but while Bonzo was stuck in a ground-floor cell they would carry on as they were. Techno had urged Bonzo to try and find a way to get himself moved to cell without a caged window.

SCREWED

# CHAPTER NINE

'Razor, Razor. Wake up sleepyhead.'

Razor forced his eyelids open and squinted. The light was burning his retinas. Where was he? His head was pounding, but he felt like he was awakening from a pleasant dream. Who was Razor? His eyes finally came into focus. There, straddling his chest with not a stitch on, was Deborah. Wow, it was real. He smiled as she bent forward and kissed him passionately.

'Come on Raz-or. Check out was over an hour ago.'

He pushed her off him and eased on top of her. It was another hour before they finally left the hotel.

Luckily for Razor, his next shift at the prison didn't start until 6.00 p.m. on Monday evening. After he'd left Deborah his Sunday seemed to have gone rapidly downhill. He felt awful, waves of depression kept washing over him, and he couldn't understand why. He'd just had one of the best weekends of his life, yet he felt like he could cry at any moment. Deborah had promised to call him in the week. He should feel on top of the world. Maybe it was the cocaine; Razor had to admit to himself that he'd taken an awful lot. He'd heard people say that it could give a downer that was equal to the high. He'd never touched any drugs before, and it was just a one-off, he assured himself, although his mind did keep drifting back to the feeling of elation he'd experienced, a sense of complete invincibility, and to top it off was the sex, he'd felt like the world's greatest lover, and if Deborah's responses were anything to go by, maybe he was.

Monday morning came and he found it nearly impossible to get out of bed. He felt sluggish and had no appetite. He considered phoning in sick, but as the day wore on, he began to feel a little more human. He managed a late lunch around three and was feeling more or less back to normal by the time he entered the prison at half five.

Deborah sent him a couple of text messages during the week. She always called him Razor, and, he had to admit, he quite liked the sound of it. She was all that he thought of; he couldn't get her out of his mind. He received another text on Thursday morning, which read:

*Hey Razor, fancy partying after work on Sat? D x*

It took Razor all of five seconds to make up his mind. He finished work at midnight at the weekends, so if he took his going out gear to work,

# SCREWED

he could change there and be in the Living Room by around 1.00 a.m.

Razor was on the two till twelve shift on Friday and Saturday night with Lucy. She had commented that he seemed to have an extra spring in his step. While they were having coffee, between cell checks, he'd told Lucy that he'd met someone and had a hot date that Saturday night. If Lucy thought that it was odd to be meeting someone for a date at one in the morning, she didn't let on. But she did say that if he wanted to get off an hour earlier, she'd cover for him. After all, the prisoners were locked away, and Lucy could manage the cell checks on her own. Razor readily agreed and promised to repay the favour if she ever needed to bunk off early.

Razor checked his watch, just after midnight, escaping early had been a nice little bonus. He now had an hour to kill but was more than happy to spend it in the comfort of a VIP booth in the Living Room. When Razor approached the VIP side of the door, a different doorman was standing there.

'VIP only sir. Do you have a card?'

Shit, he'd given Deborah her card back. What was the name of that gay manager? Claudio, that was it.

# SCREWED

'Sorry I don't have one, but if you radio up to Claudio and tell him...' began Razor.

The doorman cut him off before he could finish his sentence.

'In you go sir and enjoy your evening,' said the doorman, dipping his head slightly.

Razor walked directly to the VIP room feeling pretty pleased with himself. As he approached the double doors, he recognised the bouncer as the guy who was on the main door last week.

'Back again sir? I take it you had an enjoyable evening last Saturday,' said the doorman with a grin, as he opened the door for Razor.

'Great night, cheers. Er, is Claudio about? I'd like a quick word.'

'No problem sir. I'll send him to your booth.'

Razor hadn't noticed just how polite the door staff were last weekend, but he had to wonder if this level of politeness was reserved solely for VIPs.

Just as Razor settled into the plush leather sofa, Claudio appeared. Again he was wearing a black tuxedo, although this time, an electric-blue dicky bow completed the look. Smiling warmly, he offered his hand.

# SCREWED

'Mr Razor, fantastic to see you again.'

'Just Razor, please,' he insisted, wondering how Claudio knew his recently acquired nickname, which, to his knowledge, only Deborah knew. She apparently came here quite a lot, and Razor felt a twinge of jealousy. Did she bring other guys here? He checked himself. They'd only spent one night together; they were just two single people enjoying one another's company.

'You wished to see me?' prompted Claudio, snapping Razor from his thoughts.

'Yeah. Well, last week, I had a great night, but Deborah picked up the tab. This week, I'd like to repay the favour.'

Claudio said that he understood and explained that if Razor allowed him to swipe his debit or credit card, he would then charge the evening's drinks to him.

'Thus avoiding the vulgarity of needing to ask for the bill,' added Claudio.

*And knowing what you've spent*, Razor thought.

Claudio also explained that if he signed up for a VIP card, he'd be able to view his bills online and have thirty days' credit on everything he purchased. Razor thought it would be a good idea so gave Claudio a few details, who told him that his card would arrive in the post within the next few days.

# SCREWED

A waitress had already placed a bottle of Bollinger on the table and Razor began sipping his first glass.

'Was there anything else I can help you with before I leave you to enjoy your evening?' Claudio asked.

Razor hesitated, but then decided that the way that Claudio had said the words made it clear he could ask for anything.

'I hope you don't think me to be presumptuous, but I was wondering if you knew where I could get something...' began Razor, leaving the question hanging but giving his nose a slight touch. Claudio responded with a broad smile and a wink.

'Definitely a friend of Deborah's. Leave it with me,' he added, before flouncing off.

Razor drained his first glass of Bolly and was halfway through his second when Claudio returned.

'This should keep you going for now. The container is a gift, but the contents aren't. We'll charge that to your account,' he explained, as he handed Razor a silver vial identical to the one Deborah had used the week before. Razor had given a lot of consideration to snorting cocaine again but concluded that so long as he kept it strictly social, it would be OK.

# SCREWED

By the time Deborah arrived just after one, Razor had already consumed the entire bottle of Bollinger and at least one snort of coke. He found that the alcohol didn't seem to affect him the same when he combined it with cocaine.

'Hey, you've started the party without me,' said Deborah, her words sounding slurred.

'Sounds like I'm not the only one. Now come here.' Razor pulled her into a long embrace and slid his hand up her inner thigh.

## CHAPTER TEN

'Please Mum. I'll be sixteen on Monday, and all my mates are going,' pleaded Katie Jones to her mother.

There was a house party taking place on the upcoming Saturday night, a guy called Gary, from the sixth form, had just rented a house and was holding a house-warming party. Mrs Jones looked at her daughter, fifteen years old going on twenty-five. She was amazed at how much older girls looked nowadays.

'I don't know, honey. You're only fifteen. No doubt there will be drink, drugs and boys looking for only one thing.'

'Mum, I don't do drugs and I ain't no slag, and anyway you and Dad let me drink at home.'

Katie was right about that, her parents did let her drink at home. They knew she was going to drink anyway, so they figured it was best to let her do it where she was safe, and they could keep an eye on her.

'We'll see what your dad says,' said Mrs Jones, becoming weary of the constant badgering that hadn't let up for nearly two weeks.

'Thanks, Mum.'

Katie gave her mum a big hug, knowing that it was as good as yes. She could wrap her dad around her little finger.

# SCREWED

They had only lived in Doncaster for three months. Before that, they had lived in a small village on the outskirts of Gloucester. Her dad's job had forced them to relocate, making him feel guilty about taking Katie out of school in her final year when she would be sitting her GCSEs. She had found it extremely difficult leaving behind her old friends, and so he spoilt her to try and compensate.

As expected, Katie's father agreed that she could go to the party, on condition she was home by midnight. After some persuading, Katie got the curfew extended until 1.00 a.m. On Saturday afternoon, two of Katie's new friends came to her house with their overnight bags. Katie had told her parents that they were having a girly afternoon, painting their nails and doing each other's hair ready for the party. The real reason for the girls coming over was that they both had very strict parents, they knew that by staying at Katie's, they could wear what they liked, stay out later and be able to have a few drinks. Katie had said that her mum had got them a bottle of Lambrini to share before going to the party. The girls giggled, laughed, chatted about boys and made fun of some of the teachers from school. They felt grown up getting ready with a glass of Lambrini in their hands.

# SCREWED

'So, you fancy the Attic tonight Katie?' asked Sarah.

'What? As in the Attic nightclub?'

'Yeah. We're not going to stay at some lame house party all night,' chipped in Britney.

Katie had never been to a nightclub before, or even a bar without her parents. Despite looking older than her years, she'd yet to experience pubs or clubs. She enjoyed the odd glass of wine that her parents allowed her to drink in the house but, unlike a lot of girls her age, wasn't bothered about getting drunk.

'How much will it cost? My parents are quite strict with my allowance, and I can't exactly ask them for money to go clubbing.'

Katie was quite mature for her age and liked to think things through.

'That's the great thing about it. It won't cost *us* anything,' said Britney in a cocky tone.

'I don't get it. Are the drinks given away for free or something? And what about the admission fee?'

'Oh Katie, you're such a country bumpkin. If we get to the Attic before eleven, it's free to get in. Plus once we're in there, it will be full of guys dying to buy us drinks,' Sarah explained with a giggle.

## SCREWED

'And the other good thing is that Gary's house is only a couple of streets away, so we don't even need a taxi,' continued Britney.

Katie felt uneasy but didn't want to appear square in front of the girls. They were the only friends she'd made since moving here. It had been difficult for Katie because they moved to Doncaster at the start of the summer holidays, so for eight long weeks Katie only had her parents and younger brother for company. Within the first few days of school, however, that all changed and she'd hooked up with Sarah and Britney. They'd hit it off immediately and been inseparable ever since.

They decide to go to the party at around half eight and enjoy the free booze laid on by Gary, then leave around half ten and go straight to the Attic. Katie's house was only a ten-minute walk from Gary's place, but her dad still wanted to drop them off and pick them up again. Katie had argued against this as she wouldn't be seen dead getting dropped off by her dad at the party, after all, she was nearly sixteen, not ten. They finally compromised, and her dad agreed to drop them off a few doors away and give them the money to pay for a taxi home. He also insisted on having the address of the party and a contact number for Gary.

## SCREWED

Katie's father was sat at the kitchen table reading the newspaper when the three girls entered the room.

'Hi Mr Jones,' said Sarah and Britney in unison

'Hi, girls,' he replied, amazed at how quickly his little girl had grown up. They could all have easily passed for twenty.

'Bet you're glad I'm giving you a lift, eh girls? I can't imagine that you'd want to walk far in those,' he said, looking down at their platform shoes.

'Yes thanks, Mr Jones. It's very good of you,' said Britney.

'Come on then. Get your coats, and we'll be off.'

'We don't need coats, Dad.'

Before he could respond, the three were out of the front door. *Kids*, he thought as he grabbed his car keys and followed them out. He made the short drive to Gary's street and pulled in.

'Are you quite sure you don't want me to pick you up later?'

Sarah started to speak, but Katie cut her off sharply.

'Dad, we'll be OK with a taxi. I've got the number stored in my phone and money in my purse.'

## SCREWED

'OK, OK. But home by one, not a minute later.'

'Bye Mr Jones,' chorused Sarah and Britney.

Katie slammed the car door.

'Your dad's kind of cute,' said Sarah.

'Eww, you're gross,' replied Katie.

They walked down the street, then knocked on the front door that was promptly opened by Gary.

'Come in ladies,' said Gary, leading them to a room at the back of the house where there were three or four other lads sat around. There was a stereo in one corner that was playing heavy rock music that none of the girls liked one bit.

Without saying a word to Gary, Sarah walked straight to a table stocked with booze. She poured three large glasses of wine and handed them to her friends.

'My brother's out the back, doing the BBQ,' Gary said, gesturing to a set of open patio doors.

'Thought there'd be a few more here, Gaz,' said Britney.

'The night is young,' said Gary optimistically.

The doorbell rang and Gary, giving a relieved smile, headed to the front door. A minute or so later he returned carrying a jacket.

# SCREWED

'That was your dad, Katie. You'd left your coat in the car.'

Katie fumed and snatched the jacket from him. It was her dad's sneaky way of checking up on her. He annoyed her as she'd never been in any trouble, so why did her father feel the need to check up on her? She would be sixteen on Monday and in Katie's eyes, this was as good as being an adult. She gulped down her wine.

'I need a refill, Gaz,' she said, thrusting her empty glass at him. She'd show her dad that she wasn't a kid. By nine thirty Katie disappointedly counted twelve people at the party, and that included her and her friends. She was on her third glass of wine and was beginning to feel tipsy.

'Told you this would be a lame party,' said Britney.

'How much money have you two got?' asked Katie.

Sarah had thirteen pounds, and Katie had the twenty-pound note that her dad had given her for the taxi. Britney had no cash, but said she had a debit card in her purse that her mum insisted she carry for emergencies.

'And this definitely is an emergency,' she said, much to the amusement of the others.

'Right then girls, we've got enough for a drink or two, so let's get out of here and go to a bar for a drink before the Attic,' suggested Katie.

# SCREWED

They all agreed, left the party and headed into Doncaster town centre. Ten minutes after leaving Gary's, they were walking past two burly bouncers and into Yates's Wine Lodge. The place was packed, and the music was pumping. They worked their way towards an empty table, as they did, they attracted looks from various groups of men.

'Who's going to the bar?' Sarah asked.

'Think they'll ask for ID?' added Britney.

'I thought you pair did this all the time?' Katie asked, sounding surprised.

'Err no, it's actually our first time in a bar too,' replied Britney.

Katie, feeling full of confidence now she wasn't the odd one out, took the initiative and said, 'Look girls, they've let us in, so they've got to serve us. I'll go to the bar.'

Katie squeezed her way to the bar while Sarah and Britney waited at an empty table by the fruit machine.

'Alright sexy? Not seen you in here before.'

Katie glanced to her right to see a man, who looked about her dad's age, trying to look down her top. She ignored him and tried to make eye contact with the bartender.

'How about I buy you a drink?' said the man, just as the barman appeared in front of him.

# SCREWED

'Yes mate?' asked the Australian behind the bar.

'Pint of Foster's...' he began.

'And three large white wines,' chipped in Katie.

The Aussie glanced at the man to confirm this.

'You offered,' said Katie with a cheeky grin.

The man nodded to the bartender, figuring that now there was potentially a choice of three girls for him to try his luck on. Katie was planning to take the drinks and walk away, but as the drinks were placed in front of her, she knew that she wouldn't be able to carry them all. She realised that the guy would now have to come back to the table with her and could be hard to shake off.

'What's your name? I'm Brian.'

'Katie. Can you help me carry the drinks?' she blurted.

While Brian paid for the drinks, Katie picked up two glasses and headed back to the table. She was relieved to see only one vacant seat.

'Where's the other drink?' asked Sarah perplexed.

'Your date's got it,' said Katie with a laugh.

Right on cue, Brian appeared with the other wine and his pint of lager. Sarah looked him

## SCREWED

up and down distastefully, taking in his cream chinos and slip-on shoes. Brian glanced around trying to locate a spare seat, but to the relief of the girls, couldn't see one. So he remained standing.

'Brain got us the drinks girls,' announced Katie.

'Thanks, Brian,' chorused Sarah and Britney mockingly.

Ignoring Brian, the girls began chatting amongst themselves. Brian tried without success to join in their conversations. After his third attempt, he was starting to get annoyed.

'I bought you lot a drink, the least you can do is talk to me.'

'No offence Brian, but if we'd wanted to talk to our dads we'd have stayed at home,' said Britney.

Now Brian lost his temper.

'I know your type, fucking prick-teasers,' shouted Brian, banging his fist on the table.

The three stopped talking and looked at him with alarm.

Playing on the fruit machine next to the table was a guy in his early twenties, well dressed and in good shape.

He turned to Brian and said, 'Look, mate, they're not interested. Now fuck off before I knock you out.'

# SCREWED

Brian looked at the guy for a second or two, weighing up his options. He decided to cut his losses and walked off grumbling to himself, feeling bitter and humiliated.

Katie looked at the guy and smiled.

'Thanks,' she mouthed.

He returned her smile and went back to playing the fruit machine.

SCREWED

# CHAPTER ELEVEN

Razor finally crawled into bed at four o'clock Sunday afternoon; this was the fourth weekend on the trot. He'd been awake since eight on Saturday morning, thirty-two long hours, sixteen of which he'd spent drinking champagne, snorting cocaine and screwing Deborah. When his alarm sounded at 8.00 a.m. Monday morning, he felt dreadful. He was due to start work at twelve and was feeling severely depressed. He wished he hadn't changed his shift, working the day shift was the last thing he needed. He hit the snooze button three times, unable to face getting up. He pulled the duvet up over his face and began to sob. What the hell was wrong with him? Everything in his life was great, but this morning he felt borderline suicidal. The alarm sounded again, as he reached out to hit it his hand connected with something else. Focusing his eyes, he saw the silver vial that he'd got from Claudio. He remembered giving it back to Claudio at some point during the night for a top-up; this was a first, as normally, combined with Deborah's supply, one was enough. Desperately wanting to feel better, he grabbed the vial and tapped out a small amount of cocaine on to his hand. He paused briefly; surely a little wouldn't do any harm, just a bit to pick him up? Coming to a decision, he

# SCREWED

snorted it deeply up his left nostril. He felt instantly better, jumped out of bed and straight into the shower.

Looking in the mirror at his bloodshot eyes, he told himself that the cocaine was just an aid to a good night out.

'Control,' he said out loud.

But he knew if it weren't for the special white powder, he would have phoned into work sick. As it was, he was now strolling across the prison car park, just after eleven, feeling pretty good. Just as he was about to enter the building his phone rang. Looking at the display, he saw it was Deborah and immediately answered.

'Hey, sexy.'

'Hey, Razor. How's it going?'

'All good. Just heading into work.'

'When did you say you were off?'

'Thursday. How come?'

'Oh shit, there's a party tomorrow night. Can you change your shift? It's going to be a big one,' she purred.

'There's no chance, babe, too short notice and we're understaffed as it is. Anyway, who has a party on a Tuesday?'

'Doesn't matter. I'll take someone else,' she said abruptly.

Razor's stomach dropped, and he was hit with an overwhelming sense of jealousy.

## SCREWED

'Count me in. I'll throw a sickie,' he quickly replied.

'Meet me at nine in that new wine bar on Friars Gate and dress sharp, Razor. Razor sharp,' she said playfully, before hanging up.

The sensible part of Razor was telling him that a party on a Tuesday night was not a good idea, but the stirring in his trousers told him to worry about work later.

## CHAPTER TWELVE

Matthew Dunford had always liked fruit machines, sometimes he lost, but more often than not he won. He'd read a few books and spent many an hour on the Internet doing research on fruit machines. Matthew could now watch one and work out roughly when it was due to pay the jackpot, thus making a pretty good living out of them. He would usually sit in a bar for two or three hours, drinking only soft drinks, watching the machines. He hadn't been watching the machine in Yates's as tonight he wasn't 'working' as he called it, tonight he was on a lads' night out. He'd completed his A levels and was taking a year out, making his money from playing and beating fruit machines. He'd managed to bank a little over twenty grand during the last year. Now, at the age of twenty, it was time for university. In two weeks' time, he'd be leaving Doncaster and starting a degree in maths at Oxford. So tonight was a night with his mates, a grand send-off before student life. Even though he wasn't technically 'working', he couldn't resist a quick fiver on the machine. He'd been enjoying the gameplay when he'd heard the exchange between the man and the girls at the table. He'd already noticed the first two girls, who were lookers, but it was the third one who caught his eye. He'd

## SCREWED

guessed that she was his age, or maybe a year or two older, with long, dark hair, deep hazel eyes and a curvy figure. He was quite pleased that the older guy had been a pain in the arse, it had given him the chance to play the knight in shining armour. He'd felt electrified when she'd smiled at him. He decided he'd play his last credit then see if he could buy her a drink. An arm suddenly draped over his shoulder.

'Come on Matty; we're moving on.'

*Just my luck*, thought Matthew to himself, as he played his last credit and drained his pint. They headed to another bar for a swift one, before heading off to the Attic. Katie watched disappointedly as the mystery man at the fruit machine left the bar with his mates.

The three friends were having a fantastic time; they'd finished their drinks and were on the dance floor. They hadn't given a second thought to Brian, and it certainly hadn't put them off getting drinks from other drunken guys. Britney had been dancing in the middle of four guys when minutes later, shots appeared. All three were well on their way. Sarah checked her watch; it was ten forty-five. She grabbed the other two and dragged them toward the door, they were protesting loudly.

# SCREWED

'Come on, we've got to be in the Attic before eleven. We've got fifteen minutes,' said Sarah firmly.

Britney and Katie lagged behind laughing and joking, as Sarah led the way to the Attic. Luckily, the queue was quite short, and they managed to get free entry. As soon as the girls got into the club, they hit the dance floor. Before long, three lads were dancing with them and buying them drinks. Katie loved the club, the drink and all the attention. For the first time, she felt pleased that they'd moved to Doncaster. After a while, they all retreated to a couple of fake leather sofas to enjoy their drinks with the lads. Sarah was engaged in some serious snogging with one of the lads, and one of the other guys had his hand on Britney's leg, the third was saying something to Katie about his job, or something, but she wasn't listening to him, her mind kept jumping back to the guy at the fruit machine in Yates's. She noticed that Britney's lips were locking on to her man and Sarah still hadn't come up for air. Katie certainly had no intention of swapping saliva with the bore trying to charm her. She stood, telling the guy that she was off to powder her nose. She'd heard the line in a film that her mother liked and found it quite funny. The lad nodded, looking dejected.

# SCREWED

Matthew Dunford and his mates entered the Attic and headed straight for the bar.

'More shots, boys?' asked one of them.

They consumed a few shots before moving on to the dance floor. Matthew saw the lights from the corner of his eye, up against the wall between the bar and the dance floor, next to the door to the toilets, was a Fireball club fruit machine with a five-hundred-pound jackpot. He left his mates on the dance floor and went straight to the flashing machine.

'Hello again.'

He looked up from the machine to lock eyes with the girl from Yates's.

'Hi,' he replied. Feeling his cheeks start to flush, he was suddenly glad of the dim lighting. He'd never really had a lot of success with women, despite his good looks.

'I'm Katie. Thanks again for earlier. That guy was really starting to creep me out.'

'No problem. I'm Matt. Er, would you like a drink? I promise I won't shout if you don't want to talk to me afterwards,' he grinned.

They got drinks and then found a settee in a dark corner of the now packed club. They drank, chatted and kissed. The alcohol had gone to Katie's head, and she was feeling pretty drunk.

'Come on Katie; we're here.'

# SCREWED

Katie looked around feeling disorientated; she realised that she was sitting in the back of a taxi.

'Where's here?' she asked.

'My place. Are you OK? You do want to come in, don't you? It's OK if not. I can get the taxi to run you home.'

'I'm fine. Yeah, course I want to come in.' Katie couldn't recall how they'd got from the club to the taxi, but she felt safe with Matthew. As she got out of the taxi and followed Matt into the house, it suddenly dawned on her that they were going to have sex. Katie was still a virgin and not given much thought to sex. Sarah and Britney had talked about it a lot, but then again, they had talked a lot about pubs and clubs.

*Shit, what about Sarah and Britney? Had she told them she was leaving? And what about her dad?* she wondered.

Katie concluded that it was still early so she'd text them later. The only thing on her mind now was sex.

'Where is she? Her dad will go mad,' said Sarah with tears welling in her eyes.

It was 1.00 a.m.; they'd been walking around the club for the past half hour and couldn't find Katie anywhere. They'd both tried ringing her, but the phone had rung then gone to

## SCREWED

voicemail. The two girls, who'd been quite drunk earlier, now felt suddenly sober.

'What if someone has kidnapped her?' said Sarah.

'Come on Sar, that's a bit OTT. People don't get kidnapped from nightclubs.'

Mr Jones was pacing the living room; it was one thirty. The girls weren't back, and Katie wasn't answering her phone. Mr Jones was not happy. He knew that his daughter was probably proving a point because of the trick he'd pulled earlier with the coat. Although his intentions had been good, in hindsight, Mr Jones realised that it probably wasn't the best idea. He waited another ten long minutes before snatching up his keys and leaving the house.

He pulled up outside the house that he'd visited earlier. All seemed quiet, and there were no signs activity within the property. He pounded on the front door. Nothing. He banged again, and a light came on in an upstairs window. Then a light went on in the hallway, and the front door slowly opened, revealing a guy in his twenties wearing just his boxers.

'Where's my daughter?' demanded Mr Jones.

The guy turned and shouted into the house.

# SCREWED

'Gary, get your arse down here.'

Gary came to the front door and asked, 'Hi, Mr Jones. What's up?'

'Where's Katie?'

'She left with Sarah and Britney hours ago,' explained Gary.

'What time and where did they go?'

'Err, about half nine I think. They didn't tell me where they were going.'

Fuming, Mr Jones got back into his car and grabbed his mobile. He dialled Katie's number again and again, each time leaving a message. Next, he phoned home. His wife picked up, and he proceeded to tell her what he'd just discovered.

'Just stay where you are, and I'll try and get Britney or Sarah,' said Mrs Jones.

Britney looked down at her phone, the display read: *Katie Home calling*.

'Katie?' said Britney.

'No, it's her mum. Where are you and where's Katie?' said asked calmly.

Britney began to sob as she told her of how they'd gone to the Attic nightclub in town and lost Katie. Mrs Jones told Britney to calm down and then wait outside the Attic, her husband would be there to get them in five minutes. A few moments later, the girls climbed into the back of Mr Jones's car. He was annoyed with the girls for not looking after each other, but held his tongue as they were

# SCREWED

both very upset. Glancing at the clock on his dashboard, he saw it was one fifty, only ten more minutes till throwing out time. He figured that if they just sat tight, eventually Katie would come walking out of the club. They watched as the last dregs of people left, some getting in taxis, other standing around in groups chatting. The last people left the club and the heavy double doors slammed to behind them, there was still no Katie. Mr Jones was frantic; he decided to drive home and call the police. As he pulled into his driveway, he glanced in the rear-view mirror to see Britney and Sarah, their make-up smeared from their tears. They no longer looked like grown-ups but exactly what they were, two worried, young schoolgirls.

They all sat in the front room while Mr Jones called the police. The duty sergeant said he'd put out a radio alert and a PC would be round to take a statement. Britney and Sarah sat in silence. A thought suddenly struck Britney.

'Katie's got a new iPhone,' she said out loud.

'Yes. I got it for her birthday, but Katie insisted on having it early for the weekend,' said Mrs Jones.

# SCREWED

'Well, it's got an app called Find My iPhone. If it's lost or stolen you can track its location,' explained Britney.

'Do you have a laptop?' asked Sarah.

Like a shot, Mr Jones grabbed his laptop and booted it up. Britney instructed him on how to get on to the phone locator website. He then entered the phone details. Luckily, Mrs Jones had insisted that Katie gave her the password for the phone. A box appeared on the screen with the word 'tracking' flashing in the centre. After a few seconds, it changed to 'phone located'. A map appeared on the screen showing a red dot on a street on the other side of town. The tracker gave a location radius of up to six metres; this meant the phone's location was only accurate to within three houses. Mr Jones snatched up the laptop and headed back out to his car. Before leaving, he instructed his wife to call the police and give them the address.

Mr Jones's car roared down Duke Street; he was looking out for eighty-one, eighty-three and eighty-five that were roughly halfway down the street. Seventy-seven, seventy-nine, but no eighty-one. He screeched to a halt, jumped out of the car and began banging on number seventy-nine. Just then a police car turned on to the street, lights flashing and siren blaring.

# SCREWED

'What the fuck's going on?' demanded the annoyed man who opened the door.

One of the police officers had now joined Mr Jones in front of the house.

'Are you alone in the house sir?' asked the officer calmly.

'No, my wife and two kids are in bed,' replied the guy.

The second officer was already knocking at door number eighty-three when another squad car arrived on the scene. A man in his early twenties opened the door to number eighty-three.

'Is anyone in the house with you sir?' asked the second officer.

'Why?' asked Matthew Dunford.

A WPC had joined the second officer and added, 'Just answer the question, sir.'

'Well, OK. I've got company, but she's in bed.'

'Have you been to the Attic nightclub tonight?' asked the WPC.

'Yes, but…'

Before he could finish his sentence, the WPC had barged him out of the way and was charging up the stairs. She entered the bedroom and hit the light switch, her eyes slowly adjusting to the bright light.

'Katie?' she asked.

# SCREWED

'Yeah, why?' came the muffled response from under the duvet.

The WPC sat down on the edge of the bed and proceeded to ask Katie some questions. Had she come here of her own accord? Had she had sex? Was it consensual? Was she drunk? Had she told the man how old she was?

Once Katie was dressed, the WPC escorted her downstairs and into the open arms of her dad. While the WPC had been upstairs with Katie, the male officer had taken Matthew into the kitchen at the back of the house. Once they were able to establish that nothing non-consensual had taken place, the WPC told Katie's father to take her home, someone would be around in the morning to get a statement.

Mr Jones and his daughter drove home in silence.

The WPC joined Matthew and her colleagues in the kitchen of the house. He was sat at the kitchen table wearing just a towelling dressing gown and looking pale and confused.

'Mr Matthew Dunford, I'm arresting you on suspicion of having sex with a minor.' Matthew leapt out of his chair and vomited into the kitchen sink, without missing a beat, the officer continued to read him his rights. Matthew couldn't process

# SCREWED

what was happening. He'd met her in a club; she had to be over eighteen, how could he possibly know that she was under age?

'Do you understand, sir?' asked the WPC.

'What? No, er yes.'

'Sir, do you understand what I've just said to you?' she repeated.

Matthew nodded vacantly. He was then driven to Doncaster police station and put into one of small holding cells to await the formal interview.

## CHAPTER THIRTEEN

Eight thirty Tuesday night, Razor sat at a table in the window of Gatsby's wine bar. He was feeling a little edgy and wanted to have a few drinks before going to any party. His silver vial was now empty; he'd sniffed the last few grains while getting ready earlier. He wasn't exactly sure why, but the thought of meeting some of Deborah's friends tonight was making him feel a little nervous. He'd noted Deborah's parting words and opted for the full three-piece suit with tie. When he'd first put it on and sniffed the coke, he'd looked in the mirror and decided he looked better than James Bond. Now, studying his reflection in the wine bar window, he was starting to feel self-conscious, the effects of the coke beginning to wear off.

After a second large vodka and tonic, he finally began to relax. He gazed around the plush interior of the wine bar; this was a far cry from the places he used to frequent before meeting Deborah.

'Looking sharp, Razor,' said Deborah, interrupting his thoughts as she joined him at the table.

He smiled like a little boy as she adjusted his tie and then gave him a lingering kiss.

'Have we got time for a drink?' asked Razor, as their lips parted.

# SCREWED

'Definitely. We're not being picked up till half past; I'll have glass of Bolly.'

They clinked glasses as Razor leaned in close and whispered in her ear, 'Have you got any party powder with you, babe?'

He hated calling it cocaine or coke, to Razor calling it by its name made him sound like some druggie, whereas party powder made it sound harmless.

'Jesus Razor, I thought you topped up before we left the bar on Saturday. Those vials hold two grams; you can't have got through all that.'

Razor was a little taken aback by the look of disbelief on her face. She was the one who'd introduced him to it, and now here she was getting all high and mighty about how much he was using. Or was he overthinking things?

'Hey, relax. You think I've got a problem or something?' he replied nonchalantly. 'Look, the truth is I hadn't put the top back on properly, and when I took it out of my pocket I dropped it, and it went all over the floor.'

Her face softened, he wasn't quite sure why he had to lie to her.

'I thought I was going have to start calling you Hoover for a minute,' she laughed. 'And in answer to your question, lover boy, we're good for party powder.'

# SCREWED

Just then she gazed down at her watch, a silver Rolex with diamond bezel. Razor hadn't noticed the watch before, and it made him wonder, not for first time, exactly how much money she made taking her clothes off for drunken men.

'Time to go,' she announced, ending his silent speculations.

They walked out of the wine bar, where Razor was expecting to see a taxi waiting for them. Instead, there was a black Range Rover with blacked-out windows, at the side of which stood a man dressed in a full chauffeur's outfit, complete with hat. Razor instantly recognised him as one of the doormen from the Living Room. He opened the door and waited for them to get in, and without a word, he closed it behind them before climbing into the driver's seat and pulling into the traffic. Razor was speechless. Who sends a chauffeur-driven Ranger Rover to bring guests to a party on a Tuesday night?

'Johnny sent the car. That's whose party we're going to,' explained Deborah, as if reading his thoughts.

'Who's Johnny?'

'Oh, didn't I mention? Johnny is my boss. He owns the lap dancing bar, the Living Room and a few other bars and club here and there,' she explained.

# SCREWED

'So he does this for *all* his staff?'

'No. There's two good reasons he's looking after me,' she giggled.

Razor couldn't help looking at her chest and grinning. She caught his stare and laughed.

'Nothing like that.'

'Tell me then,' he asked with all the bravado he could muster.

'Well one, I earn his club a shitload of cash.' She paused, so Razor prompted.

'And two?'

'I've got you,' she said, rubbing her hand up the inside of his thigh.

Her words made Razor feel slightly uneasy.

'What's that meant to mean?' he asked, his voice rising a little with concern.

'He just wants to meet you, that's all. Now just relax and enjoy the ride.'

Before he could ask anything else, she'd undone his fly and slipped her hand inside his trousers. Razor let his head fall back on to the leather interior, while the driver didn't take his eyes off the road.

The drive took about twenty minutes. They had left the city and were now surrounded by countryside. The Range Rover slowed, made an abrupt left turn, and then stopped in front of a pair of black, wrought-iron gates. The gates were

# SCREWED

at least ten-feet high, topped with menacing-looking, golden-coloured spikes. An equally high wall adjoined the side of each gate, which reminded Razor of the prison where he worked, although, he suspected, that this wall and gate were designed to keep people out and not vice versa.

The driver pointed a key fob at the gates, causing them to open. Razor leaned forward, noticing the lights that ran along either side of the drive, it seemed to go on forever. As the Ranger Rover rounded a curve in the driveway, the house appeared, or maybe a mansion would have been a more accurate description. The place was huge, it was three storeys, and Razor counted at least twelve windows running around the top floor. There were two hand-carved stone columns flanking the double, solid oak, front doors. Every window in the house happened to be lit up. In front of the house was a large roundabout with an elaborate water feature in the middle. The Range Rover stopped directly outside. The driver remained behind the wheel while a man, who Razor assumed was the butler, opened the back door.

'Good evening sir, madam,' said the butler in a clipped tone.

As the servant led them into the entrance hall, they were greeted by the sounds of loud

## SCREWED

dance music and the smell of cooked pork. A sweeping staircase, leading to an open landing some twenty feet above floor level, dominated the spacious foyer, which had at least eight doors leading off it.

'The door at the far end, if you please,' said the butler, nodding towards the only open door.

Without another word the butler had disappeared, to no doubt greet other guests. Razor took Deborah's hand and proceeded to the door and into the room beyond. The place was like a stately home, walls covered in paintings that were hundreds of years old. Razor began to get lost in his thoughts, building a mental picture of Johnny. He imagined the earl from the TV programme, *Downton Abbey*. Johnny was probably like that, but then again, did that image fit with bars and strip clubs? No doubt he'd find out soon enough.

They headed in the direction of the music and ended up in another room that was a complete contrast to the one they'd just left. This room was about the size of the VIP area at the Living Room and kitted out identically. A waitress appeared and handed them both a glass of champagne. The room was packed, and Deborah seemed to know everyone there. She worked the room smoothly, introducing Razor to everyone, although he struggled to remember a single name, that was until he met Ishmael.

# SCREWED

'Or Ish to me mates,' he said, slapping Razor on the back and draping one arm over his shoulder.

Ish was a black guy in his late teens or early twenties. His physique was that of someone who spent a lot of time in the gym. Ishmael had the talent to continue a conversation, while successfully assessing every female in the vicinity. The way he acted around Deborah made Razor feel that there was maybe a bit of history there.

'Hey, I got a little something for you,' said Ish with grin.

As they followed him over to the settee in a far corner, Deborah whispered to Razor, 'Ish is a Donny lad; he makes his money selling party powder for Johnny. He's good to know because he's local and he sells a bit on the side for 'loyal' customers,' she paused before adding, 'and at a lot better rate.'

Ishmael slumped down into the middle of the settee and pulled the table closer.

'Come on, sit down. I won't bite,' he said, patting the cushions on either side of him.

They obediently obliged. Deborah sat a little too close for Razor's taste. Ish then produced a silver tube from his jacket pocket, which was easily big enough to hold a Cuban cigar. He unscrewed the end and tapped out a large pile of cocaine on to the gleaming glass table top. Then

## SCREWED

taking out a gold credit card, he cut six thick lines that were at least four-inches long. Ish then produced a crisp fifty-pound note from his bulging top pocket, rolled it up and handed it to Deborah.

'Ladies first.'

She expertly snorted a line up each nostril, before handing the note back to Ish who did the same. After two long snorts, Ish passed the fifty to Razor, who paused while taking in the size of the two lines in front of him. He didn't think he'd ever done this amount in one hit before. Not wanting to be outdone by Ish, he bent down and quickly snorted both lines. Razor felt fireworks instantly explode in his brain, as his eyes began to roll back in their sockets.

'Fuck!' gasped Razor.

Ish was grinning like a Cheshire cat.

'That's me private stash. Only came in yesterday. Not even been cut,' he laughed.

'Come on Razor, let's dance,' Deborah said, pulling Razor to his feet.

He stood, only just maintaining his balance, much to the further amusement of Ish.

'Give me a call if you need anything. Payphone only though,' said Ish, handing him a card then holding out an outstretched fist. Razor stared at the closed fist, not quite knowing what to do.

'Bump me man,' laughed Ish.

## SCREWED

Razor finally got it, gave a smile and touched his fist against Ishmael's. Deborah stood by watching with great amusement. They hit the dance floor, Razor's head was spinning, everything was starting to blur.

'I need air.' And without further explanation, he left Deborah amongst the throng of cavorting bodies on the dance floor. He staggered towards a set of patio doors that were open and led on to a large terrace. The terrace overlooked an Olympic-sized swimming pool, where fifteen or twenty people were jumping around. A woman wearing just a G-string was being chased down one side of the pool by a guy wearing black dicky bow, crisp white shirt and a pair of boxers. She let out a playful scream as he caught her and they both fell into the pool. Razor slumped down in a chair on the terrace. After just a few minutes, the fresh air seemed to do the trick, and he was beginning to feel on top of the world again. Who would have thought that just a month ago he'd be dating a top stripper, frequenting VIP areas drinking champagne and getting chauffeured to exclusive parties on large country estates?

The building surrounded the terrace and pool area on three sides, and unlike the front, most of the windows at the back were in total darkness. Razor

## SCREWED

was about to go back inside when a movement in one of the only lit windows at the back caught his eye. Through the window, he could see the back of a large chair, but the seat obstructed the view of who was sitting in it. The chair sat behind a solid, wooden desk, and the movement that had caught Razor's attention was someone entering the room and standing in front of the desk. The person looked vaguely familiar, but Razor couldn't quite place him. Within a couple of seconds it suddenly hit him. It was Paul from the stag do. What was he doing here? He very much doubted it would be police business at this hour, so he must also be a guest. Razor continued to watch with casual interest as he took in the cold night air. He then saw the person behind the desk hand something to Paul, who quickly slipped it into his inside jacket pocket.

'Mr Razor, what are you doing out here when that sexy girl of yours is inside?'

Startled, Razor turned to come face-to-face with Claudio, the manager of the Living Room, with a glass of champagne in each hand. With a coy smile, he offered one to Razor, while gently taking his arm and casually turning him away from the window to face the shenanigans taking place in the pool.

'Good to see you, Claudio. This is some place.'

# SCREWED

'That it is, Mr Razor. Have you had the pleasure of meeting our host yet?'

'Not yet and, to be honest, I'm a little nervous about it. All of this is new to me, and I'm a bit overwhelmed.'

Reaching into his pocket, Claudio produced an envelope and handing it to Razor said, 'Your VIP card and account details.'

'I thought it was coming in the post?'

'Special treatment,' he smiled. As he turned, he gave the slightest of nods towards the lit window that minutes before Razor had been peering at. 'Right, I have lots of schmoozing to do, so run along, darling, and find the delightful Deborah, and if you require anything remember, I'm always at your service.'

Before Claudio had the chance to leave, Razor had whipped out the empty silver vial. Without a word, and with the swiftness of a magician, Claudio took the container, switched it for an identical one and handed it back to Razor.

'What about payment?' asked Razor quietly.

'Don't worry; we'll charge your account. Now relax and enjoy the evening.'

Before he could respond, a well-groomed Eurasian man of no more than twenty, sidled up to them and slipped a long, slim arm around Claudio's waist.

# SCREWED

'Aren't you going to introduce me, Claudie?' asked the man, eyeing Razor from head to toe.

'Mr Razor, allow me to present my partner, Simon.'

Razor shook his limp hand and felt his cheeks burn as Simon kept hold of it for a little longer than was necessary. Sensing Razor's unease, Claudio hustled Simon back to the party.

After one last glance at the now darkened window, Razor headed back inside. He scanned the dance floor and spotted Deborah dancing with Ishmael, a little too closely for Razor's liking. He needed a drink, so decided to go in search of the bar. Like the rest of the room, the bar was a carbon copy of the one in the Living Room, with the one exception being no cash register. Still smarting from seeing Deborah dancing with Ish, he ordered a large vodka and tonic, downed it in one and ordered a second.

'I thought you'd run off,' said Deborah, planting a kiss firmly on his cheek and sliding her hand into his trouser pocket.

He pulled away abruptly.

'You seemed to be doing OK without me,' he snapped and downed the last of his drink, keeping his focus firmly on the bar.

'Seriously? You're not jealous of Ish? God Razor, he's only eighteen.' She laughed.

'If you say so,' he snorted.

# SCREWED

'You are a soppy git. Now smile Razor, our host is coming over.'

Razor followed her gaze and did a double take. He was expecting some distinguished old guy, wearing a dinner suit, like you'd expect to see at the captain's table on some expensive cruise liner. Instead, the man walking towards them couldn't be further from that image. He was somewhere between forty and forty-five, five foot nine and at least twenty stone. His enormous beer gut strained the white T-shirt that hung over his tatty jeans.

'Debbie baby.' Johnny embraced her in a rough bear hug.

This was the first time since meeting her that Razor had heard anyone address her as anything other than Deborah and was not quite sure how he felt about this. He was slightly surprised when Johnny released her from his grip and kissed her on each cheek. He did this with the finesse of a continental gentleman that Razor had only ever seen on the TV.

'Looking good, Debbie,' said Johnny, giving her a hearty slap on the bum. His voice was deep and gravelly.

Razor looked at Johnny's thick, muscly arms; there wasn't an inch of skin without a tattoo. He could just imagine the man before him stood on the terraces at an England game, hurling

# SCREWED

abuse at foreigners and causing havoc. Johnny then turned his attention to Razor.

'So this is the lucky fella is it Debbie?' he asked, as he ran a large hand over his closely shaven head, before thrusting it in Razor's direction.

Johnny broke into a huge grin as he pumped Razor's hand in greeting. Razor did his best not to stare at Johnny's mouth, every tooth was gold, and it didn't stop there, he was covered in the stuff. A gold chain hung around his neck; it was as thick as something that you'd use to chain a bicycle to a lamp post. He wore a matching chain on each wrist and every fat finger donned a gold ring.

'It's great to finally meet you, Razor. I've never had a friend who works in a prison before.' He was still smiling and gave Razor's hand an extra squeeze.

'Well I guess you do now,' replied Razor with a nervous laugh, as Johnny finally released his hand.

'Now, if there's anything you need, just give me a shout. After all, that's what friends do, don't they? Favours.' Johnny gave Razor a nod, giving him the feeling that he would be asking for a favour way before Razor needed one from him. 'Anyway, I'm neglecting my other guests. Enjoy yourselves.' Johnny turned and lumbered off.

# SCREWED

Razor could just about make out a Union Jack tattoo peeping out from the top of Johnny's T-shirt.

'Isn't he a sweetheart?' gushed Deborah.

'You've certainly got some interesting friends,' added Razor, as he continued to watch the as other guests treated Johnny like visiting royalty.

The same Range Rover dropped Razor off at home around six the next morning. He'd suggested accompanying Deborah home, but she had insisted that she was tired and had a busy day ahead of her. They'd had sex in the back of Range Rover on the way home and, if he was honest, he was looking forward to sleeping in his own bed.

## CHAPTER FOURTEEN

At 9.00 a.m. the next morning, Mr Jones opened the front door to find the WPC and her colleague from the night before. He was a little surprised to see the same two officers. As he showed them through to the living room, he commented on the long hours they apparently worked.

'Well technically we finished our shift an hour ago, but I'm quite passionate about this type of thing,' explained the WPC firmly.

'What exactly is this type of thing?' asked Mr Jones.

'Older men plying young girls with booze then taking advantage of them.' There was an edge to the WPC's voice as she said this.

Mr Jones nodded. Katie had refused point-blank to speak to him or his wife last night. He had hoped that someone hadn't taken advantage of his daughter, the very thought made him shiver, she was still his little girl after all. He made coffee for the officers while his wife went to fetch their daughter from her room.

'I don't want to speak to the police, Mum. I've done nothing wrong, and neither has Matt.'

'Come on, Katie. You're not in any trouble; they just want to ask you a couple of questions.'

# SCREWED

Reluctantly, Katie entered the living room and slumped down in a chair opposite the two officers. Her parents stood awkwardly next to her, not looking forward to hearing what their daughter was about to say.

'My name is WPC Barrymore and this is my colleague, PC Davies,' began the WPC.

'Do they have to be here?' asked Katie.

'Katie, in the eyes of the law you are a minor. Therefore you have to have at least one parent present while we talk to you,' explained Barrymore.

Mr Jones decided it would be easier if he were the one to leave, so mumbling something about the Sunday papers, he walked out of the room.

'Now Katie, in your own words, tell us about what happened last night,' prompted Barrymore. 'And remember, you've done nothing wrong and we're not here to judge,' she continued with a reassuring smile.

PC Davies opened his notebook and was poised to write down everything Katie said. Katie began the narrative, starting from the time her dad dropped her off at Gary's. Barrymore would stop her at various intervals to clarify certain points.

'So you never told him your age, and he never asked?'

## SCREWED

'No,' confirmed Katie.

'But he did buy you alcoholic drinks?'

'Yes.'

'And he invited you back to his place?'

'Yes.' Katie decided it was best not to mention the fact that she couldn't remember leaving the club or getting into the taxi.

'Did he ask your permission before having sex with you?'

'No.'

WPC Barrymore cut in.

'So you didn't give him permission to have sex with you?'

'No, it just happened.'

'Katie, you do know that it's a criminal offence for an adult to have sex with someone under the age of sixteen?'

Katie nodded glumly, tears welling in her eyes.

'It's OK, Katie. I think we'll call it a day now,' said PC Davies, snapping his notebook shut.

Katie ran out of the room sobbing. Mr Jones returned to show the two officers out. PC Davies walked directly to the squad car, but Barrymore hung back.

'What will happen now?' Mr Jones asked the WPC.

'He'll get interviewed, cautioned and then released to get another schoolgirl drunk.'

## SCREWED

'But he broke the law, surely he can't just get away with it.'

'The thing is Mr Jones, and this is off the record, it's all about money. Our sergeant has to weigh up the chances of getting a conviction should it go to court. Dunford would probably only get a suspended sentence anyway. So Sarge will probably just go for a caution and save the expense. If it were down to me, I'd throw the bloody book at him,' she explained bitterly.

'That's not justice.'

'Well, the only way he'd see the inside of a courtroom would be if you were to insist on pressing charges. Normally it would be down to the victim, but as she's under age it comes down to you,' she continued.

'And that would get him jailed would it?'

'Well that's all down to the court, so probably not, but it would make the papers and hopefully get him to think twice before doing it again.'

Before leaving, Barrymore advised him that if he did want to press charges, it would be best to visit the station today, while Dunford was still in custody. He thanked her, and she left.

At 8.00 a.m. that same morning the door to holding cell seven, that housed Matthew Dunford,

## SCREWED

was opened by an overweight custody sergeant carrying a polystyrene tray.

'Breakfast,' he announced. Matthew didn't respond, so the sergeant placed the tray on the floor then asked, 'You sure you don't want a solicitor?'

Again Matthew said nothing, so shrugging the sergeant turned and left. At 9.00 a.m. the door was unlocked again, and Matthew was led off to a small interview room. The room was windowless and contained just a table, with two chairs on each side. On the table sat a tape recorder. The officer who brought him into the room left, so Matthew sat down and waited. A few minutes later two officers entered the stale-smelling room.

'Morning Matthew, or is it Matt?' asked one of the officers in a friendly tone.

Matthew shrugged. He was numb. He'd never been in any trouble before, and now here he was under arrest for sex with a minor.

'OK then, Matt. I'm PC Ryan, and this is PC Butler. Can we get you a coffee or something before we start?'

Matthew shook his head feeling nauseous.

'I understand you've waived your right to a solicitor. Are you absolutely sure about that?'

'I've done nothing wrong,' retorted Matthew.

# SCREWED

'OK, it's your choice. Now here's what's going to happen. In a minute we're going to turn that tape on and ask you a few questions. OK?'

'Then what?' asked Matthew.

'All depends on if you tell the truth or not,' said Butler, speaking for the first time.

'You ready to start?' said Ryan in a friendlier tone.

PC Ryan then pressed record on the double tape deck. Both tapes began to roll simultaneously.

'The time is 9 a.m. on Sunday the twentieth of September 2014. This interview is taking place at Doncaster police station. My name is PC Alan Ryan, also present is PC James Butler. We are interviewing...' Then pausing and nodding at Matthew, he continued, 'Please state your full name, date of birth and current address.'

In a low, barely audible voice, Matthew gave the requested information. He then proceeded to answer all the other questions put to him. PC Butler made detailed notes. After just thirty minutes the interview was concluded and the tape turned off.

'So what now?' asked Matthew nervously.

Both Ryan and Butler had conducted enough interviews to know when someone was lying. They were both confident that Dunford was

# SCREWED

telling the truth and the whole thing was a case of unfortunate circumstances.

Ryan, feeling sorry for the poor sod, decided to level with him. 'Look Matt, for what it's worth, you're not the first guy this has happened to, and I'm sure you won't be the last. So as long as the girl's statement confirms what you've told us, I'm sure the sarge will just let you off with a caution and that will be the end of it. So come on, let's get you home.'

Matthew was then bailed to return to Doncaster police station at 3.00 p.m. on Wednesday the twenty-third of September. He was told that if he failed to surrender to bail, or made any attempt to contact Katie Jones, he would be arrested and taken into custody.

Matthew slammed the front door behind him, ran upstairs, fell on to his bed and sobbed.

SCREWED

# CHAPTER FIFTEEN

Razor wasn't at work again until Thursday, so he didn't bother setting the alarm clock. He slept until four the next afternoon and woke feeling pretty shitty. He reached for the silver vial and was disappointed to find it empty.

Shit, did he have a problem?

Wanting to sniff first thing in the morning wasn't right, but then again, it wasn't morning, and it wasn't like he was taking it daily. His last daytime sniff was a week ago, well Sunday, and that was technically last week, and after all, it was only a little pick-me-up. So no, Razor finally concluded that he didn't have a problem. He did, however, need picking up today. He grabbed his suit jacket from the back of the chair and checked the pockets. The first thing he came across was the envelope from Claudio. Putting that to one side, he carried on searching. Then he found it, the card that Ish had given to him. He stared at the card in his hand, one side was completely blank, while on the other was simply printed a mobile number.

Razor quickly dressed, grabbed his wallet, then remembering Ishmael's words, picked up a few coins. He then left the house and headed down the street to the nearest phone box. Razor hadn't used a phone box in years and wondered how long

## SCREWED

it would be before they disappeared altogether. He entered the putrid-smelling box, slotted in twenty pence and began to dial. The display flashed 'sixty pence minimum'.

'No wonder people stopped using 'em,' he said under his breath.

Then inserting a pound coin into the slot, he dialled again. The line connected and after eight rings was answered.

'Yo.'

'It's Razor. I need...'

'Woah, no names man. You're in luck though; I'm in town. Meet me outside Greggs in thirty.'

The line went dead, and Razor cursed his stupidity at using his name. He didn't want Ishmael thinking that he was some idiot.

The town centre was a twenty-minute walk which Razor just couldn't face; he didn't fancy getting behind the wheel either. Instead, he made the short walk home and ordered a taxi. As he waited for the taxi to arrive, he wandered around his house. Entering the bathroom, Razor paused to look at his reflexion in the mirror; he looked like shit. He splashed cold water on his face, which did little to improve how he looked or felt.

# SCREWED

The taxi finally arrived and dropped him outside the NatWest bank on the High Street. He wasn't quite sure what the deal was with Ish. Did he pay him cash, or did it go on the account? It suddenly struck that he didn't know what the party powder was costing him. He went to the cash machine and withdrew three hundred pounds, the maximum the card would permit. He was about to request a mini statement when he saw Ish walking down the street towards Greggs, just three doors away from the bank. They bumped fists.

'Razor, you look shitty, man,' said Ish as way of a greeting.

Ish was looking fresh faced and full of energy.

'Feel like shit too, Ish, and in serious need of a pick-me-up.'

'How much ya after?'

'Well I normally just get Claudio to top this up,' replied Razor, flashing Ish the silver vial.

'Tell you what; I've just had a punter let-down. I've got six grams on me, that's three of dem vials. That should keep you going a bit.'

'Does that go on the account?' asked Razor innocently.

Ish grinned. 'Yes and no. No, it does not go on your VIP Johnny account, but yes it can go on the Ish account. You settle Ish accounts in cash at the end of each month,' Ish explained. 'It's just a

# SCREWED

little sideline, and my shit is a lot cheaper than Johnny's, but don't tell him I said that,' he continued.

'OK, deal.'

'Good choice. That'll be five hundred and this stays between you and me.'

Razor took the small plastic bag from Ish and slipped it into his pocket. He figured that the bag should last him at least three weekends of partying with Deborah. He needed somewhere private, so he could have a little sniff, just to pick himself up. He walked into Wetherspoon's and headed straight to the gents. He went in the nearest cubicle and tapped out a small pile on to the back of his hand. Within seconds, just like that, he was back to normal. His head felt clear; his body energised. As he was already there, he decided to stay for a drink. He was on the four till midnight shift tomorrow with Lucy, so it wasn't like he had an early start or anything.

Razor checked his watch; it was half five. Not wanting to stand in the pub on his own, he decided to give Tony a quick text and see if he was free for a swift drink. He hadn't seen him since the stag do and had missed a few calls from him over the past couple of weeks. He'd meant to get in touch so now was as good a time as any. Before he'd got halfway down his first drink, his phone buzzed. Checking the display, he saw a text from Tony.

*Thought you'd died, mate. Just knocking off. Be with you about six.*

Razor sipped his pint, thinking about how Tony had acted in the lap dancing club. He'd never seen him behave aggressively before. Razor had just ordered a second pint when Tony joined him. He was about to order Tony a pint too, but Tony stopped him and insisted on orange juice.

'Game of squash at eight,' he explained. Then looking at Razor he said, 'A bit of exercise may do you some good, you look like shit.'

'Just a bit of a cold mate,' Razor replied defensively.

'If you say so. So come on then, Gilly, what happened to you in Leeds?'

'A gentleman doesn't kiss and tell,' said Razor with a smile.

'Who was it? Not the stripper?'

Razor's face said it all.

'Bloody hell, you old dog. She was a right stunner. I can't believe it.'

'Don't sound so surprised,' Razor said, feigning deep hurt.

'Sorry mate, it's just. Well… Jesus… She's a stripper and all that.'

'Her name's Deborah,' he retorted.

'What? You seeing her or something?'

# SCREWED

'Or something,' Razor smiled.

'Well, as you're obviously in good spirits, I suppose it's a good time to tell you that you owe me a hundred and sixty quid.'

'Fuck me! What for?'

'Taxis, hotel, paintballing. We had a square up on Sunday morning, but someone had better places to be,' Tony said light-heartedly.

Razor got out his wallet and paid Tony the cash. Pocketing the money, Tony then pulled an envelope from his pocket and handed it to Razor.

'What's this?'

'Open it. I've been trying to get hold of you for two weeks to give you this.'

It was a wedding invite.

'I didn't know you were seeing someone, but if you want to bring her along you're more than welcome. Just let me know for sure, cos of the seating plan and all that shite,' continued Tony.

'Cheers Tone, we'll both be there. Although it may be bit awkward, me knowing that you've seen her tits,' he said, with all the bravado he could muster.

'To be honest mate, I was so pissed; I don't recall much about it.'

'OK, sound. Is your friend Paul going?' asked Razor casually.

'You mean my boss, Paul?'

# SCREWED

'Boss?'

'Yeah, Paul's the chief super. Why do you ask?'

'No reason, just thought he was a good laugh that's all,' said Razor, changing the subject.

Half an hour later Tony left, and Razor decided to call it a night. He texted Deborah, telling her about the wedding a week on Saturday and then fell asleep in front of the television.

SCREWED

# CHAPTER SIXTEEN

Brian Barber was in a foul mood. He'd had a blazing row with his wife, and it had made him late for work. He figured that if he cut through the new Pickwood Park housing estate, he'd avoid the town centre and shave a few minutes off his journey. What he didn't realise was that since the builder had finished the development, the council had installed speed bumps on every road through the estate, so now he'd be even later.

'Come on Katie, your dentist appointment is in ten minutes.'

Mr Jones was stood by the car waiting for her to leave the house. He was planning to take her to the dentists then nip into town to buy his wife a gift for her up-and-coming birthday. He'd promised Katie that if she helped him choose a gift, she could have the whole day off school. So when she finally came out of the front door, she was dressed casually, but wearing a full face of make-up. Mr Jones shook his head.

Brian Barber had slowed to ten miles per hour in anticipation of the next speed bump. He glanced casually to his right. Jesus Christ. Coming out of one of the big detached houses was that tart from

# SCREWED

Yates's, who'd got him to buy her and her friends a drink then blanked him.

Brian buzzed down his window and shouted, 'You cheap fucking slut,' before accelerating off feeling pleased with himself.

'Was that him, that Dunford lad?' demanded Mr Jones.

Katie had caught a fleeting glance of the driver and instantly recognised him as the guy from Yates's, but she wasn't about to explain that one to her dad on top of everything else. So she simply got into the car and slammed the door. Mr Jones decided that he wouldn't push the issue with her, but he made up his mind to report the incident to the police.

PC Ryan approached Sergeant Duffield's desk.

'We've got the Dunford lad answering his bail this afternoon, Sarge. Are you going to caution him?'

The sergeant looked up from the file he was reading. The statements from Katie Jones and Matthew Dunford matched almost word for word. The sergeant thought they were both telling the truth and the girl's age had never come up. She'd willingly gone back to his house, and the sex had been consensual. That said, she was still only fifteen and that made it an offence. Weighing up

## SCREWED

all the facts, the sergeant had decided the best course of action would be a caution. He was just about to sign the paperwork when the phone on his desk buzzed. He picked it up and listened for a couple of minutes before putting it down and looking at Ryan.

'That was Mr Jones on the phone. Turns out Dunford has just driven past their house shouting abuse at his daughter. He wants to press full charges, and on top of that, it puts Dunford in breach of his bail conditions.'

PC Ryan was taken aback. He genuinely didn't think Dunford was like that.

'That means we're going have to charge him with sex with a minor and breach of bail,' Sergeant Duffield said grimly.

Matthew Dunford walked into Doncaster police station at five minutes to three, convinced that he'd be leaving with a caution, then he could put this nightmare behind him. By ten minutes past three, however, he had been rearrested, charged and was on his way to the holding cells, ready for an appearance at Doncaster Magistrates' Court at 10.00 a.m. the following morning.

## CHAPTER SEVENTEEN

Razor awoke early Friday morning feeling a little down, but not as bad as he sometimes did. He'd only had three pints and one line of party powder. By only having one line he had proved to himself that he was in control, only losers became addicts. He glanced down at his phone to see that he had received a text message. It was from Deborah and read:

*Wedding sounds fun. How about lunch on Sat? D. x.*

*Lunch is good for me*, he immediately texted back.

*I'll pick you up at one. D x*, she replied.

Razor pulled into his usual space at work at three thirty, Friday afternoon, ready for his 4.00 p.m. start. As he got out of his car, he saw Lucy walking towards him.

'Hey, Lucy. How ya doing?'

'Good thanks. Listen, Gilly, I need a favour.'

Lucy explained that it was her friend's birthday that evening and her jealous boyfriend was insisting on picking her up at one to take her home. If she finished work at midnight, she'd barely have time for one drink, so she wanted Razor to cover for her so she could leave work early.

# SCREWED

'No one would notice. They didn't know when you left early, did they?' she added, giving a winning smile.

Razor said it wouldn't be a problem so long as he could bunk off early the following night. This arrangement suited both of them, and after all, what harm was there? All the cons were safely locked away by 6.00 p.m.

Lucy and Razor walked on to wing 1A at five minutes to four to relieve Dave and Martin from their shift. It was all quiet on the wing as all the prisoners were locked away for afternoon bang up. They signed the log and noted down the time of their shift start. Martin and Dave repeated the process, noting down their departure time.

'Anything to tell us?' asked Lucy.

'Yeah, we've got a new boy in 308. Ridgley, a small-time dealer who thinks he's Al Capone. So keep an eye on him,' replied Martin.

Four thirty on the dot, Razor and Lucy began unlocking the doors for feeding time. They had to open each cell, wait for the prisoners to vacate, then relock the door to prevent anyone else entering the cell. It was twenty minutes before they returned to their table and the newspapers that they knew would be left behind by the last shift. It was the general opinion of the staff on 1A that the pay wasn't good enough to deal with the

# SCREWED

lowlifes who resided there. The consensus was that so long as they only fought amongst themselves, the staff were happy.

The chaotic scrum quickly formed around the serving hatch, as the prisoners pushed and shoved each other to get their food. Lucy gave Razor a nudge and nodded towards cell 308. A prisoner had just walked out wearing a red dressing gown and flip-flops. He failed to shut his door, as was required, and left it wide open.

'308 close your door,' shouted Lucy.

The prisoner glared at Lucy, then turned and slammed his door to. He then walked toward the servery and three other YO prisoners fell in line behind him. YOs, or young offenders, were prisoners between the ages of eighteen and twenty-one and were a pain in the arse. Officially, young offenders were under the age of eighteen but in some prisons, prisoners were classed as YOs up until the age of twenty-one. The four walked straight past the queue and thrust their plates at the guy serving the meals. They came away with plates piled high with food. Razor looked up, shook his head and returned to the back page of *The Sun*. The four sat at a table on their own. Red dressing gown said something while looking over at Lucy and Razor, the clan

## SCREWED

high-fived and burst into laughter. Razor checked his watch, four fifty.

'Ten minutes to bang up,' he bellowed.

By ten past five everyone was locked back in their cells, and all was quiet. Now for the next six hours, from 6.00 p.m. onwards, all they had to do were the cell checks every two hours. The cell check consisted of the officer opening the flap in the cell door and looking in to check that a prisoner hadn't harmed himself or his cellmate. However the two-hour intervals were often ignored, and in reality, during the six-hour period, the officers would only check twice. They decided that, as with last time, they would adhere strictly to the rules and do the required three checks. Razor would do the 8.00 p.m. check, Lucy the 10.00 p.m. and then Razor the final one just before midnight. While one was checking the cells, the other would remain sat at the officers' desk. The reason for this was simple; the CCTV cameras had a blind spot where the officers' desk sat. So if anyone happened to replay the tape, they would see one person cell checking on an alternate basis, it could then be explained that the other person was sitting at the officers' desk.

Lucy carried out her cell check a few minutes before ten then signed herself out on the log, stating the time as midnight. She then left to get to the party. Razor did the final check at

# SCREWED

eleven forty-five. Most of the prisoners were asleep with lights off. At exactly midnight, the door to the wing swung open and the twelve till eight came on to take over. Midnight until eight was the graveyard shift and the staff rarely had contact with any prisoners, normally these were the rookies who were new to the job or those who just wanted a quiet life. Razor glanced up from his paper to see who was working tonight.

'Evening Gilly.'

'Alright Steve. How's it going?'

Steve had worked at the prison since it opened nearly twenty years ago. He was ex-military and was approaching his sixty-fifth birthday. He'd worked the graveyard shift for the past five years. At his age, he'd no desire to mix with prisoners.

'All good. Where's Lucy tonight?' replied Steve.

'You've just missed her. Her boyfriend was picking her up, and she wanted to get out bang on time. You know what he's like,' explained Razor.

'Don't know why she stays with him. I'd be happy to keep her warm at night,' grinned Steve.

'You dirty old goat. Anyway, who's your new mate?' asked Razor, nodding his head towards the young guy stood just behind Steve. 'Have you noticed that they never leave you alone

# SCREWED

with a young woman?' continued Razor, to which Steve gave a hearty laugh.

'This is Pete. Pete meet Gilly. It's his first night.'

'Still time to change your mind, you know,' said Razor as he shook Pete's hand.

They exchanged banter for the next few minutes, before Razor left for the night. Razor toyed with the idea of stopping for a few pints on the way home, but decided against it, as he planned to have a big night tomorrow.

Steve pointed to where the tea and coffee were kept then, leaving Pete to make the drinks, he picked up his novel.

'So, what exactly do we do, Steve?' asked Pete, placing two steaming mugs of coffee on the desk.

'Nothing really, drink coffee, read, sleep if you want. Then at two, four and six we do a cell check.'

'Cell check?' said Pete, sounding concerned. He imagined that he might have to go inside the cells during the night.

'Relax, it's nothing major. Just open that little flap on the door and have a peek to see that they haven't hung themselves. Then at eight, we're out of here before anyone is even unlocked. Proper cushy this son and we get paid the same as the poor sods who have to break up the fights and have piss thrown at them.'

'Don't get why it takes two of us though.'

'Health and safety son. Plus, if I was on my own, I may decide to go into one of those cells and dish out a beating or two.'

Pete couldn't work out if Steve was serious or not. He finished his coffee and picked up a newspaper that was lying on the desk. He read a few articles then checked his watch, twelve forty-five; this was going to be a long night.

*Bang, bang*. Pete physically jumped and looked to where the sounds were coming. The sound came again; it was coming from a cell on the top landing. He looked at Steve, whose eyes hadn't moved from his book.

'Just some dickhead kicking his door. Ignore him, he'll soon get bored,' explained Steve, giving a yawn.

*Bang, bang* again.

'Shut the fuck up,' a voice boomed from behind another door.

All went quiet, then five minutes later it started again. *Bang, bang, bang*. Pete looked up to see the small, red light outside cell 308 was illuminated. The door was also moving slightly with each bang.

'Steve, the call light is on at 308.'

# SCREWED

'If you want to waste your time going up there then be my guest. But I've got better things to do.'

Pete got out of his seat, walked across the wing and ascended the metal staircase to the top landing. He opened the flap in the door at cell 308 and jumped backward. There was a face pressed up against the window behind the flap. Pete composed himself and stepped back towards to the door.

'What's the matter?' asked Pete.

'Fuck you,' replied Ridgley, before laughing and jumping back on to his bunk.

Pete reset the light and returned to the desk.

'It's all a game, Pete. You've got to just ignore them.'

All remained quiet, then at 2.00 a.m. Steve put down his novel.

'Come on then Pete, time we did a bit. Cell check time; then it's your turn again to make the coffees.'

They walked around the cells on the bottom landing first, flipping open the flaps for a quick glance. They repeated the process on the top landing that was until they reached cell 308. Steve gave Pete a sly grin, then took a small torch from his belt. He then opened the flap and shone it into the cell. The intense LED light lit up the

## SCREWED

tiny cell like Blackpool. Steve then proceeded to wave it up and down, causing Ridgley, who'd obviously been asleep, to wake and lift his head.

Steve then moved his mouth to the gap at the side of the cell door and growled, 'Fuck you!' He then slammed the flap closed. He winked at Pete and said, 'We'll do that again at four and six; then tomorrow he'll be quiet as a mouse. All a game, son, all a game.'

## CHAPTER EIGHTEEN

Matthew Dunford sat nervously next to the duty solicitor in the waiting area outside court three at Doncaster Magistrates.

'It's OK Matthew, this is just a formality. You'll be back home by lunchtime,' said the solicitor in a reassuring tone.

Matthew wasn't convinced; he still couldn't understand how he'd ended up in this position. He glanced over to the seats on the opposite side of the room. A man and woman, both wearing shell suits, were having a heated argument. It was apparent they were both under the influence of either drugs or alcohol. Matthew watched them for a few minutes until the court usher appeared and called his name.

Matthew was guided into the dock, where he stood taking in his surroundings. The courtroom was traditional and in Matthew's opinion, old-fashioned, exactly like he'd seen many times on the television.

The clerk of the court stood and, facing Matthew, said, 'Please state your full name.'

'Matthew Andrew Dunford.'

Matthew then gave his address, occupation and date of birth.

# SCREWED

'M'lord, the defendant is charged with sex with a minor, contrary to common law,' began the prosecuting solicitor in a clipped tone.

'How does the defendant plead? Guilty or not guilty?'

Matthew glanced at his solicitor, then in a timid tone replied, 'Not guilty.'

The judge scribbled a note on his pad and then announced, 'This case will now be passed to the Crown Court for trial. The Crown Court will convene in thirty days from today, which I make to be the twenty-fourth of October. Any objections to bail?' said the judge.

'Yes, M'lord,' began the prosecution's solicitor, as he got to his feet.

The judge raised an eyebrow and stared expectantly at the solicitor.

'On the twenty-third of this month, the defendant breached his bail conditions by driving past the victim's property and shouting obscenities. We therefore request denial of bail,' he continued.

The duty solicitor allocated to Dunford stood.

'M'lord, my client categorically denies this allegation.'

'Of course he does. Bail denied. The defendant shall be remanded in custody until the twenty-fourth of October,' snapped the judge and banged his gavel.

SCREWED

# CHAPTER NINETEEN

Razor slammed the front door behind him at 1.00 p.m. Standing on the kerbside, he looked impatiently up and down the street. A Range Rover Evoque turned and drove up the road; it was black with a red roof and made him think of Deborah's Louboutin shoes. Admiring the vehicle, Razor thought that if he ever had a spare forty grand he'd buy one in an instant. The sun was hitting the windscreen, making it appear golden in colour, and obscuring the view of the driver. The Evoque then came to a standstill in front of him, and a black, tinted window buzzed down.

'Hey sexy, want a lift?' grinned Deborah from behind the wheel.

'Wow, is this yours?' said Razor, surprised to see her driving a car like this. He jumped in and leant over for a kiss.

'No, I just nicked it. Course it's mine, you dope. I picked it up this morning.'

'No way. How much?'

'The bargain price of forty-two, fully loaded. Buy me lunch, and I'll let you drive it back.'

'Deal,' said Razor, grinning like kid on Christmas morning.

# SCREWED

They had a long lunch at a country pub overlooking the River Don on the outskirts of Doncaster. The food was good, and the conversation flowed. It struck Razor that this was the first time since they'd met that they weren't either drunk, high, or recovering from the aforementioned.

'This is pleasant, Razor. Do you think we're partying too hard during the weekends?' she asked, looking into his eyes.

'It's only Saturday nights,' he said dismissively.

'It was Tuesday night too, remember.'

'That was a one-off. I can take it,' he said, trying to play it down.

'Well if you're sure Razor, but just be careful. OK?'

'What do you mean?' he asked, surprised at the change in conversation.

'Look. Ish and Johnny, I love them both to pieces, but they're not people like you, and I just worry that's all.'

'I am a big boy. No need to worry about me.' He leaned over and kissed her.

She smiled at him, giving him a knowing look and said, 'How about we christen my new car?'

# SCREWED

As promised, Razor drove the Evoque to the prison. Getting to drive the vehicle was worth the walk home after his shift, which he was due to start at four. It did feel amazing, rolling up in a car like this. He was enjoying the envious looks he was getting from the other staff arriving for work. As he pulled into his space, he spotted Lucy getting out of her car. Razor jumped out of the driver's side, allowing Deborah to get back behind the wheel. She gave him a quick kiss, and then sped off out of the car park. Razor noticed Lucy staring, so walked over to her.

'I can see why you want to rush off on Saturday nights, Gilly,' she said with a hint of envy in her voice.

'Speaking of which Lucy...'

'Yeah, yeah. I'll cover for you.'

'Cheers Lucy. Eleven will do, it's only an hour. Anyway, how was your night?'

'I was having a blinder till one of my friends took me to one side and said she'd heard rumours about Greg. She reckons he's having a fucking affair.'

'Yeah?'

'Oh, I had him about it alright when he picked me up.'

'What did he say?'

## SCREWED

'Denied it, of course. Then things turned quite nasty,' she said, rolling up her sleeve and showing him the marks on her arm.

'Jesus Lucy, you can't let him do that. You need to get shut,' he said, feeling sorry for her.

'I'm going to try and catch him out next Friday. If you cover for me, I want to slip off a couple of hours early and see exactly what he's up to.'

'Course I will. But what he's done just ain't right. Now come on, let's get inside.'

The shift was relatively uneventful apart from a scuffle involving Ridgley, or Beef as he was referred to by his fellow gang members. It was over as quickly as it began and, as a result, there was no need for any intervention from Razor or Lucy. Not that Razor liked to get involved, he was more than happy to look the other way while the prisoners knocked lumps out of each other. After bang up, they followed the same routine as the previous evening, but this time it was Razor's turn to bunk off early.

'Have fun stud and see you Monday,' called Lucy, as Razor left the wing at ten thirty.

Steve and Pete were on again and arrived on the wing a couple of minutes before midnight.

# SCREWED

'Evening, Luce. Missed you last night. This is the new boy, Pete.'

Pete's eyes widened as he took Lucy's hand and shook it. She took the opportunity to chat to Pete about the job for a few minutes, thus avoiding any talk of her absence last night.

'Gilly's just shot off to the gents. He looked a little peaky,' she explained with as much sincerity as she could muster.

Steve eyed her, then simply picked up the clipboard and signed the log.

'Pete, run down to the toilets and see if Gilly's OK,' instructed Steve.

Lucy visibly paled. Pete hesitated, wondering about the exchange.

'Now son,' said Steve sternly.

Pete promptly left the wing in search of Gilly.

'Are you going to tell me what's going on Lucy?' asked Steve.

'Nothing. I'm sure Pete will find him throwing up in the bogs or something,' she said unconvincingly.

'Look, Lucy, I ain't stupid. I've done this job for twenty years. We both know Pete won't find Gilly.'

Lucy stared down at the floor sheepishly.

'I know the score. But be careful, Lucy. I won't be doing this again,' said Steve, as he signed

# SCREWED

Gilly's name and wrote 12:05 in the blank space on the register.

Lucy was unable to meet Steve's eyes as she silently cursed Gilly for forgetting to sign out.

'If anything happens, you'll both be in serious shit,' warned Steve.

'No sign of him in the bogs. He must have got straight off,' said a breathless Pete, as he came back on to the wing.

'Not to worry. I'm sure he'll be fine,' replied Steve. 'Here, don't forget to sign in,' he continued, handing Pete the clipboard and giving Lucy a brief stare.

Feeling chastised, Lucy left the wing telling herself that once she'd caught her cheating boyfriend next week, she was going to play strictly by the book, no more covering for Gilly and no more sneaking off early. They'd got away with it for too long now and she couldn't believe he'd forgotten to sign out, he was getting sloppy.

Razor arrived home, showered, changed and grabbed his wallet. He was just about to walk out of the door when he remembered the envelope that Claudio had given to him; he'd meant to look at it all week. Deciding there was no time like the present, he went back to his bedroom and opened the envelope. Inside were two sheets of paper. The

# SCREWED

first listed all the establishments where the VIP card was valid. Reading down the list, he counted fifteen places where the card could be used. Surely Johnny didn't own them all? There were also extensive details of the privileges that were available to VIP members. Razor was quite impressed by what he'd read so far and turned to read the second sheet. This one was entitled 'Account Details' and contained his account number, along with login details so that members could monitor their accounts online. He made a mental note to check out the state of the account after the weekend. Attached to the bottom of the sheet was his very own shiny, gold VIP card. He held the card for a brief moment, feeling like he finally was someone. He slipped the card into his wallet and headed out.

Razor left his Vauxhall Astra in the hotel car park. Driving his car was a disappointing experience compared to being behind the wheel of Deborah's Evoque. He called a taxi and ten minutes later, was walking towards the VIP entrance of the Living Room bar in Leeds' city centre. He nodded to the doormen, but instead of heading to their usual booth, he went in search of Claudio. In his haste to get out of the house, he'd left his silver vial on the side. He'd already topped it up with the stuff he'd bought from Ish and was

## SCREWED

now feeling gutted that he'd forgotten it. It didn't take him long to find Claudio, at the end of the bar, dishing out some stern words to a young waitress. Upon seeing Razor, his demeanour changed and he broke into a welcoming smile. He adjusted his dicky bow and moved to join Razor.

'Good to see you, Mr Razor. I trust you enjoyed the party on Tuesday evening.'

'Yeah, cracking night and I've told you before, it's just Razor, drop the mister.'

'Of course, if that's what sir prefers. Now, what can I do for you tonight?' asked Claudio, turning to business.

'Bolly of course.'

'Anything else?' prompted Claudio.

'Actually, I left home without my...'

Razor hesitated, and Claudio instantly saved him the embarrassment of finishing the sentence by saying, 'Of course. But allow me to get it before you go to your booth.'

'No rush, just bring it along with the champagne,' said Razor casually.

'I think it may be wise if I get it for you now, Mr Razor.'

'Why's that, Claudio?' Razor asked, genuinely intrigued.

'Because you have a guest waiting for you, my dear man,' he explained, before disappearing through a door marked private.

# SCREWED

Less than a minute later, he swept back through the door and handed Razor a shiny silver vial.

'Now don't keep your guest waiting any longer. I'll send the champagne over.'

Razor thanked him and headed directly to the booth. As he approached, he could make someone out, sitting at the far end, looking out on to the dance floor. He slid into the booth next to the current occupant who immediately broke into a huge grin. His teeth appeared to glow in the dim light.

'Ish, how's it going?' said Razor surprised.

'Good man. Real good,' he replied.

'I wasn't expecting to see you so soon. You did say the end of the month for that cash?'

Ish pulled a face, trying to look hurt.

'This is social, Razor man. I was in da area and wanted to look at some hotties. So I thought I'd call in here and have a drink with my new friend,' he said, putting a hand on Razor's shoulder.

Razor noticed that Ish didn't have a drink but, as if on cue, Razor's Bollinger arrived with two glasses. It was served by a waitress in her early thirties with a massive cleavage, long legs, but a little too much make-up. Ish was watching her every move as she uncorked the bottle and poured. As she handed him his glass, Ish leant forward and whispered something in her ear. The waitress giggled like a schoolgirl then was gone.

'I love da older totty, innit.'

'Cheers Ish. Great to see you,' said Razor, holding up his glass.

Ish clinked glasses before draining the lot.

'I love this shit. You've got good taste, Razor man.'

Ish then eyed Razor for a moment, as if weighing up what to say. Razor felt a wave of uneasiness wash over him. After a few uncomfortable seconds, Razor retrieved the vial from his pocket.

'How about a livener, Ish?' Razor asked, trying to lighten the atmosphere.

The look on Ish's face changed again, from cold to friendly, as a wide grin spread across it. Razor tapped a pile of party powder on to the back of his hand and snorted it, then passed the vial to Ish, who tapped out a thick line on to the table and, using a crisp fifty, took in the lot in one long snort. He then tapped out another line for his other nostril. Razor watched in horror, thinking that at least fifty quid had just disappeared up Ishmael's nose. With a big smile, he handed the vial back to Razor.

'You haven't used all that stuff you bought off me, have you Razor man? That's some serious going man,' laughed Ish.

# SCREWED

Razor was momentarily confused then realised that Ish could tell the difference between the stuff he sold and the stuff that he'd just snorted seconds before.

'God no. Left the house in a hurry and forgot it,' laughed Razor.

Chill, Razor man. You don't have to explain yourself to me. It's all cool.'

Ish picked up his glass, drained it, then helped himself to a top-up.

'So you mentioned on Tuesday that you work at Doncatraz.'

Razor didn't recall saying anything to Ish about where he worked. His mind suddenly whipped back to Deborah's warning, or was he just being paranoid?

'I've got a mate in there, a real good friend.' Ish's face was very serious again. 'Maybe you know him,' he continued.

Not sure where this conversation was going, he replied quickly, 'It's a big jail, Ish. Nearly twelve hundred inmates.'

'Twelve hundred eh? That's a lot of nasty men in one place. Anyway, time for me to find a hottie,' said Ish all smiles again, before holding out his fist.

Ish then melted away into the crowd. Razor took a large gulp of champagne, wondering what all that was about. He was lost in thought when Deborah flopped down beside him.

After kissing him, she nodded at the empty glass and asked, 'You had company, Razor?'

'Yeah. Ish of all people,' he replied.

'Ish? What did he want?'

'Nothing. Said he was just on the lookout for hotties and decided to call in here for a drink.'

Deborah just nodded, and Razor noticed that she looked a little preoccupied.

'You OK?' he asked.

'Fine. Just a long night, that's all. Had a bunch of drunken dickheads in.'

Razor decided that it wasn't the best time to ask how Ish may have known where he worked. Instead, he waved over the waitress and requested a clean champagne flute for Deborah.

SCREWED

# CHAPTER TWENTY

'Welcome to Doncatraz,' sneered the screw.

The processing of Matthew Dunford into HMP Doncaster was slow and laborious. As he wasn't expecting to be going to prison, Matthew had no belongings with him. The only thing in his possession was the charge sheet given to him at Doncaster police station the previous day. He was issued with prison clothing and taken to a cell on induction wing 1D. Matthew looked around the small cell and felt sick to the pit of his stomach. How had he ended up in here? Matthew threw his charge sheet on to the metal table, collapsed on to the bottom bunk and cried himself to sleep. He awoke sometime later to the sound of the cell door opening. He wasn't sure of the time, but there was no longer any daylight coming through the tiny, barred window. Another prisoner got ushered into the small, cramped cell. The guard tossed two plastic bags on to the desk containing a carton of milk and some cereal.

'How's it going man? I'm Bonzo innit,' said the young, black guy as he held out a clenched fist by way of a greeting.

Matthew just stared at him then turned over; he didn't want to talk to anyone. Bonzo shrugged, then jumped on to the top bunk and turned on the TV.

# SCREWED

Ten thirty the next morning the cell door swung open.

'Get your shit together gents; you'll be moving in twenty minutes.'

Matthew didn't move, he had nothing to get together. Bonzo jumped down from his bunk. He'd known full well where he was coming to and had packed accordingly.

Looking at the unmoving figure on the bottom bunk, he asked, 'You want your cereal man?'

'Take it,' came a weak reply.

Bonzo sat at the desk, ate both packs of cornflakes, and then rolled a cigarette. As he took a deep pull on the roll-up, his eyes settled on the single sheet of paper that lay on the desk. Name, address, arresting office and details of charge; 'Sex with a minor contrary to common law'. It was all there in black and white. Shit, he was in a cell with a nonce, a fucking kiddie fiddler. This made Bonzo feel sick to the pit of his stomach. The heavy lock slid back, and the door abruptly opened.

'Come on gents, we're off to 1A.'

Bonzo grabbed his large plastic bag and left the cell. Matthew got off the bunk and followed him. As there were no double cells available, Bonzo was doubled up with a fellow smoker, who was currently in hospital, leaving Bonzo with the double cell to himself, while Matthew ended up in a single on his own. Single cells were considered a privilege, so this would only be a temporary measure.

At eleven thirty Matthew's cell door was opened for lunch. He didn't realise it was lunchtime until he'd noticed other prisoners walking past carrying their plates. Realising that he hadn't eaten for more than twenty-four hours, he slowly walked over to the scrum of men at the serving hatch and waited patiently. He felt isolated and intimidated as he was pushed and shoved. He was about to turn and go back to his cell, when he spotted the black guy who he'd shared the cell with the night before. Seeing a familiar face made him feel more comfortable, so Matthew gave him a nod and was planning to sit with him and eat his lunch.

'Don't look at me you fucking paedo,' he hissed and barged past him. Luckily for Matthew no one else in the noisy queue heard what Bonzo had said. Matthew's appetite suddenly left him, and he trudged back to his cell door.

SCREWED

# CHAPTER TWENTY-ONE

Razor and Lucy began their shift at 4.00 p.m. Friday afternoon.

'You OK, Gilly? Not coming down with a cold?' asked Lucy, as they walked on to the wing.

'Just a sniffle, Luce.'

The truth was that Razor had been out with Deborah the night before and hadn't made it to bed until gone six that morning. He'd not risen until just over an hour ago and had taken a little snort of dancing dust to pick him up. This evening shift was going to be his last for two days, as he'd got Tony's wedding tomorrow and he'd booked the following day off as well. They signed in as Dave and Martin signed out.

'Anything happening?' Razor asked.

'Two newbies on today. One's in 312 with Turner. He's a drug dealer.'

'Isn't Turner in the hospital?

'Yeah, another few weeks apparently. Poor old bastard's in a bad way.'

'And who's the other?'

'He's in 311. He's a non-smoker, so I had to stick him in the single. He's on remand for a month,' explained Martin.

'And he's a wrong'un,' added Dave in disgust.

# SCREWED

'Why isn't the dirty bastard on 3A with the other nonces?' asked Lucy.

'No room,' replied Martin.

'Word's not out yet either, but keep an eye on him,' said Dave.

'Yeah, imagine the paperwork if he gets lynched in the showers,' added Razor.

Dave and Martin then left the wing, while Razor made the coffees before the four thirty unlock.

At four thirty Lucy began opening the cells on the first landing, while Razor took the top. He undid the door to cell 308. Just as he put his key into 309, he heard a voice behind him.

'Afternoon Razor.'

Razor froze. No one in prison called him Razor. He'd always been Gilly; it was Deborah who'd first called him Razor and only people in her circle knew that. He turned around and came face-to-face with Ridgley, or Beef as he liked to be known.

'We have a friend in common innit,' said Beef with a wink.

Razor stood motionless for a moment. Then it hit him, Ishmael. That's who he must have been referring to on Saturday night. A feeling of foreboding spread over Razor, and he wished he hadn't snorted that line before coming into work.

# SCREWED

Coke was great in a party atmosphere but now, in this environment, it was making him feel edgy and paranoid.

Cell 311 was the last to be unlocked and by the time Matthew had got downstairs the queue for the servery had died down. A prisoner slopped the food on to his plate; then he made his way to an empty table. Matthew didn't notice a foot shoot out from a table as he passed by and he tripped, falling face down, his food hitting the floor.

'Fucking nonce,' someone shouted.

'Shit Lucy, let's go,' shouted Razor, running to where Dunford lay.

Food was now being thrown at him as he lay on the floor. Four other prisoners were now on their feet and were clambering over tables to get to him. Other cons were banging the tables and chanting 'Kill the nonce'.

One of the four prisoners managed to get to Matthew before Razor could and placed a hard kick to his ribs. Razor managed to drag Matthew to his feet; Lucy was now at his side.

'Get the fuck back,' she snarled.

Razor reluctantly dragged Matthew up the stairs and roughly threw him into his cell. In all honestly, he wished he could have left Dunford to the mob.

# SCREWED

'You'll be on the nonce wing tomorrow with your own kind,' snapped Razor, before locking the door.

'I've done nothing wrong. I'm not a fucking nonce!' screamed Matthew at the closed door.

The wing was extra noisy after the little kick off so at four fifty, ten minutes early, Razor and Lucy began locking everyone away. One or two prisoners on the top landing had gone to Matthew's door and were banging on it and shouting threats. After ten minutes everyone was locked away and the noise level had returned to normal. Razor put in a radio call to 3A, the nonce wing, to see if they could take another prisoner that evening. Unfortunately, due to staffing problems on 3A, they wouldn't be able to take Matthew until 9.00 a.m. the next day. Razor then filled out a report form. He'd let Steve know about the prisoner at the shift change at midnight.

'Why didn't they just wait until the kiddie-fiddling bastard was in the shower? They would of have had a good few minutes with him then and it would be off camera.'

'Good question that Lucy. Suppose they just couldn't wait.'

'I just don't get why they keep trying to mix them in on regular wings and causing us more shit,' said Lucy.

# SCREWED

'Problem is there are more nonces than places on the nonce wing. Make us a coffee Lucy, it's your turn.'

Before Lucy had finished making the coffees the banging started, followed by shouts of 'Kill the paedo'. The shouting went on for about an hour, until the prisoners got bored and returned to their TV sets.

'You still sneaking off early tonight?' asked Razor.

'Yeah, if you're still OK with it. But I think we need to calm it down a bit then. Steve has sussed out what we've been up to.'

'It's fine with me. But you're right, we shouldn't push our luck. Do you really think Greg is cheating on you?'

'I wouldn't put it past him.'

At 9.00 p.m., three hours early, Lucy left the prison and headed home to hopefully catch her boyfriend in the middle of some extracurricular activity. Razor carried out the cell check just before 10.00 p.m. Everything was quiet and in order. His mind kept returning to Ridgley and the look in his eyes during their brief exchange. He made up his mind that he'd square Ish up then have nothing more to do with him. Razor checked his watch, eleven forty-five. A quick cell check then it would be time for Steve and Pete to come

## SCREWED

on at midnight. He checked the bottom landing first then moved up to the top. He started at cell 311. Razor opened the flap and looked in. Holy shit, Dunford was practically lying on the floor with his head tilting toward the door and eyes his bulging. He had rolled up his bed sheet to form a makeshift rope, then tied one end to the bed's metal frame and the other end around his neck. By lying on the floor, the weight of his body had caused the sheet to choke him.

*What the fuck should I do?* he nearly said out loud.

He knew the procedure, but self-preservation was kicking in, and he could only think about saving his own skin. He'd taken cocaine before his shift and knew that prison officers were automatically tested for drugs and alcohol after any major incident. A drug test would end his career, and Lucy's absence would also be discovered, thus ending both their careers, all because of this worthless nonce. Razor tried to gather his thoughts; he knew he had to move. Suddenly Matthew's eyes flickered, fuck he wasn't dead. If he opened the door, he could untie the sheet and save his life, but in doing so, he'd screw himself and Lucy. Razor stood watching for a few seconds longer when Matthew's eyes suddenly closed. Razor strained to see his chest, no movement; he wasn't breathing. Fuck him.

# SCREWED

Next door in cell 312, Bonzo lay awake on his bunk staring up at the ceiling. He'd heard heavy boots walking down the corridor as the cell checks were getting performed. The boots had come to a sudden stop, and now there was only silence. It was at least a minute before the boots started to move again. Bonzo racked his brains wondering what the screw could have been doing for all that time. He'd have to keep his ear to the ground, sometimes the smallest of things could be used to one's advantage.

Razor finished the cell check and returned to the desk. He slumped down shaking like a leaf. He desperately wanted some party powder, just to calm his nerves. Razor subconsciously ran a hand over his forehead, when he looked down at it he noticed it was soaked with sweat. The wing door opened and in walked Steve, closely followed by Pete.

'Evening, Gilly. Have I missed Lucy again?'

'Yeah, Steve she's just...'

'Don't bother,' said Steve curtly, cutting him off.

'I know the script Steve, and this is the last time, OK? We've both had a few things that needed sorting.'

## SCREWED

'I'll keep the favour in the bank. At least Lucy remembers to sign out,' said Steve, his voice softening.

'Oh yeah, before I forget, we've got a wrong'un in 311. We had a bit of aggro earlier. I've tried 3A, but they're full till morning. Just give them a buzz first thing, and they'll take him. I've done the paperwork. Now I'm off for the weekend, so I'll see you two on Monday night.'

Razor moved towards the door then turned.

'I did the cell check about ten minutes ago, so you're good for a while.'

He needed to get out of the prison; he wanted to run. What the hell had just happened? He'd watched a man die. Jesus Christ. He snatched his coat from his locker and left; he needed to be the other side of the prison walls as soon as possible. Razor jumped into his car and raced out of the car park. He was shaking again; he needed a drink. No, he needed more than drink. Luckily, he'd put his silver vial in the glovebox of his car 'just in case'. He pulled over and tapped out a small pile on to the back of his trembling hand and snorted greedily. The cocaine hit the brain instantly, now he needed that drink.

He headed straight to a pub that he knew served until 2.00 a.m. Razor was relieved to find the bar wasn't particularly busy, so he got served immediately. He ordered a pint and large vodka,

## SCREWED

no ice, no mixer, and downed it in one. As the fiery liquid slid down his throat and into his bloodstream, he felt his nerves begin to steady. He fished out his mobile and keyed a text to Lucy.

*I need to talk to you. Call me urgently.*

Twenty minutes later, Lucy was sat opposite him in the corner of the bar. She'd called him more or less as soon as he'd sent the message. Lucy had been in floods of tears and asked where he was, but not what it was he wanted. She'd only said she was on her way. From the minute Lucy had met him in the bar, she hadn't stopped crying. She explained how she'd arrived home to find her boyfriend in bed with another woman. Lucy had thrown them both out of the house then spent the following two hours bagging all of his belongings into bin bags and dumping them outside on the front lawn. Finally, the penny dropped, and she remembered that it was Razor who'd texted her.

'Razor, I'm so sorry. I've been going on and on about that tosser. Is everything OK?'

'That nonce, Dunford. He's dead, Luce,' he said, panic rising again.

A look of absolute fear spread across Lucy's face. Her career would be over at the very least, and she could end up facing criminal charges. Her eyes began to well up, and then she started to cry hysterically.

# SCREWED

'Lucy, calm down,' he said taking her hand.

'But how? Did someone get to him? Or was it an accident?' she sniffled.

'He committed suicide, Luce.'

'But what about security and medics, what did they do?'

'Do you really think I'd be sat here if anyone knew? I'd be stuck in there for hours doing the paperwork,' he continued.

Now the reality began to dawn on her. Razor had saved her skin. She breathed a huge sigh of relief.

'So how are we going to play this?' she asked.

'As I see it, Dunford will be found by either Steve or Pete. It will go on the record as happening on their watch. I doubt that anyone will even be arsed to speak us.'

They spent a good half hour discussing their version of events in the unlikelihood of anyone asking.

'Just one thing bothers me, Gilly. Steve.'

'What about him?'

'Well, he knows we've been sneaking off early. So what if he suspects something?'

'I can't see why he would. I told him I'd done the cell check at ten to twelve, so why would he doubt me?'

# SCREWED

'I can't believe you're willing to do all this for me, Gilly. I can't thank you enough. I owe you big time,' she said feeling relieved, yet flattered by his loyalty and the fact that he was willing to put his neck on the line for her.

Razor felt a pang of guilt for allowing Lucy to believe that his motives were purely selfless, but didn't dwell on it. His actions would, after all, save both their skins.

# SCREWED

# CHAPTER TWENTY-TWO

Steve was engrossed in a novel as usual, while Pete sat beside him lost in thought. He had guessed that the two officers from the previous shift were taking it in turns to bunk off early and it didn't sit well with him. Pete was debating whether or not to broach the subject with Steve. All thoughts left his mind when Steve announced that he was at a crucial point so told him to toddle off and do the 2.00 a.m. cell checks on his own.

Pete relished the task and was taking his time to look into each cell, as opposed to the quick glance that he'd seen Steve do. He'd already read the paper cover to cover, and there were another six hours until shift change. Pete saw this as a way to pass the time; maybe Steve would let him do all the cell checks on his own from now on. He had to admit that having the opportunity to peek into each cell fascinated him. Each cell varied, some were kitted out with all manner of things, from curtains fashioned out of bed sheets, tablecloths on the desks and bookshelves piled high with books and files, whereas others were very basic. Maybe the cells represented how these men lived on the outside. Pete slowly walked up the metal staircase to the top landing and checked his watch. It had taken nearly fifteen minutes to check the twenty-seven cells on the bottom landing, another twenty-seven more cells up here and that should be a whole half hour killed off. He walked along the top landing and began checking the cells one by one. As all of the other cell lights were turned off, he thought it unusual to see a glimmer of light from under the door as he approached cell 311. Thinking he may catch the occupant doing something he shouldn't, Pete eased open the flap carefully so as to make as little noise as possible. Busting prisoners could be a good way to boost his career. As he peered through the flap, he recoiled and then froze to the spot.

'Steve! Steve!' he called out in a quivering voice.

Frustrated by the interruption, Steve put down his book and looked up to where Pete was stood rigid.

'What's up son?'

'Just get up here,' replied Pete, trying to compose himself

Pete was fumbling with his keys as Steve joined him breathlessly outside cell 311. He peered through the glass to see Dunford dead on the floor.

'Fuck, just what I need. Right, get on your radio and call in a code nine,' Steve barked as he unlocked the door. As he entered the cell, the stench hit him. Dunford's bowels had emptied as was common after death. Although Steve knew it was futile, he followed protocol and checked for a pulse. No pulse and the body was cold to the touch.

*He must have done it right after Gilly did his last cell check and just into my shift. Bloody typical,* thought Steve to himself and then silently cursed as his mind drifted to the piles of paperwork he would have to complete.

The wing door flew open, and two medics rushed up the stairs and into the cell.

SCREWED

# CHAPTER TWENTY-THREE

Razor found sleep difficult; his mind was whirling. Not because of the suicide, one less nonce in the world was never a bad thing. He knew it could never be proven that he'd done nothing to prevent it, plus Lucy was onside, and in her eyes, she was the guilty one, not him. The thing that was bothering him was that kid, Beef, calling him 'Razor'.

His alarm sounded at 8.00 a.m., just four hours after he'd finally got to sleep. It was the day of Tony's wedding, and he felt dreadful. He decided it would be unfair to Tony if he were to turn up to his big day looking like doom and gloom, so he'd better do something about it. He groped around on his bedside table, finally putting his hand on the plastic bag containing the party powder that he'd bought from Ish. He cut a small line; he didn't want to go mad at such an early hour. The buzz hit him instantly. He hit the remote on the TV, and MTV filled the room, now he felt human again. He was now looking forward to the wedding and intended to have a ball. He'd managed to reserve a room for himself and Deborah at the venue of the reception. It would cost him an arm and a leg, but he'd decided to push the boat out.

# SCREWED

Razor pumped up the volume on the TV and hit the shower.

At 10.00 a.m. on the dot, Deborah was outside in her shiny, new Evoque. As he approached the car, she jumped out and threw him the keys.

'You're driving,' she grinned.

She was wearing an electric-blue, off-the-shoulder minidress, her trademark Louboutin shoes and a clutch bag that probably cost more than he earned in a month.

'You're not meant to outdo the bride,' he said, looking her up and down in appreciation.

The wedding was very traditional and held in a country church. The bride wore white, had lots of bridesmaids and the church was swamped with flowers. Razor had never given much thought to marriage, but the way Deborah held his hand throughout the service made him feel that it was something he would consider in the future.

The reception was at an exclusive country club on the outskirts of Leeds; it was very lavish. Obviously, money was no object. Champagne flowed like tap water during the gourmet, five-course meal. Razor and Deborah sat at a table with three other couples who he'd not met before. They were good company, and everyone got on well. However, Razor was sure that the men

# SCREWED

around the table kept taking sneaky glances in Deborah's direction when their wives weren't looking.

Razor had noticed Paul sitting on an adjacent table and tried to catch his eye, but Paul, who seemed engrossed by the other people on his table, had failed to see Razor. Razor decided he'd catch up with Paul later. He was intrigued to find out what a chief super was doing at the party at Johnny's mansion.

After the meal and the speeches, Razor and Deborah spent a few minutes congratulating Tony and his new wife. They then slipped off to their room to consume a few lines of power party in preparation for the evening do.

They entered the ballroom, just as the band had begun playing, and headed straight to the bar. Deborah ordered and paid for a bottle of Bollinger. Razor was relieved that she'd insisted on paying. He was paying for the hotel room and still hadn't got round to checking his bank balance, he vowed to check it on Monday before work. He was aware that it would be depleted somewhat due to the level of spending he'd been doing lately, but wasn't quite sure by how much.

The bar area was quite busy when Paul walked up to the bar, and he didn't notice that he'd inadvertently positioned himself next to

# SCREWED

Razor. He ordered a pint and a glass of wine, as he did so, Razor turned, and their eyes met.

'Thought I heard your dulcet tones,' said Razor.

'Ah, Gilly. How are things? You recovered from the stag do?'

'Yeah, just about. What a blast, eh?'

'Yeah, great weekend. I've not been out since. The wife likes to keep me on a short leash,' Paul said with a laugh.

'Not been out? I could have sworn I saw you last Tuesday night.'

'Didn't know you were a member of the squash club,' Paul retorted.

'I'm not. It was at...'

'In that case, you definitely didn't see me,' said Paul abruptly, cutting him off mid sentence.

'Are you going to introduce me to your friend?' purred Deborah, turning away from the person she'd been chatting to. Paul's face instantly softened.

'Of course. Deborah, this is Paul. Tony's boss.'

Paul kissed her on each cheek, and then his eyes seemed to stay locked on to hers for just a second longer than they should have.

'It's a pleasure to meet you, Paul,' she said with a warm smile.

# SCREWED

'The pleasure is all mine. Would you care to join my wife and I at our table?'

Before Razor could decline the offer, Deborah jumped in and said, 'Yes, thanks. We'll be over in a moment.'

Paul collected his drinks from the bar and joined his wife at a round table to one side of the room.

'Have you met him before?' asked Razor with a hint of suspicion.

'Razor, you've only just introduced us.'

'You looked like you recognised each other,' he said, his voice raised.

'Maybe he remembered me from work and was too polite to mention it, and do you really think that I remember every man that walks through the door?'

With that, Deborah picked up the two champagne flutes and sauntered over to where Paul was sitting with his wife. Feeling silly, Razor followed behind carrying the ice bucket. As they sat, Paul introduced them to his wife. Victoria was a classically attractive woman, well spoken and obviously educated. Razor guessed that she was in her early forties. Victoria complimented Deborah on her dress causing a ten-minute conflab about shoes and bags. Victoria spent considerable time talking about the various charities she worked with before asking Deborah what she did for a living.

'I'm in hospitality,' Deborah replied calmly.

Razor noticed a thin smile appear on Paul's lips as she said this.

Victoria, seeing that the men weren't saying much, switched her attention to Razor. Paul seemed more than happy to chat away to Deborah while Victoria spoke in depth with Razor about her volunteer work with young offenders. As Razor topped up the champagne flutes, Victoria commented on how much Paul loved champagne too.

'It's all he drinks at home, although he's more of a Dom Pérignon man.'

Once they finished the champagne, Deborah announced that she wanted to dance and dragged Razor on to the dance floor. Razor welcomed the distraction, lovely as Victoria was, he really didn't want to spend his evening talking about work and wanted at least some time alone with Deborah.

After a few songs and some close dancing, Deborah said that she was going to the ladies.

'Wait for me outside. Won't be long,' she said to Razor.

He took the opportunity to nip to the gents and headed straight for the nearest cubicle. He took out the silver vial and tapped a small mound on to the back of his hand. He wasn't going to cut a line on a toilet seat, no matter how beautiful the place was. He snorted the coke and was just about to leave when he heard the toilet lid slam down in the next cubicle. He noticed that the occupier's feet were still facing forward. Listening, he heard the familiar tap, tap sound of a credit card against a hard surface, followed by two long sniffs. Razor flushed the toilet, left the cubicle and stopped at the row of sinks in front of the huge mirror that sat in a gilded frame. He turned on the taps but kept his eyes fixed on the cubicle door. After a minute or so the door opened and out walked Paul, the chief superintendent of Doncaster police force. Razor stared at him in the reflection.

'Maybe we could play a game sometime... at that squash club of yours,' said Razor.

'Maybe,' said Paul as he hurried out of the toilets.

Next morning Razor and Deborah enjoyed breakfast in bed before leaving the room at ten. Razor went to the reception desk to settle the bill, while Deborah waited on a large comfortable chair nearby. The man behind the counter tapped efficiently on his keyboard, and then handed Razor an itemised bill. The total balance, including breakfast and champagne that room service had delivered, was £524.00. Razor visibly paled, five hundred quid was a lot more than he intended to spend, but it was a one-off. He inserted his debit card into the small machine on the counter.

'Enter your PIN number please, sir,' prompted the receptionist.

Razor entered his PIN and waited.

'There appears to be a problem, sir. Do you have another card?' asked the receptionist.

Looking down, Razor noticed that the machine had announced 'unauthorised transaction'. He didn't have another card, he only had a debit card.

'Try again, there's obviously a mistake,' he snapped, his face turning red with embarrassment as a queue was beginning to form behind him. The receptionist tried again with the same result.

'I'm terribly sorry, but we can't accept this card. Do you have any other means of payment?'

A feeling of dread spread over Razor, and he merely stared at the card machine not quite knowing what to do or say. Deborah then walked over to see what was taking so long.

'What's the hold-up, babe?' she asked.

'There must have been a mix up at the bank and my card's not working.'

'I'll deal with it,' she said looking put out.

Razor stepped to one side; his head bowed so as not to have to look at the queue behind them. Without another word, Deborah produced a gold card from her bag and settled the bill.

On the way home, she'd asked Razor, more than once, if he was having any money problems. He'd assured her that it was simply a mistake and that he'd be calling the bank first thing Monday morning.

'I only checked my account yesterday and everything was OK then,' he lied.

She could tell that he was embarrassed by the whole episode and decided to change the subject.

'I'll have to drop you straight off. I've promised to meet my friend for a drink this afternoon,' she said pleasantly.

When Razor walked through his front door, he felt lonely and rejected. Still reeling from the episode at the hotel, he decided to log into his online banking and find out once and for all exactly how much he had been spending. What he saw when he logged in made Razor feel a whole lot worse. He stared at the balance in shock, funds available '£146.18'. What was going on? He always kept at least five thousand pounds in his current account. He received twelve hundred a month from the prison, and he kept an additional three thousand eight hundred as a reserve. He kept his savings locked away in a five-year, high-interest bond. With a shaking hand, he clicked the statement icon and scrolled through the list of transactions. Listed were his usual direct debits of rent and other household bills. He saw the twelve fifty that he'd spent on his new clothes at Meadowhall and a payment from the prison for his wages. The last transaction was on Friday 25th for two thousand six hundred pounds. Next to the word 'debit' was the transaction's details: The Living Room, Leeds. Jesus, how could he have spent all that? In a blind panic, he rummaged for the envelope that Claudio had given to him. He needed to log into his Living Room VIP account to see where the money had been spent. Using the details in the envelope, he logged in and selected account activity. His eyes moved down the statement. There were just nine items listed. The first five listings were for Bollinger champagne, at two hundred pounds per bottle, and the next four listings were for vodka with a Coke mixer, costing four hundred pounds each. He was momentarily confused.

*He didn't drink vodka and Coke. Was there a mistake?* he wondered.

Razor looked again at the list, no mention of the vials that he purchased from Claudio. Then it hit him like a train, vodka and Coke had to be code for the cocaine that the Living Room supplied. He couldn't believe how stupid he'd

## SCREWED

been. How could he not ask the price of something before buying it? No wonder Johnny could afford to live in a mansion, he was charging double what Ish was. Then he remembered that he owed Ish five hundred quid and it was due on Tuesday. He tried to remain calm and think of a way out; he got paid on the tenth, so surely Ish could hang on for a few days. After paying Ish that would only leave him with seven hundred quid that month to cover his bills and his nights out with Deborah. Feeling utterly distraught, he reached for the silver vial. The moment he'd snorted the coke, he wished he hadn't.

## CHAPTER TWENTY-FOUR

It was Monday afternoon and as Razor and Lucy entered the prison, there were two members of the security team waiting for them. Razor felt a knot forming in his stomach. They took them both into the manager's bubble that overlooked the wing and explained that there had been a suicide on Friday night and, while it didn't happen on their shift, they still needed to be interviewed. They asked Razor to step outside and wait while they spoke to Lucy first. Although she knew this would happen, she was still feeling nervous as she sat across the table from the two security personnel.

'There's nothing to worry about,' the first officer assured her.

'We've just got a few routine questions,' added the second.

They wanted to know why Lucy did the first cell checks and Razor did the second two. She explained that it suited them to take it in turns; one would make the coffee while the other did the checks. One of the officers made a note on his pad, and then asked if she ever used drugs or alcohol before a shift. She gave a firm no. Then he asked the question that she'd been dreading.

'At any point during the shift did you leave your colleague alone on the wing?'

# SCREWED

Again she gave a firm no. With that, they thanked Lucy for her time and asked her to send in Officer Gillmore. She left the room feeling relieved. They were going to get away with this.

Razor was faced with the same set of questions and gave virtually identical answers. Just as he thought they'd finished, they hit him with something that he hadn't considered.

'When we watched the CCTV tapes of that night, we noticed that you spent roughly five seconds at each flap, but at cell 311 you spent thirty-eight seconds. Can you explain why?'

Razor hadn't given this a thought and was amazed to learn that he'd spent that long at the door. Thinking on his feet, he proceeded to tell them his version of what had happened.

'When I opened the flap Dunford sat up and started mumbling something to me. I couldn't hear what he said, so I asked him to repeat himself. He didn't, he just lay back down. I asked him if he was OK to which he responded yes. So I told him to get some sleep.'

'And at that point, you had no reason to believe that he was a danger to himself?'

'No, or else I wouldn't have left him.'

Both officers nodded, seeming happy with Razor's answers and dismissed him.

# SCREWED

Back on the wing, Razor slumped down at the officers' desk next to Lucy and breathed a sigh of relief. He was confident that they were in the clear, and now, hopefully, things would get back to normal.

During the shift Lucy mentioned that after everything that had happened, she was considering changing jobs. Her boyfriend was gone, despite begging for forgiveness, so maybe it was time for a new start.

# CHAPTER TWENTY-FIVE

It was Tuesday, month end had arrived, and Razor knew that Ish would be expecting his money. He decided it would be best to give him a quick call and ask for a few extra days. The last thing Razor wanted was for Ish to come looking for him. He walked to the phone box at the end of the road and dialled. No answer. Razor looked at his watch. Half nine, maybe it was a little early for Ish, so he decided he'd try again in a couple of hours. Razor arrived home, with time on his hands, and decided it was time to apply for a credit card. Just for emergencies, he never wanted to repeat the performance at the hotel. He fired up his laptop and checked a comparison site for the best deals. He found two cards with reasonable interest rates and applied for both. A few minutes later he'd been accepted for both, and the two cards would be with him within a couple of days. Razor felt suddenly at ease, knowing that his short-term financial problems would soon get resolved, then he would cut back on the coke and curb his spending a bit. As he still had time to kill, he decided to do a little Internet research on Paul, the chief super. A couple of clicks on the South Yorkshire Police website and Razor was looking at Paul's life story. He'd been educated locally, before leaving Doncaster for Oxford University. On

# SCREWED

leaving Oxford with a first in law, he joined the police force. He soon fast-tracked up the ranks by making a name for himself implementing a zero tolerance drugs policy. This last piece of information Razor found amusing, as he thought back the gents toilets at Tony's wedding. Razor left the house at midday to try and contact Ish again. This time his call was answered:

'Yo.'

'It's me. Can we meet?'

'You're learning, my man. Same place in about an hour.'

The line went dead. Razor decided to make the twenty-minute walk into town, as the only exercise he was getting recently was in the bedroom. He got into town and walked around a few shops before heading to Greggs to meet Ish. Ishmael broke into a wide grin when he saw Razor waiting alongside the pie shop. They bumped fists.

'Yo, Razor. Great to see you man. Wish all my clients were like you.'

'Like me?' said Razor with genuine interest.

'Yeah, it's not often people call me to settle their accounts, it's normally me threatening to break their legs,' he said with a sinister laugh.

'Listen Ish, er, about that. I've got a slight problem.'

The smile vanished from Ishmael's face.

# SCREWED

'I hope your problem ain't financial.'

'No, er yes, but I will sort it in a couple of days. Just a cock-up with my wages,' said Razor quickly.

'I don't give a fuck about your wages; you owe me five ton, cash, today,' spat Ish, before leaning in closer and hissing, 'unless you want to send your lady friend to see me. I'm sure she'd find a way to satisfy your debt.'

Ish put extra emphasis on the word 'satisfy'. Without thinking, Razor grabbed hold of Ishmael's coat.

'Hit a nerve have I, Razor?' laughed Ish.

Realising he needed to calm things down, he let go of Ish's coat and stepped back a pace. Ish eyed him for a moment; then the smile returned to his face.

'As it's you, maybe we can work something out. Let's grab a drink and see.'

They walked into a nearby Costa Coffee, and Ish nodded to a vacant table.

'Sit there. I'll get the coffees seeing as you're skint,' laughed Ish, as he walked to the counter.

Ishmael returned with two steaming coffees in cardboard cups and placed them on the table top.

# SCREWED

'Two regular coffees in this shop cost £1.95 each. How much profit do you think they make on each coffee?'

Razor was taken aback, wondering where this was leading and merely shrugged.

'Come on, Razor man, how much? Have a guess.'

'I don't know, a lot, maybe one pound fifty.'

'Nah, nah, you're way off, man,' laughed Ishmael.

'I give up. Just tell me.'

'Three pence. Three *whole* pence on a £1.95 cup of shitty coffee. Can you believe that, man?'

'Amazing,' replied Razor, trying to humour him but still confused as to what this had to do with anything.

'And do you know why they only make three pence?'

'Enlighten me Ish.'

'Overheads man. Staff, rates, advertising. People never consider that shit. They pay £1.95 and think the Costas of this world are making a shitload of profit.'

'What's your point, Ish?'

'I'm coming to that, chill out man. Now take a large coffee with a vanilla shot. That costs £2.95. How much profit now?'

'Fuck knows, six pence?'

# SCREWED

'Nah, nah, you're way off again. They make £1.03. Now throw in a blueberry muffin at £2.25, and the profit jumps to £3.23. Now that's why they make millions. No one comes in and buys just a standard coffee.

Razor nodded at the two regular coffees that were sitting on the table in front of them.

'Ah, my point. I'm the exception to the rule. It's just like the drug game. Once the overhead is covered the rest is gravy.'

Razor was still unsure why Ish had spent the last few minutes waffling on about the economics of coffee shops. Figuring his mood had improved, he decided to steer him back to the matter at hand.

'Look Ish, if you can give me ten days I'll make it six hundred instead of five, for your inconvenience.'

'Nah, nah, Razor man. Look we are friends, and friends do favours. So as a favour to you I'm going to give you the extra time, and you only need to give me what's owed.' Razor felt relief wash over him, however, it soon evaporated as Ish continued, 'But Razor, my man, I want you to do a favour for me.'

A sudden chill ran down Razor's spine, but he knew that whatever the favour, he had no choice. He didn't have the money for Ish and had no means to get it; he'd even phoned the bank to

# SCREWED

see if he could release some cash from his ISA, only to be told he would need to give sixty days' notice.

'What do you want me to do?' asked Razor helplessly.

'Well as you ask man... Remember I mentioned that I had a mate doing time in your nick? Well he's serving a short sentence and it just so happens he's on your wing. You'll know him, Ridgley, or Beef to his mates.'

'I know him,' Razor sighed.

'Well, Beef wants to be able to talk in private, without you lot listening to his conversations.'

'There's nothing I can do about the prison phones, Ish.'

'I'm sure you can't, that's why my man needs a mobile. You deliver the phone, and I give you extra time to pay me. Simple favours for favours.'

Razor saw an opportunity open up before him. He knew how easy it was to walk into the prison carrying a mobile phone. He'd done it accidentally a couple of times with his phone, simply forgetting that it was in his pocket. Officers were meant to get searched randomly, but this rarely happened. In Razor's time at the prison it had happened once and that was carried out by an external security firm on the run-up to Christmas.

'Question for you, Ish.'

'Shoot man.'

'Do you know how much it would cost to get a phone smuggled in?'

Ish knew exactly but shook his head.

'Anything between two and two and a half grand. So here's the deal. I take the phone in, and the debt is clear. I'm guessing that you're doubling your money on the coke you sold me, so actually your mate Beef is getting a phone for two fifty. A fucking bargain.'

Ish broke into one of his trademark grins.

'Deborah was bang on when she christened you Razor. You're sharp, man.'

'I take it that's a deal then?'

In response, Ish held out his fist, which Razor duly bumped, thus sealing the deal. They agreed to meet the next day, same time, same place, so that Razor could collect the phone.

The next day, when Razor came on to the wing at 4.00 p.m., he was carrying a small pay-as-you-go phone. It was loaded with one hundred pounds worth of credit and had four numbers stored in the memory. At 4.30 p.m. it was time to begin the afternoon unlock in preparation for the last meal of the day. Razor told Lucy to open downstairs, and he'd do the top landing. He gave an involuntary shudder as he passed, the unoccupied, cell 311 and moved quickly on. At cell 308 he unlocked the door, then reached into his pocket, and placed his hand on the small mobile device with a feeling of trepidation.

'Come on Ridgley, teatime.'

As Ridgley walked out of the cell, Razor, keeping his back to the CCTV cameras, quickly tossed the phone on to his bunk and relocked the door. Job done, and it was easier than he could have imagined. He was out of debt with Ish and hadn't parted with a single penny. As soon he got paid he intended to pay Deborah back for the hotel. By 5.30 p.m. everyone was locked away for the night, and Lucy and Razor were sat at the desk enjoying a coffee. The unit manager made an unexpected visit to the wing and informed them that there were going to be some changes. As from Monday, staff hours were going to change. Instead of working a five-day week with eight hours per shift, they would only work four days but for ten hours. There would also now be three staff on the wing whenever the prisoners were out of their cells. He asked Lucy and Razor if they were willing to switch to the day shift which was now 8.00 a.m. until 6.00 p.m. They agreed to give it go. For Razor, a four-day week and no night shifts was quite appealing. The unit manager left as

# SCREWED

quickly as he had arrived, leaving them to finish their coffees.

'You had any more thoughts about leaving, Luce?' asked Razor.

'I've heard there's a job going in the offices, I may go for that. To be honest, I've had enough of wing work. That shit with Dunford was the last straw.'

'Don't let that bother you too much; he was only a nonce.'

'I know Razor, that's the only thing stopping me from walking. Anyway, I'm off for a fag.'

'When did you start smoking, Lucy?'

'Very recently,' she said with a smile and headed to the fire exit.

# SCREWED

# CHAPTER TWENTY-SIX

With the weekend approaching and payday not until the following Wednesday, Razor's bank balance was showing a measly eighty pounds. He needed to go food shopping, and his phone bill was due, there was no chance he could afford a night with Deborah. Added to that, he'd got accustomed to the good life and couldn't imagine going back to a life of the occasional lager in his local pubs. The problem for Razor was, that on his salary, the good life just wasn't sustainable. Razor's mind flicked to Ish, and he wondered if he had any other mates who needed a phone. He figured that if Ish did have any others mates needing a phone, he could make at least a grand out it. His mind was made up; he'd call Ish.

Razor was already sat in Costa Coffee when Ishmael walked in.

'Yo, Razor man,' said Ish as they bumped fists.

Ish grinned as he glanced down at the table to see two regular coffees.

'What can I do for you, Razor man?'
'Is your man happy with his new phone?'
'Yeah man, he's made up.'

# SCREWED

'I was thinking. Have you got any other mates who may want one?' asked Razor, giving Ish an expectant look.

Ish wondered what was going through Razor's mind. He thought the guy was sharp. Did he believe that HMP Doncaster was full of his mates all wanting phones at two grand a pop? Ish could see an opportunity here, but decided not to let on to Razor at that moment.

'Nah, I ain't got no one.' Ish couldn't miss the look of disappointment on Razor's face and asked, 'You short on dough or summat?'

'Do you know how much I earn, Ish?'

Ishmael didn't, but he'd heard that staff in a state-run prison were making between 35 and 40k a year, so he figured that staff in a private prison would be taking home a good chunk more.

'You must be on a decent screw. Forgive the pun.'

Razor laughed and said, 'After tax and stoppages eleven hundred quid.'

'Fuck, Razor man that's a good earner.'

'You realise that's for the whole month, Ish?'

Ish was speechless; he knew guys on benefits who made more than that. No wonder this guy was up for an extra earner.

After contemplating for a moment or two, Ish said, 'Be in the Living Room, Saturday night. I may have an idea how you can make some extra dollar.' With that Ish whipped up his coffee and left.

SCREWED

# CHAPTER TWENTY-SEVEN

The new shift pattern started on Monday, which meant that Friday was Razor's last night shift. Both he and Lucy were sat at the desk when Steve and Pete walked on to the wing.

'Nice to see you both,' said Steve by way of a greeting.

Pete gave them a polite nod but said nothing.

They exchanged small talk then Steve became grave and said, 'I hear prison security interviewed you two.'

'Yeah, just a formality,' replied Razor.

'Well luckily for you, they didn't ask me if you were both on the wing when we began our shift,' said Steve, his demeanour softening.

Razor winked at Lucy, he knew that Steve would have covered for them even if security had asked.

'Anyway, they put it down to unpreventable suicide,' continued Steve.

'How do you know that? The report isn't due until next week,' said Lucy with surprise.

'I've got a mate who works in security. He told me that the time of death was in question, but the fact that Gilly spoke to Dunford when he was doing the cell check cleared that up, so that narrowed down the time of the suicide to between midnight and 2.00 a.m. So life goes on as normal, and there's one less nonce in the world.'

Lucy and Razor signed the log and left the wing.

As they walked toward the locker room Lucy turned to Razor, 'You never said that you spoke to Dunford that night.'

'I didn't talk to him, but I needed to explain why I was standing at his cell door for thirty-eight long seconds. What else could I say?'

'I hope you're on the level with me, Gilly,' she said, before entering the ladies' locker room.

SCREWED

# CHAPTER TWENTY-EIGHT

Saturday morning and Razor got up to find two envelopes on his doormat containing credit cards. He was surprised to find that one had a limit of four thousand and the other had five thousand. He was pleased but reminded himself that these cards were just a safety net.

Razor walked into the Living Room at a few minutes before 11.00 p.m. He no longer needed to show his VIP card at the door as all the door staff knew him by name.

'Evening, Mr Razor. Will Miss Deborah be joining you later?' said the doorman with a smile on his face. Razor remembered him to be the man who had driven him and Deborah to and from Johnny's party, and he flushed as he recalled what they'd done on the way home.

'I expect she will,' he replied, hurrying in.

Razor glanced toward his usual booth to see if Ish had arrived before him. It was empty, so he walked to the bar while scanning the crowd and nodding to a few familiar faces. His mind flicking back to his bank balance, he ordered a vodka and tonic from the attractive brunette behind the marble counter and slid over his VIP card.

'Good evening, Mr Razor.'

# SCREWED

Razor turned to see Claudio standing behind him.

'Not on the Bollinger tonight?' enquired Claudio, although the way he said it made Razor feel as though he meant to say: 'Can't you afford our overpriced champagne, you cheapskate?'

Razor was planning to stay on the cheaper drinks until Deborah arrived, but Claudio's tone pricked Razor's ego, so he replied, 'Of course, I'll be having champagne, Claudio; I just needed a quick thirst quencher. Send a bottle over as soon as my guest arrives.'

'Certainly. Will you require anything else, Mr Razor?'

Razor had put the last of the cocaine that he'd got from Ish in the silver vial. Although it was only half full, he was hoping it would last him the night.

'No, that will be all, Claudio, thanks.'

Claudio hurried off through the door marked private.

'That's one puff I don't like.' Then looking at the brunette behind the bar, 'I'll have what he's having,' said Ish, nodding his head towards Razor.

The barmaid set Ish's drink in front of him, as she did so he leant over the bar and whispered into her ear. The girl giggled and moved on to the next customer.

'Hotties, I love 'em, man. Come on let's sit.'

# SCREWED

They walked to the booth and sat on opposite sides, facing each other. Seconds later a waitress appeared with an ice bucket containing the Bollinger and two glasses. She set the bucket down but didn't pour, as Ish had waved her off.

'Now Razor man, to business. As we're mates, I've got a plan that could earn us both a few quid.'

'I'm listening,' said Razor, hoping he'd get straight to the point. He didn't want another lecture on the economics of coffee shops.

'You know how much an ounce of weed costs on the street?'

*Here we go again*, thought Razor.

'Look, Ish, I've got no idea. Just cut to the chase,' he replied with a hint of annoyance in his voice.

'Chill, Razor man. An ounce on the street sells for £90 - £120. In prison, it's three or four times more, so let's say £400 an ounce on the inside or £25 for a joint. You with me?'

Razor nodded.

'Demand is high, and supply is difficult. A lot don't even get to the wing, and a lot of the stuff that does gets confiscated. This drives up the price to a level that most cons can't afford. Still following?'

'Yeah, go on.'

# SCREWED

'Now my man, our mutual friend, and his gang have been supplying, but it's been a bit hit and miss.'

'What on my wing?' Razor hadn't known there was dealing on the wing, but that said, the only time he saw prisoners was during the half hour unlock at teatime.

'On your wing and every other wing. But that's for another day. Now another problem with weed. There's someone else bringing it in and with more success. So...'

'He's selling it cheaper?' chipped in Razor.

'Spot on, Razor. Sharp man. Basically, our friend can't compete.'

'So what's the solution?'

'You heard of Spice?' grinned Ish.

'Yeah, we had a memo about it just last week. It said, it's a sedative used for transporting carp. They sprinkle it on the top of the water, the carp eat it, and it reduces the stress. But, according to the memo, people have started to smoke it because it has a similar effect to cannabis. By the sound of it, the side effects can be quite nasty.'

'Fucking hell, Razor, you sound like an encyclopaedia. A simple yes or no would have done.'

'Says you,' retorted Razor with a laugh.

# SCREWED

'Nasty or not, man, it's legal. Legal to use, legal to buy, legal to sell and legal to possess. And the cherry on the cake is it's cheap. Do you know how much it is for an ounce from the Internet?'

'No.'

'£38. Then we can knock it out for £1,100 an ounce on the inside. Now that's profit and who gives a fuck if we lose the odd ounce.'

'You sure, Ish? That doesn't seem right to me.'

'That's the rate, Razor man. Although we won't be selling much by the ounce, it will be mainly single joints at fifteen quid a go.'

Razor liked what he was hearing, and he wasn't doing anything illegal, that was until he stepped inside the prison. But with the profit involved, he figured it was well worth the small risk.

'How much can your man shift?' asked Razor.

'To start with I think two ounces a week, split into two drops. A fag packet will hold four ounces, but with just an ounce in there the weight is right. That would give us just over two grand per week, and that's just for starters man.'

'What's the split?'

'Three ways, equal man.'

Razor wasn't happy with the split. He argued that it was him taking all the risks. What exactly was Ish doing for his share? Ish shot back that it was his man on the inside and he also had to sort out the collection of the money. Razor hadn't considered this side of things and wondered how the money would get collected. Ish assured him that that side was under control. Although he didn't voice it, Razor wondered if the guy on the inside would actually see any of the cash. After ten minutes debating, they agreed that the money would get split three ways. Razor would receive £350 for every ounce he took into the prison; Ish would look after the rest. This would give Razor an extra £700 a week in cash; he was more than happy. Time to celebrate; Razor poured two glasses of champagne while Ish cut four lines of coke. They clinked glasses and took a line up each nostril.

'Here's to Doncatraz,' said Razor.

They clinked glasses again and downed the champagne.

'What are you two so pleased about?' asked Deborah, as she joined them in the booth.

She was wearing a low-cut, red minidress and looked stunning. As she bent forward to pick up Razor's champagne glass, both men adjusted their positions slightly to take in the view of Deborah's cleavage. They caught each other looking and broke into childish hysterics.

# SCREWED

'You pair of perverts,' she pretended to scold.

'Think we better have another bottle,' grinned Razor.

'I presume you sorted your bank issue then?' she whispered so only he could hear.

'Yeah, just as I suspected, a balls-up with the bank. But it's sorted now. So how about tomorrow I buy you lunch and I'll give you that money back too.' He winked at Ish as he said this.

'Forget about the money, you can treat me to a night in a posh hotel instead,' she replied.

'You can count on it,' grinned Razor, as Deborah stood to leave for the ladies.

Ish told Razor that he'd drop the first ounce of Spice off on Sunday night.

'I thought you needed to order first?'

'Yep, it came this morning.'

'But you didn't know I'd agree.'

'Yes, I did,' grinned Ish.

# SCREWED

# CHAPTER TWENTY-NINE

Monday morning, Razor walked into HMP Doncaster carrying a pack of Embassy cigarettes, but instead of cigarettes, the package contained one ounce of Spice. The previous night Ishmael had carefully undone the cellophane wrapping, removed the cigarettes and replaced them with the Spice. He'd then stuffed cotton wool into the packet to stop the Spice rattling, should anyone shake the pack. He'd then slid the cellophane back over the packet and sealed it on the underside. The packet now looked unopened, and even the weight was the same. Ish had also advised Razor to always carry an additional pack containing just two or three cigarettes, that way, if he got searched, it wouldn't look strange having an unopened box on his person. Despite Ishmael's reassurances Razor was nervous, he could feel the sweat running down his back as he entered the prison.

*Was that security guard staring at him?*

Razor decided he was just being paranoid, he wished he hadn't snorted that little livener before work.

When Razor unlocked cell 308 at 8.30 a.m., he threw the unopened packet on to the bed. Beef quickly slid the cigarette box under his pillow.

# SCREWED

'Cheers, Razor,' he said.

'Don't ever call me that,' snarled Razor.

'Whatever you say... Razor,' Beef retorted sarcastically.

Razor moved to unlock the next cell muttering under his breath. The thought of the £350 he'd just earned, made dealing with Beef a little easier. He repeated the exercise again on Thursday, the nerves gone, another £350 in his pocket; this was too easy. The one thing that was beginning to annoy him was that some of the other cons had started calling him Razor. This was obviously down to that arsehole, Beef. He made a conscious effort not to respond whenever anyone used the name, however, this didn't stop them. Since the changes to shift patterns, he was now seeing a lot more of the prisoners. He had observed Beef while sitting at the desk. The guy was an idiot, always huddled with his gang and trying to stir up trouble. The other thing that grated on Razor was how Beef strutted around the wing in his red dressing gown. Razor had to keep reminding himself that, like him or not, Beef was earning him money, so he tried to look the other way whenever he stepped out of line. Martin, who had always worked days, seemed happy to ignore most things too. He said, more than once, that they didn't get paid enough to get involved. As long as the cons didn't kill each other, Martin was happy to leave them be. That was all right with Razor.

That afternoon, when the prisoners were locked away, the unit manager came on to the wing and took Razor and Lucy to one side.

'The prison security report was released today, and it concluded that Dunford's suicide was unpreventable. So that means case closed.'

'That's good to know. Thanks for keeping us in the loop,' said Lucy.

'How are the new shifts suiting you?' asked the unit manager.

They both agreed that things were OK so far. The unit manager told them to keep up the good work then left the wing.

Razor was looking forward to his up-and-coming three-day weekend. Deborah was not working on Thursday evening, so they'd arranged to visit a swanky new restaurant that had opened in the centre of Doncaster. He was looking forward to having her to himself for a change. He only really got to see her on Saturday nights. Last Saturday Ish had been there, and the Saturday before was the wedding. Razor had called the restaurant and got informed that there was a six-week waiting list. When he'd mentioned this to Deborah, she told him to leave it with her. She called him back twenty minutes later and said that they had a table at 8.30 p.m.

Deborah arrived at Razor's in her Evoque a little earlier than expected. Instead of sounding the horn as she normally did, she knocked and walked in.

'We'll get a taxi into town. Will my car be OK outside?'

'What are you implying?' asked Razor with a laugh. 'Of course, it'll be OK,' he continued, as he left for the bedroom to do his hair.

This was the first time she'd ever been inside his house, and he wondered if there'd be any other firsts tonight. Maybe she'd end up in his bed this evening.

'Razor, you really need to decorate,' she called from the living room.

'It's only a rental.'

'Have you thought about buying somewhere?' she asked, as she walked into the bedroom.

'Yeah, but I'm saving up. I don't want a mortgage, and I'm about halfway to being able to buy one for cash.' He could tell she wasn't going to ask where his money had come from so he explained, 'I had a decent payout from the police and working nights my social life was zero, so that helped.'

# SCREWED

Just then a horn sounded outside signalling the taxi's arrival.

The taxi dropped them outside the glass-fronted restaurant. The windows were tinted so that passers-by couldn't gawp in at the diners. Above the door, on a subtly lit sign, was the restaurant's name, 'Pascal'. The restaurant was ultra-modern, lots of glass and shiny chrome, but with an intimate ambience. The dining room wasn't exceptionally spacious; it housed around twenty tables. Most tables had customers already seated, and those that didn't were set, waiting for guests with reservations. The maître d', without even asking their names, guided them over to their table and offered them a complimentary glass of champagne. Razor glanced down at the table; it had a crisp, white linen tablecloth and a vast array of cutlery. A waiter appeared and handed them both a menu.

'Bonsoir Madame, Monsieur.'

Then the waiter, in one fluid motion, whipped the folded linen napkin from the table, shook it and laid across the knees of Deborah and then Razor. Deborah said a few words to him in French, and he was gone.

'I didn't know you spoke French,' said Razor with genuine surprise.

# SCREWED

'There's a lot you don't know about me, Razor,' she said playfully.

Another waiter presented himself at their table, introduced himself as the sommelier and handed Razor a thick, leather-bound wine list. Noting the look of dread that spread over Razor's face, the sommelier suggested the wine pairing. Razor nodded gratefully, so the sommelier proceeded to explain the various wines that would complement their food. With a slight bow of the head, the sommelier turned on his expensive heel and left. Razor turned his attention to the single sheet of heavy, embossed paper that displayed an array of culinary delights.

'How come there are no prices on here?' asked Razor.

'If you need to ask how much then you probably can't afford it, not that that applies to us,' said Deborah cryptically.

Razor ignored the comment and turned his attention back to the menu.

His knowledge of food was equal to his knowledge of wine, so turning to Deborah, he asked, 'What would you recommend, Deborah?'

'Oh Razor, it's a tasting menu.'

'So what's good?'

'It's all good, and we get all of it,' she said with a laugh.

'Jesus, we've got to eat eight courses?'

# SCREWED

'Oh, Razor, you're so funny.'

Razor forced a laugh and decided not to ask any more questions. He'd sit back and follow Deborah's lead.

The first course duly arrived, and Razor stared in disbelief at the oversized plate with only a mouthful of food artistically placed in the centre. The waiter explained the dish in great detail before being replaced by the sommelier. He poured the wine and then launched into a long monologue about the wine's vintage, provenance and character. Razor had switched off by the end of the first sentence.

'Please tell me we haven't got to sit through that another seven times,' groaned Razor once the sommelier had left.

Deborah ignored his whining and with a slight edge in her voice said, 'Try the scallop, Razor. It's divine.'

Razor had never tasted scallop before, let alone knew the correct way to eat it. He watched Deborah cut the scallop into four then select a piece and gently dab it into a scattering of green crystals that decorated the place. Razor did the same and popped the tiny morsel into his mouth. The taste was sensational; his tongue was alive with the mixture of flavours. He'd never experienced such unusual flavours and textures.

# SCREWED

'Wonderful isn't it? Now try a sip of the wine,' prompted Deborah.

He took a small sip, the taste of the wine had changed, it was even better now he'd tried the food.

Noting the look of appreciation on Razor's face, Deborah said, 'You wouldn't think Johnny had such good taste, would you?'

'Johnny?'

'Yeah Johnny, big house, gold teeth. Do you know he worked alongside the chef designing the menu and selecting the wines? It's actually a hobby of his,' she said with amusement.

'I'm amazed; I thought lap dancing bars were more his thing.'

Razor couldn't imagine Johnny, with his tattoos and draped in gold, in a fancy restaurant and certainly not designing the menu. He thought him more suited to a greasy spoon café, wolfing down heart-attack-inducing fry-ups.

'So why is Johnny designing the...' Razor stopped mid sentence, suddenly knowing the answer to his question. 'This is Johnny's place, right?' he continued.

Deborah winked then put another piece of scallop into her mouth. It all now made sense to Razor, how Deborah succeeded in getting a table and the price didn't matter because they weren't paying. What didn't add up was why. Was Johnny just very generous or was it another case of favours for favours? Razor suspected it would be the latter.

# SCREWED

# CHAPTER THIRTY

Johnny leant back in his leather, captain's chair and put his feet up on the antique, mahogany desk. His eyes remained fixed on the large, flat-screen TV that displayed the images from the restaurant downstairs. Using the remote control, he could move the cameras to monitor any one of the twenty-five tables. He also had the capability to listen to what his customers were saying. Johnny was a great believer in the old saying 'information is power'. He already had police officers in Doncaster, Leeds and Sheffield on his payroll and now, thanks to Deborah, he'd soon have a screw inside HMP Doncaster. Johnny hit the zoom command; Razor's face appeared on the screen.

Johnny allowed himself a broad, gold-toothed smile and said out loud, 'It's going to be a pleasure doing business.'

Johnny clicked another button, and the image of Razor changed to a view of the whole restaurant. A total of sixty people occupied the restaurant, all paying an average of £150 per head, a total of £9,000 and it was only a Thursday night. Pascal's was open five nights a week and fully booked every one of those nights. In addition to that, there was a six-week waiting list to get into the place.

## SCREWED

The idea for the restaurant hadn't been Johnny's, an old friend and business associate gave him the idea. The friend had told Johnny that a restaurant would be an ideal way to supply cocaine to his high-end clients and launder the proceeds at the same time. That friend was now in the unfortunate position of spending the next couple of years at Her Majesty's pleasure for masterminding a multimillion-pound VAT scam. He was also currently residing in HMP Doncaster.

SCREWED

# CHAPTER THIRTY-ONE

Lucy and Razor were sat at the officers' desk when the unit manager came on to the wing brandishing a copy of the *Doncaster Star*. He placed the paper on the desk and turned it to face Lucy and Razor.

*Prison Suicide Unpreventable?* screamed the headline on the front page.

The article began with a brief bio of Matthew Dunford including details of how his bail had been revoked due to breaching the conditions, namely shouting abuse at the victim. The paper was questioning Dunford's breach and claimed that an undisclosed source had admitted to driving past the victim's address and yelling at Dunford's victim in an unrelated incident. Had the source come forward then Dunford would never have been remanded into custody. The paper asked why the police hadn't done more to ascertain whether it was indeed Dunford who had driven past the victim's house.

It then went on to give quotes from the report that had cleared the wing staff.

*Officer Ian Gillmore had spoken to the prisoner for approximately thirty seconds during his nightly cell checks just before midnight. At the time Officer Gillmore noted no suicidal tendencies, and therefore it was concluded that the prisoner*

## SCREWED

*had planned to take his life between the midnight and 2.00 a.m. cell checks.*

The paper went on to describe the previous attack on Dunford and the intention to move him to another wing for his safety. It then raised questions as to why Dunford hadn't been immediately moved from his current location if his safety was in question.

'Not pleasant reading, but I think the police have more to worry about than us,' sighed the unit manager.

'Well the report cleared the prison, didn't it?' said Lucy.

'The report was only an internal security report, and it did conclude that the staff were not to blame, but now the papers are involved there may be an independent inquiry,' said the unit manager glumly.

Lucy looked at Razor, but he couldn't meet her eyes.

'Five minutes to bang up,' he shouted, trying to divert her attention from him.

'Fuck off, Razor,' shouted an unseen prisoner.

Razor froze, this was getting beyond a joke; if his new nickname was becoming common then what else was?

# SCREWED

The prison staff weren't the only ones to read the *Doncaster Star*. Prisoners were permitted to buy both daily and local newspapers from their earning accounts. Bonzo was one of those prisoners. He wasn't in education and didn't have a prison job, so he had plenty of time to read the papers and liked to keep on top of what was going on locally. Each day he'd have a *Sun*, and a *Doncaster Star* delivered to his cell. As he lay on his bunk, he read the article on the front page of the *Doncaster Star* for the third time. He kept returning to one part and rereading it over and over again. *Officer Ian Gillmore had spoken to the prisoner for thirty seconds*. Bonzo's mind kept flicking back to that night in question, three weeks ago. He remembered hearing the footsteps; he remembered hearing his flap open, then the steps stopping outside the one next to his cell, Dunford's. He had recalled the pause before the footsteps continued again. What was bothering him was that he hadn't heard Gillmore talking to Dunford as the paper had stated. At that time of the night, everything was silent, and it would be impossible not to hear someone talking. It was Bonzo who'd spread the rumour around the wing about Dunford having sex with kids, but now he'd read the article it was apparent that the guy was just unlucky. When had he ever asked a girl's age in a pub or club? He felt a little bad for the guy,

## SCREWED

not that he was going to dwell on Dunford at all, he had other things on his mind. His weed business wasn't doing quite as well as it had been. His supply channel was working a treat, but that was irrelevant if the demand wasn't there. At first, he'd had customers queuing, but then he didn't have any real competition. Beef was selling Spice but having supply issues. Now that seemed to have all changed, Beef had an unlimited supply of Spice and could sell it a lot cheaper than Bonzo's weed. Bonzo had considered switching from marijuana to Spice and had mentioned this to Techno on his last visit. Techno had convinced him that it would be a bad idea. The market wasn't huge, so splitting it between two dealers would drive down the price and still cause a turf war on the wing. All in all, it wasn't worth the hassle. Techno also reasoned that Beef's unlimited supply had to be the result of a bent screw. Having a crooked officer on the other side could also lead to all sorts of problems for Bonzo. Techno figured that the only solution was to get Bonzo on to another wing, ideally one with a high percentage of young offenders. The only problem now was how to get moved.

As Bonzo lay on his bunk with the *Doncaster Star*, an idea began to form.

## CHAPTER THIRTY-TWO

It had been a long day on the wing, there'd been two fights, and a prisoner had taken an overdose of Spice causing him to vomit and lose control of his bowels. Lucy had suggested a couple of drinks after work and Razor had eagerly agreed.

'I feel terrible about this thing in the paper, Gilly,' said Lucy, taking a large gulp of wine.

'Look, I feel a little guilty too, but what can we do? What's done is done.'

'Look, Gilly, if it was any other con, say a burglar, and he got attacked, we'd have paid far more attention and checked on him more often, wouldn't we?'

'It's irrelevant, Luce; the guy still had sex with a minor.' Razor wasn't sure if he was trying to convince Lucy or himself.

'She was two days off her sixteenth birthday and in a nightclub for fuck's sake. She knew exactly what she was doing by agreeing to go back to his place. There's no way he deserved to be banged up. Gilly, he was only twenty, no wonder the poor sod couldn't cope.' Lucy's eyes were glistening with tears.

'It's tragic, Luce, but we didn't bang him up. He would have done the deed whatever we did or didn't do.' Razor closed his eyes and massaged

## SCREWED

his temples as the image of a dying Dunford overtook his thoughts. He knew that if it had been anyone other than someone he believed to be a nonce he would have opened the door and saved his life, no matter what the consequences. Razor opened his eyes and looked at Lucy. 'No matter what, Lucy, we're in the clear. Nothing else matters.'

Then Lucy threw a potential spanner into the works.

'What about Greg?' she said.

'Who?'

'Greg, my ex.'

'Yeah, I mean, what about him?'

'Well, I was throwing him out of my house while I was supposed to be at work providing a duty of care, making sure innocent men don't fucking hang themselves.' Her voice had risen, and the tears were flowing.

Razor held her hand and tried to think of something to say. Greg was a control freak and hadn't taken rejection well, but surely he wouldn't use this against her.

'He won't do anything, Luce.'

'You don't know him, Gilly. This is such a mess; we could both end up in prison.' She drained her glass with trembling hands.

'He probably hasn't even made the connection.'

## SCREWED

Razor picked up her empty glass and headed to the bar. He needed a few minutes to gather his thoughts. While he waited for the drinks, he ran the possibilities over in his mind. If Greg had realised the significance of that night, he was probably the type of guy who would say something to Lucy first. Razor concluded that the best course of action would be to wait and see. To his relief, Lucy agreed with him.

'Do you think I should take a few days off sick to sort my head out?' she asked.

'That's the last thing you should do. It may look dodgy if you suddenly go off sick the day after that newspaper report. There's obviously someone tipping the press off, and the last thing we need is them digging any further.'

Razor lay awake in bed, Deborah had texted him wanting to go out, but he just couldn't face it. The last thing he wanted was to let Deborah see him in this state. Razor didn't want her thinking that he was passing up on a night with her, so he'd replied back saying he wasn't feeling too well and was turning in early. In reality, there was no chance of that. Every time he closed his eyes Mathew Dunford was there. Lucy's words had really got to him. The only crime Dunford committed was going to a nightclub and not asking a girl her age.

# SCREWED

Next morning Razor was relieved to see Lucy's car parked up when he arrived for work. She was already on the wing when he walked in, and she seemed to be in good spirits.

'Morning, Luce. How's you today?'

'I'm good, Gilly. Guess what?'

'Go on, tell me.'

'I've got myself a job interview,' she beamed.

'What, you're leaving Doncatraz?'

'No. Remember that job I mentioned in admin?'

'The one that deals with prisoner categorisation?'

'Yeah, that's the one. It's a grand a year less, but it gets me off the wing. The interview's later on today.'

'I'll keep my fingers crossed for you.'

Razor checked his watch, time to lock the prisoners up or take those who wanted it, on to the exercise yard.

'Exercise or bang up,' he bellowed.

A few cons moved to the wing door so that they could be let out to the yard. Most went to stand by their cell doors so they could be locked away until lunchtime. Only Beef and four of his gang remained leaning against the pool table. Razor was getting tired of Beef's attitude. He'd enjoyed picking up the £700 from Ish on Saturday night, and he'd already dropped off the first of this week's packages so was due another £700 this weekend, but dealing with Beef was getting under his skin and, to make matters worse, Beef knew it and was taking great pleasure in pushing him to his limits. As Beef's release date got closer, he began to take more liberties with what he was saying. The guy was a fucking idiot and was breaking the rules to the extreme. Ish had mentioned a replacement for Beef, once he was released, but at the rate Beef was going it would all be out in the open before the new guy came on board. Maybe this was Beef's plan, a final fuck you to Razor as a parting gift. He'd have to have a serious chat with Ish about it.

Not in the mood for another confrontation with Beef, Razor grabbed his jacket and headed for the yard to supervise the exercise period. He'd leave Lucy to deal with Beef.

Bonzo had nearly got to his cell door when he noticed Razor going to the yard in his coat. He knew that Razor would be the only prison officer out there, so it would give him that long-awaited opportunity for a chat. He changed direction and joined the small group waiting to be let out on to the exercise yard. Once out in the yard, Razor stood by the door and watched the prisoners

# SCREWED

walking round and round. Bonzo had done two laps before coming to a standstill beside Razor. The other prisoners carried on circling the yard and paid no attention to Bonzo or Razor.

'Alright, Mr Gillmore?' said Bonzo.

'You can't go back in yet if that's what you're after,' said Razor, in no mood to talk.

'I just fancied a chat, is all.'

'Maybe I don't feel like talking, and you're supposed to be out here to exercise, so exercise,' Razor snapped.

'OK, if you don't wanna chat. How about I talk, you listen!'

Razor didn't respond. Instead, he shifted his attention to a pigeon sat on the barbed wire fence.

'Interesting article in the Donny Star the other day.'

Razor ignored him and said nothing.

'Funny, you stop at the door talking away to suicide boy, while I'm right next door and I don't hear a thing. Why do you think that is?'

Razor turned his head and glared directly at Bonzo.

'What's your point?'

'Point is, Mr Gillmore, you say you were talking, I *know* you weren't.'

'Nobody is going to believe what you think you did or didn't hear. You think they'd take the

# SCREWED

word of a drug dealing lowlife over that of a respected prison officer?' he hissed, trying to keep his voice calm.

'You feel brave enough to take that chance, Mr Gillmore?' taunted Bonzo.

Razor certainly didn't want to take that chance, but he didn't want to show Bonzo his hand. He wondered what exactly he was after. He decided attack was the best form of defence.

'How about we security toss your cell tonight?'

Bonzo grinned and said, 'Go right ahead; you won't find nothing in there.'

Razor was about to respond when a small group of prisoners came into earshot. He waited until they'd passed before saying, 'You're very sure of your fucking self, Bonzo.'

'That I am. Now listen up. I don't give a fuck about suicide boy or you for that matter. What I do give a fuck about is getting moved to 3C.'

'The YO wing?' asked Razor, genuinely surprised. The move was something he could sort with relative ease but couldn't understand why Bonzo would make such a simple request. Having Bonzo on another wing would suit him just fine. Out of sight, out of mind. Bonzo didn't respond so Razor asked, 'Is that it?'

# SCREWED

'Yeah. I want to be with all those young offenders. Bigger market for my product.'

Razor agreed, a little too quickly. Bonzo picked up on this and realised there was a greater opportunity to be had.

'I also want a good write-up so I can get a nice single cell. It's been quite nice while Turner's been away in the hospital, and I've got quite used to my own company.'

'OK, so I do that for you, and you forget everything you did or didn't hear.'

'That's the deal, Mr Gillmore,' said Bonzo pleasantly.

'You'll be gone Monday.'

Bonzo gave Razor a toothy grin and resumed his laps of the yard.

Razor called an end to exercise and herded the prisoners back inside. Within ten minutes everyone was locked away and the wing was quiet. Lucy was sat at the desk drinking coffee. Razor walked over to her and told her he was off to see the unit manager.

'How come?' she asked him.

'Nothing exciting, just that kid in 312 wants off the wing. He's getting a bit of shit apparently.'

'Not like you, Gilly, to give a toss.'

# SCREWED

'After Dunford, we can't take risks. Can we?'

He left the wing, found the unit manager and put forward the case for moving Bonzo to 3C. As Bonzo was only in his early twenties, Razor explained that he'd be better suited being with prisoners closer to his own age. In normal circumstances, a report would need filing and a mountain of paperwork filled in, but in light of the story in the *Doncaster Star*, the unit manager didn't want any problems. After a few clicks on his computer, the unit manager said there was a single cell free, so he signed off the move there and then.

*Perfect*, thought Razor not believing his luck. Lucy could take Bonzo to 3C on her way to the job interview that afternoon, and then after today he'd never have to clap eyes on him again.

Back on the wing, Razor headed off to give Bonzo the good news. Although he was pleased that Bonzo would now be off the wing, Razor was beginning to worry about him. He wasn't convinced that Bonzo would be able to keep quiet. The more he thought about it, the more he became convinced that Bonzo was a liability.

At 1.30 p.m. Lucy unlocked the cell door. Bonzo had his belongings packed into a single, large plastic bag and was sat on his bunk waiting. He followed her through the maze of corridors and the series of locked, barred doors until they reached wing 3C.

Techno had already found a new vantage point that overlooked Bonzo's new home. There was another bonus of not being on the ground floor, that being, there were no cages over the windows, so they could now get larger packages into the jail. Bonzo glanced around the wing at his new customer base and smiled. As well as selling Spice, Techno had told Bonzo that they would soon be running Doncatraz's first branch of Carphone Warehouse.

After depositing Bonzo in his new cell, Lucy headed eagerly to the Amenities Block for her job interview. An hour and a half later she was back on the wing.

'I got it, Gilly, they gave me the job. Starting Monday. Can you believe that?'

'They don't mess around, do they? Seriously, Luce, I'm made up for you.'

'Well, to be honest, there was only me that applied. Apparently, they've got massive backlogs on security and such, so they needed someone ASAP. Anyway, who cares, I'm off the wing. No more prisoners.'

They agreed to go for a few drinks after work to celebrate. Three hours later they were sat

## SCREWED

in the same pub as the previous night, but tonight the mood was a lot lighter. Lucy was in high spirits. What a difference twenty-four hours had made. A few other officers from the wing came and went over the course of the evening, but by last orders, it was just Razor and Lucy.

Leaning across the table to Razor, she slurred, 'I think this new job is going to be a new start for me, but I'm going miss working with you, Gilly.' Then turning serious she continued, 'I could never forget about what happened if I was still on that wing.'

Razor was going to miss working with Lucy too, but he had to admit that it was a good thing for both of them. He'd been worried about Lucy's state of mind and was concerned that her conscience would eventually get the better of her. That was the problem with wing work; it could be a constant reminder. Once she was tucked away in the offices, she'd be busy and have less time to think.

Neither Razor nor Lucy had any reason to rush home. Both their houses would be empty, Lucy was now single, and Deborah was working until late. They decided to have one more drink then head off to a curry house.

They ordered wine with the curry, and by now they were both feeling quite drunk, giggling

# SCREWED

like a couple of teenagers. Suddenly Lucy's phone chimed indicating that she'd received a text message. The blood drained from her face as she read the message and her whole persona changed.

'What's up, Luce? Has something happened?' asked Razor.

'It's a text from Greg.'

'What's up with him now?'

She proceeded to read the text out loud: 'Didn't know you could be in two places at once! Ring me.'

'Come on, Luce, that could mean anything. He's an arse. He's just after a reaction,' said Razor, not actually believing his own words.

'You don't know him like I do, Gilly. He may be cruel, but he's not stupid. He will have seen the paper and put two and two together.'

'Just ignore him, Luce. If he thinks you're not concerned, he'll soon get bored and go away.'

'And what if he doesn't?'

'We'll cross that bridge when, and if, we come to it.'

'I've lost my appetite, Gilly. Let's call it a night.'

Razor paid the bill, and they shared a taxi home. When the taxi stopped outside Lucy's house, she asked Razor if he'd like to come in for a drink. After polishing off another bottle of wine, Razor announced that he should be getting home.

# SCREWED

Lucy placed a hand on his knee and asked him to stay. Seeing the look on Razor's face, she instantly regretted her words. Razor, not wanting to embarrass them both, made an excuse about meeting Deborah and made a hasty exit.

Once home, Razor snorted a quick line then flicked on the TV. He replayed the conversations with Bonzo. There was no question that Bonzo could cause him all kinds of problems. It was a risk he couldn't afford to take. Razor made up his mind that Bonzo was a liability and would somehow have to be silenced.

## CHAPTER THIRTY-THREE

Razor felt a little awkward as he walked on to the wing the next morning. There was a little tension between them to begin with, but thankfully Lucy didn't mention anything about the night before. Razor put her actions down to too much booze and was glad it was forgotten. His mind kept flicking back to the problem of Bonzo. No doubt Ish would have a solution.

The shifts had now been altered slightly to accommodate Lucy's move. The change meant that both Razor and Lucy had to work on the coming Friday, but Razor could then take the Monday off.

After work, Razor met up with Ish to collect the second batch of Spice of the week.

'I can hold out until next week for my cash, Ish. No need to meet up on Saturday.'

The truth was Razor didn't want to spend another Saturday night in Ishmael's company. The previous week they were meant to be meeting for a 'quick drink', but Ish stuck around all night, drinking their champagne and snorting their party powder.

'You mean, you don't want me crashing your party with Deborah,' grinned Ish.

'Well, you know how it is, Ish. We don't a lot of time together.'

# SCREWED

'Yeah man, it's cool. I've got me a hottie for Saturday night anyway.'

After a bit of small talk Razor's mind focused on his two problems: Lucy's ex-partner and Bonzo. He decided not to mention anything about Lucy's ex for now, as nothing may come of that. But the problem with Bonzo was imminent.

'Listen Ish, we've got a bit of a problem with a guy on the inside.'

Ishmael leaned in closer, a look of concern spreading over his face.

Razor had been thinking about the best way to get Ish to sort out Bonzo and decided it would be easier to imply that he was somehow going to jeopardise their little enterprise with the Spice. He proceeded to explain that Bonzo had found out about the supply of Spice and threatened to inform unless he received a cut. Ishmael's features darkened as Razor lied about Bonzo's threats.

'Da treacherous bastard. We'll have to get him sorted,' spat Ish.

'I've moved him off the wing, but that's as much as I can do, he could still fuck everything up for us.'

'Leave it with me, I'll get him sorted,' Ishmael said coldly.

# SCREWED

Razor grinned, feeling pleased with himself. It felt good knowing at least one of his problems would soon be sorted.

# CHAPTER THIRTY-FOUR

Friday morning Lucy unlocked the lower landing while Razor took care of the top landing. When he got to cell 308, he unlocked it and tossed in the fag packet containing the Spice.

'Where the fook have you been with this, Razor? I should of 'ad it yesterday,' spat Beef.

'You got a problem, get it from someone else,' hissed Razor venomously, before moving on to unlock the next cell.

As Razor opened the door, the YO who occupied the cell looked up from his bunk and said, 'Hey, Razor, know where there's any Spice going?'

Razor froze. Beef had apparently been spouting off about their business dealings. He felt his blood beginning to boil. Who else knew? He decided this was something that Ish needed to know about. He'd mention it when he collected the money next week but didn't know how Ish would react to him criticising one of his crew. Razor was sure that it wouldn't be too hard to replace Beef with one of other many drug dealers who resided at the prison, and maybe they could save a few quid in the process.

On Friday night around twenty-five prison officers gathered in the pub near to the jail to give Lucy a send-off. Razor took Lucy to one side, before she had too much to drink, and asked her if she'd heard any more from her ex. She told him that she'd heard nothing.

'We're going to keep in touch aren't we, Gilly?'

'Jesus Lucy, we're still working in the same building. It's not like you're emigrating.'

'When was the last time you ever laid eyes on anyone from admin? We've even got our own entrance.'

'Good point, but yeah, we'll keep in touch.'

'Oh and Gilly, about the other night.'

'Forget it, Luce. Let's get a drink.'

Razor was looking forward to his long weekend; he'd planned a bit of shopping on Saturday daytime, and then up to Leeds for a blowout with Deborah at night. He was hoping Sunday would then be a lazy day in bed for them both followed by a swanky meal Sunday night. The new four-day work week was suiting Razor, although he was spending a lot more money. The additional income from the Spice was proving essential. There was just one problem in his life at the moment and that was Beef, the guy was a liability and could ruin it for all concerned. Something needed doing.

Ish had contacted Razor early Saturday morning; he was going away for a couple of days so needed

## SCREWED

to see him. He suggested Razor call round to his place to collect the Spice and his share of the cash. He was now making the equivalent of three weeks' wages every week.

'Razor man, welcome into my humble abode,' said a grinning Ishmael as he opened the front door.

Razor walked into the front room and sat on one of the leather settees. His eyes rested on the huge flat-screen TV that seemed to dominate the front room.

'I see you like my TV, Razor man. Well you'll like what's behind it more,' said Ish as he moved toward the TV. He then flicked a hidden button behind the flat screen, and the whole thing swung to one side. Behind the television, and built into the chimney breast, was a large safe. Ishmael snapped on a pair of surgical gloves, removed a key from his pocket and unlocked the safe.

'Can't be too careful, Razor man.'

He then removed two plastic bags containing Spice and a thick bundle of cash. He tossed them both to an amazed Razor.

'Pretty neat eh, Razor man? Johnny had it installed for me. If the pigs ever came knocking they'd never find this.' He then locked the safe and swung the TV back into position, then said, 'I think I've sorted out that Bonzo geezer too. I've

# SCREWED

got a couple of mates on 3C who owe me a favour or two.'

Ish then tapped out a couple of lines of coke from his personal stash.

Razor left Ishmael's feeling positive, he was buzzing from the coke, had a pile of cash in his pocket and it was looking like Bonzo was going to be sorted out too. It wasn't until he'd left Ishmael's house that he remembered that he'd wanted to have a chat about Beef.

*Fuck Beef. He can wait*, Razor thought to himself.

Razor then spent the afternoon with Deborah. They hit the shops, had a long lunch and then ended up in bed back at his place. His day had got better and better.

'I'm going have to get up soon and get sorted for work,' purred Deborah, as she ran her hand up and down his chest.

'Haven't you ever considered trying something else?' asked Razor pushing her hand away.

'Are you jealous or something, Razor?' she said abruptly, sitting up.

'No, no, it's not the job, it's just the hours I don't like.'

## SCREWED

The truth was Razor was very jealous of other men leering over her, and the hours just made it worse.

'Nine till one, five days a week, and I walk out with five grand in cash. You tell me what other job pays that?'

Razor sat up.

'Fucking hell, Deborah. I'd have to work nearly a month to earn what you make in a night.'

'Yeah, but you haven't got a pair of these,' she said rubbing her breasts and laughing loudly.

Still laughing, she hopped out of bed and headed for the bathroom.

'Seriously, do you actually earn five grand a week?' he shouted after her.

Popping her head back around the door she said, 'No, Razor, not always. Sometimes I make six or seven.' She laughed again and disappeared into the bathroom.

While Deborah was in the shower the subject kept turning over in Razor's mind, and when she came back into the bedroom he asked, 'So are you going do it forever?'

She looked over at him.

'If you want to make big money you have to use whatever you have to your full advantage. I've got my body, but it won't last forever. You've got your job, and to some people that could be a significant benefit,' she said matter-of-factly and continued to get ready for work.

After she'd left, her words were ringing in Razor's ears. Had she meant anyone in particular when she'd referred to 'some people'? He was sure that he'd find out soon enough. Razor's thoughts were interrupted by a beep from his mobile. He'd received a text from Tony asking if he fancied a couple of drinks early doors. As he hadn't planned on leaving for Leeds until about ten, he agreed. He could have a few drinks then get a taxi to Leeds afterwards.

Razor was stood at the bar, halfway down his pint, when Tony joined him.

'Alright, Tone. What ya drinking?'

'I'll have the same, mate.'

'So how's married life, Tone?'

'She lets me out when she's at her night course, but that's about as good as it gets. But fuck married life, how's life dating a stripper? At the wedding she looked even sexier than I remembered. You're a lucky bugger.'

They chatted for a while about the life in general, then just after ordering the next round the topic changed to work. Tony brought up the one subject that Razor really didn't want to discuss.

## SCREWED

'Bad news about that suicide at your place. Poor chap shouldn't have even been in there.'

'That's not down to us, Tone. We're there to keep 'em...' Razor was about to say safe but thought better of it.

'Yeah well, you know that independent police enquiry that they are setting up?'

'Yeah, thanks to that newspaper article.'

'You remember Paul, from the stag do, the chief super? Well he's overseeing the enquiry.'

'Is that a part of his job remit?' asked Razor sounding surprised.

'It can be, but this one Paul has actually requested.'

Razor listened and wondered why Paul had requested such a thing. He knew that the prison and the police would take a bit of flak but everyone would come out OK.

*So why would a chief superintendent get involved?* he wondered.

It was getting toward ten, and both Tony and Razor were getting a taste for the booze. Then Tony received a call from his wife.

'What are you doing for the rest of the night, Gilly?'

'I'm off to Leeds to see Deborah. Why?'

'My curfew's just been extended. The wife is going for drinks with her night class buddies, so I think I'll make the most of it and come with you.'

# SCREWED

The drinks had clouded Razor's judgement slightly. Under normal circumstances, he wouldn't want any of his old mates mixing in his new circle. But enjoying Tony's company, he agreed. They finished their beers and grabbed a taxi. The taxi pulled up outside the Living Room, and they jumped out.

'For fuck's sake, Gilly, look at the queue. I'm not standing in that for an hour. Let's go somewhere else.'

Smiling, Razor ushered him to the VIP entrance where, to Tony's amazement, they entered without delay. They went directly to the VIP room where a doorman welcomed them. They walked over to the bar to find Claudio talking animatedly to a young waitress.

'Evening Claudio, Chloe,' said Razor with bravado.

Claudio rushed around the bar to greet them.

'I'll have a bottle of your usual sent over for you and your guest. Do you require anything else this evening?'

'No Claudio, that'll be all. Allow me to introduce my friend, Tony. He's a DS in the police force.'

Tony and Claudio shook hands. Luckily, Tony was too preoccupied with Chloe's cleavage to

# SCREWED

notice how Razor had introduced him. Razor led the way to the booth while Tony followed closely behind, taking in all the sights. No sooner had they sat down, than Claudio arrived with the bottle of Bollinger and two glasses.

'This one's on Johnny. He's in tonight and says he'll pop over later and say hello.'

Tony just stared in amazement, as Claudio filled the two flutes. Once Claudio had left, Tony picked up a glass and looked over at Razor.

'What the fuck's going on? All this VIP treatment, free champagne. Have I had a bump on the head? Are we in heaven? And what's all this Mr Razor shit?' laughed Tony.

Razor sipped his champagne enjoying the envy in Tony's voice. They'd soon finished the first bottle and, without asking, another one appeared, however, this time it came with three glasses. The waitress, who was bending over pouring champagne, gave a squeal and nearly knocked over a glass. Razor looked up to see Johnny stood behind her grinning, his gold teeth shining in the dim light.

'How's it going gents? Is Chloe here looking after you?' he said, giving her bottom a slap as she walked away.

Johnny then sat down and Razor made the introductions. Johnny started telling story after

# SCREWED

story about the time he'd spent running various strip clubs and had Tony and Razor in fits of laughter. The champagne was flowing in earnest and, without the cocaine, Razor was feeling the effects which he didn't enjoy quite as much. He excused himself and found Claudio, before heading off to the gents. Claudio had guessed Razor would be needing a little something extra and took the liberty of having a vial tucked away in his silk-lined jacket pocket. Razor went straight to the cubicle and tapped out a large pile on to the back of his hand. His mind instantly cleared as the cocaine hit his brain like a bullet. By the time he returned to the booth, the conversation had taken an altogether different tone. Tony was now enlightening Johnny on life in the police. Every so often Johnny would ask a seemingly innocent question, to a casual passer-by it would appear that Tony and Johnny were two old mates catching up, but Razor was beginning to get the feeling that with Johnny there was bound to be an angle.

'I'm off for a piss, chaps,' slurred Tony, as he unsteadily got to his feet and left the booth.

Johnny moved, shifted position and sat next to Razor.

'I'm at your place tomorrow,' said Johnny with a grin. The look of confusion on Razor's face prompted Johnny to say with a laugh, 'You know,

# SCREWED

Doncatraz? What? Don't tell me you forgot you still work there?'

'Oh yeah, right. Sorry. What you doing there?'

'Oh, I just thought I'd check in for a couple of nights of all-inclusive luxury.'

'Eh?' said Razor missing the sarcasm in Johnny's voice.

'I'm visiting an old mate, you doughnut.'

'Oh yeah, right. Anyone I know?' asked Razor, regretting asking the question as soon as he said it.

'It's a big place ain't it? Maybe you would, maybe you wouldn't. Anyway, it wouldn't be fair to mention his name without his knowledge, and I wouldn't want you to feel obliged to treat him differently.'

Just as Tony returned from the toilet, Johnny announced that he had business to attend to. He shook them both warmly by the hand and left.

'Bloody nice guy, your mate Johnny. Looks a bit rough, and I certainly wouldn't want to be on the wrong side of him, but he's the salt of the earth,' began Tony.

Razor nodded.

'He knows some of the lads at work too and he...' he continued.

# SCREWED

Deciding he'd heard enough about Johnny, he cut Tony off mid sentence.

'Listen, Tone, Deborah will be here soon, and I don't want you getting into any shit with your missus. What time did you tell her you'd be home?'

'Relax Gilly old boy, soon as your girl gets here, I'll make a move. I wasn't planning on playing gooseberry.'

Ishmael was standing at the bar chatting to the barmaid. He'd expected to call in and have a word with Razor, but seeing that he had company decided to wait until later on. As usual, his eyes were darting around the place as he chatted. He suddenly noticed Deborah enter the room, but when he saw who she was with his mood darkened. He knocked back his drink and decided he'd leave; his business with Razor would just have to wait, he had no intention of being in the same vicinity as Deborah's sneaky, white-assed bitch of a mate. He'd known Jodie, or Crystal as she now called herself, when she was a two-bit hooker working on the housing estates. She would do anything to make a few quid, and Ishmael had a serious dislike for her.

Deborah, closely followed by her friend, sauntered across the dance floor and into the booth.

# SCREWED

'Hey Razor, how's my lover?' Her lips met his, and she wriggled up close to him on the sofa, then looking over at Tony she said, 'Hey, Tony. I didn't know you'd be here tonight. Great to see you again.'

Tony didn't answer immediately, as his eyes were fixed firmly on Deborah's friend who was still standing up showing off everything she had to offer. She was a tall brunette and was wearing the tightest minidress that Tony had ever seen. Her surgically enhanced breasts were straining the white fabric of the dress. Razor glanced at Tony, whose eyes were fit to burst out of his head, and gave an exaggerated cough. Tony snapped out of his trance, and his eyes moved to Deborah.

'Oh yeah, great to see you too, Deborah.'

'You don't mind if Crystal joins us do you guys? Her douchebag boyfriend has been cheating on her, and she needs cheering up,' said Deborah rubbing Razor's leg.

Before they could answer the question, she quickly pulled Crystal into the booth next to Tony and made the introductions. Tony kissed Crystal on each cheek.

'It's a pleasure to meet you, Tony,' said Crystal, her words dripping like honey from her full, red lips.

# SCREWED

'The pleasure's all mine; it's not often I get to be in the presence of such beauty.'

'Oh, what a gentleman,' she giggled.

Razor was cringing at the exchange and felt it was time for Tony to leave. 'Tony was just about to...' Razor wanted to say 'go home to his wife' to halt the sickly flirting between the two.

Tony, sensing what Razor was about to say, cut him off mid sentence.

'...Go to the bar and get these two stunning ladies some champagne,' said Tony standing up and giving Razor the wink.

'There's no need for that, Tony. We're in the VIP area, table service,' said Deborah.

Tony sat back down unnecessarily close to Crystal, not that she put up any objections. More champagne duly arrived, and Razor decided that maybe it wasn't a bad thing after all for Tony to stick around. He didn't want to listen to Deborah and her mate chatting all night, while he sat there like a spare part. At least this way he had Deborah more or less to himself, as it appeared that Tony was more than happy to entertain Crystal.

After copious amounts of champagne, Razor had relaxed, and the four of them were now all chatting and laughing together. Before long they were in the middle of the crowded dance floor

# SCREWED

doing some very close dancing. To the delight of Tony, Deborah and Crystal began gyrating against each other like a couple of porn stars. Deborah then caught hold of Tony and pulled him in close, her legs entwining into his as they danced. Crystal put her arms around Razor's waist and began to grind against him. He wasn't in the mood for these games, so he eased her away and headed straight to the toilets. He took a glance back over his shoulder to see Tony, sandwiched between the two girls, looking like the cat who'd got the cream. Razor slammed the cubicle door shut and snorted a larger than usual pile of the white stuff. Heading back to the dance floor, he saw only Tony and Crystal. Tony's hand was lost up Crystal's barely there dress, and they were kissing with the enthusiasm of a couple of teenagers. After scanning the dance floor and not seeing Deborah, he decided to go back to the booth and hopefully find her there waiting for him. As he entered the booth, he found Deborah sat, legs crossed, refilling two champagne flutes. He sat next to her, she smiled and handed him a glass.

'Everything OK, Razor? You seem a little preoccupied tonight.'

'I'm fine, Deborah, but tell me it was just a coincidence that you turn up here with that sort, Crystal, the only time I'm here with a mate.'

# SCREWED

'What are you getting at, Razor? I told you, she just needed cheering up,' she said calmly.

'It's not right; he's only just got married. You were at the wedding, remember?' he snapped.

'Well, he's not acting very married,' she retorted, as she nodded to the dance floor where the two had their mouths locked together with no sign of coming up for air.

'Look, I'm sorry. Tough day,' said Razor, pulling her towards him for a kiss. Razor's mood was lightening by the second. He downed his champagne, took Deborah by the hand and led her back to the dance floor.

Razor's last sighting of Tony was as he was staggering towards the exit, his arm firmly around Crystal's slim waste, he was holding her as if she may run off.

Razor wasn't the only one to observe Tony leaving the bar with Crystal. From a large office at the back of the building Johnny had been watching Tony, with immense amusement, on one of the many CCTV screens. He smiled his big, gold smile, took a pull on a thick Cuban cigar and blew a huge plume of blue-tinged smoke towards the ceiling.

Johnny then leant back in his plush black leather chair, that dwarfed even his bulk, and said out loud to himself, 'Welcome to the family, Detective Tony Price.'

# SCREWED

# CHAPTER THIRTY-FIVE

Bonzo walked out of his new single cell. He leaned on the metal banister that surrounded the top landing and looked down on to wing 3C. Bonzo smiled to himself, as he watched his new batch of customers wandering around the wing with vacant expressions on their faces. The move to 3C couldn't have been any better. He was now making over two thousand pounds every week. Looking back he decided that he probably could have extracted a few quid out of that screw Gillmore, but then why be greedy? This way he was making good money and the screw was still onside, should he ever need him again. Everyone was happy.

As most of the inmates were playing cards, pool, or walking around the wing in a Spice-induced state, Bonzo decided it would be a good time to take a shower. He enjoyed having the shower block to himself. He returned to his cell, picked up his towel and shower gel, and walked towards the shower block that was located in the corner of the wing.

Two prisoners were watching as Bonzo made his slow walk to the showers. They gave a quick glance towards the two screws on duty. The officers were sat at the desk near the entrance to the wing. They were engrossed in conversation

## SCREWED

and paying no attention to what may, or may not, be going on around them. The two prisoners ascended the stairs to the top landing and entered the shower block. The shower stalls were only five-feet high, so the two could easily see Bonzo. The first guy moved into the stall next to Bonzo. In one swift movement he reached over and took hold of Bonzo's head and pulled it backwards. At the same time the second prisoner ran into the stall that Bonzo was occupying. The first thing Bonzo saw was the razor blade that had been melted into the end of a toothbrush. In one fluid motion the prisoner slashed the blade across Bonzo's exposed throat. The two prisoners then left the shower block. The whole incident lasted no more than ten seconds.

Bonzo clasped his hands to his throat; he could feel himself becoming light-headed. He managed three steps before collapsing on to the tiled floor.

Bonzo's lifeless body was discovered an hour later, after one of the prison officers checked the shower block before afternoon bang up.

# CHAPTER THIRTY-SIX

Johnny was pacing around his office, the very same office he'd occupied the night before. He'd told her to be here at one, and it was now nearly half past. He had to be at Doncatraz at three and hated to be kept waiting, by anyone, let alone someone in his employ. Just then there was a quiet tap at the door.

'Come in,' he bellowed.

A girl wearing an expensive, mauve-coloured mac entered the room. Johnny noticed that under the mac she was still wearing the white minidress from the previous night.

'You must have something good for me, Jodie, or is it still Crystal?' he said, looking her up and down with a grin.

She fished a mobile phone from one of her pockets and waved it at Johnny.

'Turn on your computer. I think you're going to like this,' she said gleefully.

Johnny ambled around his desk, sank into his chair and fired up his desktop computer. Jodie was standing next to him, as he transferred the data from the phone to the PC. As he did so, he slid his left hand up her leg and gripped her firm buttocks. Jodie slipped off the mac and let it fall to the floor. Before Johnny could go any further, the computer beeped once indicating the transfer was complete. Johnny clicked 'open', and the screen filled with a clear image showing a semi-naked Jodie draped over the detective. After viewing a further twenty-five images, Johnny came to the jackpot. It was a three-minute video clip starring Jodie and Detective Tony Price, which certainly left nothing to the imagination.

'You've excelled yourself, Jodie,' he said, as he removed his hand from her pert behind. He then opened a drawer in his desk and pulled out a thick envelope, it contained three grand in used twenties. He tossed the envelope on to the desk. Three grand was a steal for another copper in his pocket, even if DS Tony Price didn't know it yet.

Jodie leant over the desk to pick up the envelope, as she did so Johnny eased up her minidress and proceeded to undo his belt. Ten minutes later he exited the Living Room via a back door.

He climbed into the waiting Range Rover and said gruffly, 'Take me to Doncatraz.'

# SCREWED

# CHAPTER THIRTY-SEVEN

Once Johnny was out of the prison and back in the comfort of the Range Rover, he took out his mobile phone and sent a text to Deborah.

*You and your man, my restaurant tonight. 8.30 sharp.*

Johnny didn't believe in using pleasantries when they weren't needed. He looked after his people well and in return expected loyalty and commitment, so if Johnny requested your presence somewhere, you were supposed to turn up and no excuses. Johnny adjusted his large frame to retrieve a thin book from the back pocket of his jeans. He needed a date for tonight to make up the foursome. He flicked through the well-worn pages. Johnny was very old-fashioned in that respect, he just didn't trust mobile phones. He liked things written down, plus the bonus with his diary was that he was able to add a little note next to each name. After all, when you owned four lap dancing clubs, you had the pick of a lot of women. But as with most things in life, it was horses for courses. All of the girls in his clubs were great to look at, and most were blinding in the sack. But sit them in a nice restaurant, and they wouldn't know which end of a fork to use. Tonight he wanted someone who could hold a good conversation, eat with their mouth closed and one

## SCREWED

that he actually had a degree of respect for. Tall order. At times like these Johnny wished he had a wife. After ten minutes' deliberation, he selected a girl named Joanne. She held the same position as Deborah but in the Sheffield club. Joanne, however, had given up the stripping some time ago and was happy managing the girls. She was now in her early forties and had earned enough money from lap dancing to have a very comfortable lifestyle. However, she still enjoyed working with the girls and for Johnny. The £1,000 per week that he paid her was the icing on the cake.

With his fat fingers prodding away at the buttons on his phone, Johnny sent an equally blunt text to Joanne. Johnny's phone was the most basic on the market; he could make calls, receive them and text. What else did a man need? There was an increasing number of criminals serving time at Her Majesty's pleasure due to their exact locations being identified by the GPS on their smartphones. Johnny's phone had no bells, no whistles and definitely no GPS.

Johnny barked an address at his driver. His phone beeped twice. As he spoke he looked down, the first message read:

*OK, see you there. D x.*

The second read:

## SCREWED

*Pick me up at 8, and it's Cristal champagne all night big boy. Jo x.*

Johnny smiled to himself, the cheeky bint, Cristal champagne was £500 a bottle at his place, but she'd always come when Johnny shouted. He knew that she liked to feel as though she'd scored a point or two from him, he admired that about her and let her get away with it.

The Range Rover stopped outside an end terrace house. The house was in better condition than the other houses in the street. The windows were uPVC and looked new, the front door was a sturdy metal and painted a dark red. As was typical with end terraces, the house had ample room to one side that was tarmacked and flanked by a six-foot high wooden fence. In the space sat a three series BMW, no more than twelve months old, with tinted windows and alloy wheels. Even though the light was fading, the black BMW was gleaming. Johnny slowly disembarked from the back of the Range Rover and approached the red front door and gave a loud knock. There was no answer. He noticed closed curtains in the window next to the door but a light shone through a slight gap where they hadn't quite met. He knocked again with greater force. This time he noticed that the peephole in the door had gone dark, indicating that someone was looking through it. Johnny gave a broad smile, showing off his gold teeth. Two bolts then slid back, and the key turned. The door opened to reveal Ishmael wearing a bright purple onesie.

'Fuck me, have I come to the wrong house? You look like an overgrown baby.'

'It's fashion, Johnny man. Come in.'

Johnny stepped through the door into the front room. Between the sofas, that dominated the room, was a low, black glass coffee table. The only thing on it was a large, silver ashtray in which lay a thick, smouldering joint. They both sat on opposite sofas facing each other. Ish felt around for the remote and lowered the volume on the TV that filled the chimney breast. Johnny glanced briefly at the half-naked, black women singing and twerking on the screen before switching his attention to Ish.

'So, Johnny man, what brings you to me crib?' said Ishmael taking a long drag on the joint.

Johnny could tell, by the size of Ishmael's pupils, that it probably wasn't Ishmael's first joint of the day.

'I've been to Doncatraz today, Ish. An old mate of mine is doing a bit of bird there.' Johnny was observing Ishmael's features, and so far there had been no reaction to his words, so he continued. 'Anyway, my mate seems to think, although he's not entirely sure, that there's a bent screw bringing in drugs. Now obviously that can't

# SCREWED

be true, else I'd know about it wouldn't I, Ish?' said Johnny with an edge.

'Yeah, cuz you'd know. Cuz I'd know, and we don't 'av no secrets,' said Ish a little too quickly.

Johnny had noticed a vein in Ishmael's temple twitch and instantly knew he was lying.

'How long have you worked for me now, Ish? Two, three years?'

Johnny knew the answer but wanted to gauge his reaction further to be certain.

'Four years, Johnny man, innit? Look, if I heard anything about a bent screw you'd be the first to know. What wing is this bent screw meant to be on anyway?'

Johnny decided to test him now.

'Well my mate is on wing 3C, so I'd say the bent screw is on there, wouldn't you?' lied Johnny.

Ish visibly relaxed, Razor worked on 1A so he concluded there must be another bent screw working on 3C. He'd make some enquiries and hopefully score some brownie points with Johnny.

'Must be one of the other firms, Johnny man. I'll ask around.'

Johnny instantly noticed how Ishmael's body had relaxed the second he'd mentioned wing 3C. This gave him all the confirmation he needed. The treacherous bastard was doing business behind his back. Johnny stared at Ish wanting to

# SCREWED

rip out his throat there and then, but managed to keep his rage under control. He needed to be subtle and couldn't get his hands dirty. Not wanting Ish to realise how mad he was, Johnny shifted his gaze back to the flat-screen TV. That was when an idea hit him; he'd sold this house to Ishmael and knew exactly what was hiding behind that big, expensive flat-screen TV.

He stood abruptly, and fixing Ish with a hard stare said, 'Yeah, you ask around, Ish. I'd hate for anyone to be on the make without giving me my dues.'

Ishmael, not liking Johnny's tone, scrambled to his feet, eager to get him out of the house.

'I'll get right on to it, Johnny man,' he said with a slight tremor in his voice.

Johnny opened the front door and walked out without another word. His driver obediently opened the back door of the Range Rover, hopped into the driver's seat and waited. Johnny sat for a moment turning over the brief meeting in his mind. It seemed obvious that Razor was the bent screw working with Ishmael. In one respect it was a good thing, because if Razor was already bent it would save Johnny the hassle of corrupting him. But if he was bent then he should be Johnny's bent screw, not working with a fucking underling who didn't have the decency to keep his boss in the loop. On top of that was the dealer inside the prison. Johnny knew full well that Beef was serving time in Doncatraz, so it stood to reason that if Ish had a man dealing on the wing, Beef would be that man. He sat for another minute or two cementing his plans for Ishmael and Beef, before noticing the driver looking at him expectantly in the rear-view mirror.

'Home,' growled Johnny.

Ish locked the door and slid the heavy-duty bolts into place. He breathed a sigh of relief. Looking at the depleted joint in the ashtray, he decided he needed something a bit stronger. After the exchange with Johnny, he felt it well deserved. He retrieved a small plastic bag from the safe behind the TV and cut himself two thick lines of cocaine. In one swift movement, he pulled out a crisp twenty, rolled it and snorted a line up each nostril. The coke gave him an instant lift.

'Fucking Johnny seems to know everything,' Ish mumbled to himself.

Ish was making a small fortune out of the Spice. Beef was managing to sell it for around two grand an ounce, instead of the eleven hundred they'd first planned on. Out of the two thousand, Razor was getting £350, which he believed was his share, and Beef was getting £250. Ishmael got the remaining £1,200 per deal for virtually no work.

## SCREWED

At the current rate of two deals per week, he was making nearly double the amount he made working for Johnny. He couldn't afford to let this come to an end. Ish had been relieved when Johnny had mentioned wing 3C but then, knowing Johnny as he did, it was possible that saying 3C was just a diversion. Johnny liked to keep things close to his chest. Ish decided that he'd carry on as normal, he'd just have to be careful, no more meeting Razor in the Living Room. It occurred to Ish that Razor could be a problem. Now that Johnny had a mate stuck in Doncatraz, he would no doubt want to use Razor for his own ends. The question was would Razor say anything to Johnny about their business? Time would tell.

# SCREWED

# CHAPTER THIRTY-EIGHT

'Do you always jump whenever Johnny tells you?'

'I'm not jumping, Razor. Johnny invited us to dinner, and I accepted. Simple as that. Anyway, I thought you liked it at Pascal's,' she said firmly.

'Look, Deborah, I'm not having a go, but I'd prefer it if you asked me if I fancied going to dinner with Johnny and some tart, and not just told me.'

'If you don't want to go that's fine. I'll call Johnny and tell him you don't want to go.'

Before Razor could respond, his phone rang. He looked at the caller ID; 'Private Number'. He answered it anyway, glad of the distraction.

'It's me.'

'Who's me?'

'Me, man. Are you about later? Me and you gotta talk.'

'No sorry, we're having dinner at Pascal's.'

'I get it; you can't talk now. Call me.'

The line went dead.

'So do you want to call the taxi or shall I?' smiled Deborah.

They arrived at the restaurant a few minutes after half eight. The place was almost full but for one or two tables that would no doubt be occupied by nine. The maître d' guided them to the bar area that was discreetly located just off the main dining room. Johnny was standing with a beautiful brunette wearing an expensive evening dress. Her dark curls appeared to dance on her bare shoulders as she laughed at something Johnny was saying. Razor had to admit that even Johnny looked smart, he was wearing a pinstriped, charcoal-grey, two-piece suit accompanied by a burgundy tie. As if on cue, Johnny's massive frame turned to face them, and that's when Razor noticed the gold chain that was as thick as his thumb draped around Johnny's thick, bull-like neck.

'Debbie, Razor. Great to see you both. Glad you could make it at such short notice,' said Johnny before kissing Deborah on both cheeks and shaking Razor's hand warmly.

'Razor, old boy, I'd like you to meet the lovely Joanne.' Then turning to Deborah, he continued, 'No need for further introductions, I know you girls are well acquainted.'

Razor followed Johnny's example and kissed Joanne on both cheeks. The ladies also kissed and exchanged pleasantries. Johnny then handed them each a flute of Cristal champagne that he'd poured just seconds before their arrival. After a few minutes of small talk, Johnny announced that it was time to go to their table.

# SCREWED

Johnny led the way to the rear of the restaurant to a secluded alcove that housed a single table. Johnny moved to the chair with its back to the rear wall and stood behind it, from this position he had a full view of the entire restaurant. A waiter appeared and pulled out chairs for the ladies; Johnny waited for everyone to sit down before seating himself. Deborah was seated next to Johnny, facing Razor, with Joanne next to Razor, facing Johnny. The sommelier placed the ice bucket on to a stand beside the table, refilled their glasses then silently melted away. Menus were then handed out and napkins placed over expensively clad knees. Razor noted that the menu was another eight-course affair but was different from the last time he'd dined there. There were dishes on the menu that he'd never even heard of, let alone tasted, and he was glad he didn't have to choose. At least this time he had a general idea of how he should eat the food, if not how to pronounce it. As the conversation and drinks flowed, Razor was amazed at just how much he was enjoying himself. Joanne was great fun to be around and, more surprisingly, Johnny was good company too.

As the dessert plates were getting cleared, Johnny looked over to Razor and said, 'How about we leave these two lovelies to talk handbags and bugger off for a cigar and a large brandy, Razor old boy?'

The way Johnny's eyes bored into him gave Razor the impression that it was not a question.

'You'll have to excuse us, ladies. Unfortunately, I'm no longer permitted to enjoy a cigar in my own restaurant,' said Johnny, rising from his chair.

As Razor followed Johnny through the door marked 'Private', he was feeling slightly apprehensive. They entered a large, well-appointed office dominated by a large, antique, leather-topped, Edwardian desk. On the desk sat a computer terminal and two piles of neatly stacked documents. Johnny nodded to one of the green leather, high-backed chairs that sat in front of the desk, indicating for Razor to sit. He then proceeded to pour two large glasses of Louis XIII Remy Martin Grande Champagne Cognac. He placed the glasses on the desk, and then from a drawer he produced a large, hand-carved, wooden box.

'Cuban, I have them flown in specially,' explained Johnny, as he opened the lid of the box and retrieved two of Cuba's finest exports.

Johnny took out a gold lighter and began the ritual of lighting his cigar. He sucked deeply on the cigar until it finally lit. Razor sat in silence watching Johnny and waiting to find out the real reason for being brought here. He'd bet a month's wages it wasn't just to drink expensive brandy and smoke cigars, no matter what their origin. Johnny passed over the lighter and, after several attempts, Razor got his cigar to light. He'd heard somewhere how cigars and brandy were meant to be the perfect combination, he'd never believed it, that was until now.

Johnny decided to confirm his suspicions that it was Razor who was working with Ish.

'So, how are you getting along with my man, Ishmael?' asked Johnny.

Razor was slightly taken aback by the question and wasn't quite sure if he was referring to Ish as a person or their business relationship. He hadn't considered the possibility of Johnny having any involvement; he'd assumed that it was Ishmael's venture. But then considering that Ish worked for Johnny, it would make sense for him to be involved somehow.

'He's quite a character,' replied Razor cautiously.

'I know he's a character, but I was referring to work,' said Johnny still smiling pleasantly.

That confirmed it for Razor, Johnny did know, so he decided this was a good thing and he could raise his concerns about Beef.

# SCREWED

'I can't say that the money isn't coming in handy but er... the guy on the wing...' Razor hesitated, he wanted to choose his words carefully. After all, Beef was probably one of Johnny's men

'Spit it out, Razor. What you say in here stays in here, and remember you're higher up the pecking order than some lowlife on the wing,' said Johnny reassuringly before taking a slug of brandy and noisily swilling it around his mouth.

'Well, the guy who's selling, Beef, can't keep his mouth shut. Too many people on the wing know what's going and, to be honest, he's making my life a fucking misery. If he doesn't stop we'll all end up in the shit, and I could end up serving time.'

Johnny nodded as if he was acutely aware of the situation.

'Well, Razor old boy, if this guy, Beef, can't play by the rules then neither will we. It would be more convenient if he was on the outside, but I'll sort something.'

Johnny was secretly fuming that not only was Ishmael taking the piss out of him, but Beef was too. This was a massive kick in the teeth for Johnny. When Beef got handed a short term in jail for dealing, Johnny had made sure that his rent got paid and he'd got a few quid to help him out on the inside. Johnny prided himself on looking after his people, no matter how small a part they played

## SCREWED

in his organisation. In return he expected commitment and loyalty. In Johnny's eyes this was a monumental piss-take.

He managed to contain his anger and continued. 'If you happen to find out when Beef is getting released, give me a shout. I'd be very grateful.'

Johnny then paused and decided it was time to get a favour out of Razor.

'I'd hate for your income to suffer while we find a replacement so, in the meantime, how about you do a favour for a friend of mine? I'm sure he'll compensate you for your trouble.'

Razor swallowed, this was exactly what he'd been dreading.

'What's that then, Johnny?' asked Razor trying to sound casual.

'Well an old mate of mine is starting a stint at Doncatraz, and he wants a cushy job in the staff kitchen so he can at least get to eat some decent food. The only problem is, as you know, there's a waiting list for those jobs and there's a security clearance backlog. I'm sure a couple clicks on a computer would do the trick,' explained Johnny.

Razor felt relieved, he was expecting a much bigger ask, but the problem was he rarely came into contact with the prison computers.

# SCREWED

'Leave it with me, Johnny,' said Razor, although how he was going to do it, he didn't quite know. However he did it, it would be worth it to get Beef out of his hair.

'I knew I could rely on you, Razor old boy,' said Johnny, as he opened his desk drawer and pulled out a thick, brown envelope. 'Here's a little something for your trouble. Let's call it a down payment,' continued Johnny, as he handed the envelope to Razor. As Razor took hold of it Johnny retained his grip, and looking him straight in the eye said, 'I know you won't let me down.'

He then released the envelope, and a smile returned to his face. Razor desperately wanted to open the envelope and count the cash there and then, but he restrained himself and slipped the envelope into his jacket pocket.

'We better get back to the girls. You go ahead, Razor. I've got a quick business call to make.'

Razor eased himself out of the chair and walked across the thick carpet to the door. It didn't occur to him that 11.30 p.m. on a Sunday evening was an odd time to make a business call. Once Razor had closed the door, Johnny picked up his mobile and dialled a number from memory. To Johnny's frustration, the caller didn't answer immediately.

# SCREWED

'Do you know what time it is?' the voice complained after twelve rings.

'Just listen, OK,' growled Johnny.

Johnny rejoined the group and launched into a story about a mate of his who was involved in a VAT fraud to the tune of tens of millions. This friend, who wasn't named, had invited Johnny to some fancy do in London. Johnny had turned up without a dinner jacket, so his mate had got straight on his mobile and ordered a helicopter to pick Johnny up from the roof of the hotel and drop him on the helipad at Harrods.

'Some pompous git kitted me out in full tux then I got back in the helicopter and made it back in time for the starter,' said Johnny, as he erupted into raucous laughter and banged the table.

Razor wondered if maybe the guy Johnny was telling the story about was, in fact, his mate who had landed himself in Doncatraz. It was well past one by the time the four left the restaurant. Razor and Deborah fell into a waiting taxi, while Johnny guided a giggling Joanne into the back of his Range Rover.

## CHAPTER THIRTY-NINE

'Police! Open up.' Detective Sergeant Tony Price banged on the deep red painted door.

It was 7.00 a.m. The drug squad had only been given the address an hour before their morning briefing. An anonymous source had given information that a large quantity of class A drugs were at the address. According to the source, it was due to be moved to another location that very day, so they had to act fast. DS Price and three officers were at the front door, while another two waited around the back. Tony banged on the door a second time. Still no movement inside the house.

'Go and fetch the front door key,' he barked.

Two of the officers went to the back of the police Land Rover and retrieved a heavy, metal, battering ram.

'OK, open it up,' instructed Tony, standing to one side.

The officers swung the ram which collided with the door just below the handle. Nothing happened. This was not unusual when raiding the homes of drug dealers, they often had reinforced front doors. It took another four hard hits before the front door crashed open, and they stormed into the house. The living room, as expected, was unoccupied. Two of them continued through to the

# SCREWED

kitchen and opened the door for their waiting colleagues, while the other two went upstairs.

'Police! Make yourself seen,' shouted the first officer up the stairs.

As they got to the top of the stairs, one of the bedroom doors slowly opened.

'Hands on your head.'

Ishmael, wearing just his boxer shorts and wondering what was going on, moved his hands up slowly.

Tony stepped forward and said, 'Ishmael Robson, I'm arresting you on suspicion of being in possession of class A drugs with intent to supply. You do not have to say anything, but anything you do say can be used in evidence in a court of law. Do you understand?'

'Fuck you man, you ain't got nuffin on me,' spat Ishmael.

Ish knew that the only thing they stood any chance of finding was a half smoked joint, so he wasn't at all concerned when they began searching his house.

'I'm gonna sue you lot for wrongful arrest and a new front door,' said Ish in a cocky tone. As he said this, he was dragged back to the bedroom and ordered to dress.

'What, you're gonna watch me, ya fucking pervert?'

# SCREWED

The officer didn't reply and just stared disinterestedly, as Ishmael pulled on a designer tracksuit. Once Ishmael was dressed, one of the policemen put handcuffs on him and manhandled him down the stairs. His heart sunk as he was pushed into the front room to see two officers lifting the flat-screen TV from the wall.

Minutes later Ish was locked in the back of a waiting squad car.

Back in the living room, Tony watched as the large flat-screen TV was lifted from its bracket and placed on the floor. He stepped forward to take a closer look at the safe that sat in the chimney breast. The safe was two-feet square and had a single keyhole in the centre on the door. On closer inspection, Tony noticed that the TV bracket was hinged so the TV could get swung to one side and the safe easily accessed.

'Get me a photo of this and find me the fucking key,' barked Tony to no one in particular, causing a flurry of activity in the house.

The next hour was spent searching the house for the key to the safe. Losing patience, Tony stormed out of the house and got into the back of the squad car with Ishmael.

'You found any drugs yet, pig?' grinned Ish.

# SCREWED

'We both know what's in the safe. Why don't you make it easier on yourself and tell me where the key is?'

'I don't know nothing about no safe.'

Tony considered this for a moment then decided the best option would be to get Ishmael into custody.

'Fair enough, we'll do it your way.' Then turning to the driver said, 'Get this lowlife to the station.'

A dull black Mondeo pulled up outside Ishmael's property, and two forensics officers got out. Tony joined them at the front of the house and explained about the safe. To nail Ishmael, they would need to find at least one print on the outside of the safe. If they could find a print on the inside that would be the cherry on the cake. Tony left the two forensic officers with the safe to get a progress report from the rest of the team. He wasn't pleased to leave; there was still no sign of the key.

'I'm off to the station to get him processed. Give it another hour then call it a day,' instructed Tony before leaving the house.

By the time Ishmael had been processed and put in a holding cell, Tony's team were back at the station. To Tony's annoyance, there was still no sign of the safe key.

# SCREWED

Tony found a vacant computer terminal and searched for an approved contractor who could crack the safe. It didn't take long as there were only two in the whole of Yorkshire. The first was busy for the next three days, but the second had a two-hour slot available later that day at an extortionate cost. They agreed to meet at 2.00 p.m. at Ishmael's property.

SCREWED

# CHAPTER FORTY

By the time Razor awoke on Monday morning, it was 10.00 a.m. He was still feeling hungover, but thanks to the new four-day week he had all day to recover. His phone beeped once. Picking it up, he saw fourteen missed calls and five text messages. Flicking through the log, he saw all the calls and messages were from Lucy. The first call had come through at ten past midnight and the most recent at 7.30 a.m. that morning. A feeling of alarm spread over him, and he cursed himself for not taking his phone out with him to the restaurant. He opened the first text message which read:

*Please call ASAP, any time.*

He remembered that now Lucy worked in admin, she'd have her phone with her while she was at work, so he dialled. The call got answered on the second ring, and Lucy spoke before Razor had a chance to utter a word.

'Gilly, can you meet me at lunchtime? It's urgent,' said Lucy in a low tone, so Razor guessed it must be difficult for her to talk.

'Yeah, course. When and where?'

'The White Hart at one.' With that she cut the connection.

Razor stared at the phone for a second or two, thinking it couldn't be good news.

# SCREWED

'You feeling OK, Razor? You look pale,' said Deborah, as she returned from the shower.

'I'm fine, just feeling a bit hung-over.'

'OK, no problem. How about we have a drive out and have a long leisurely lunch. I'm yours all day,' she said running her fingers through his hair.

'I'd love to, but I promised that I'd meet a friend from work for lunch.'

'Oh, so I'm getting dumped for a work colleague,' she teased.

'It's just; they're having some problems and...'

'Razor, it's fine. I'm just messing. I think I'll head to Leeds then and do some shopping.'

Razor was in two minds whether or not to cancel Lucy and spend the day with Deborah, but on balance decided Lucy's problem might impact on him so he would meet her.

Razor walked into the pub at few minutes before 1.00 p.m. and was surprised to see Lucy already stood at the bar. The first thing he noticed was that she was clutching a large glass of wine.

'Alright, Lucy?'

As she turned to face him, he noticed how tired she looked. Her usually sharp, blue eyes were sunken and dark.

# SCREWED

'Sorry I didn't call sooner. I was out last night and forgot my phone. Anyway, I'm here now. What's up?'

'It's Greg. He turned up at my house last night and said he knew all about the suicide, and that I wasn't at work where I should have been when it happened.'

Lucy's eyes had welled up. Razor suggested that she find a seat while he got a drink. He needed a minute or two to think things through. He was about to order a pint, but then with Lucy on the verge of hysterics he decided he needed something stronger and instead opted for a large vodka tonic. As he waited for his drink to arrive, he suddenly had a Eureka moment. He realised that Lucy now worked on the computers all day and the favour for Johnny involved 'just a couple of clicks'.

Razor joined Lucy at a table in the corner of the pub. She was staring into space and subconsciously fiddling with a beer mat.

'OK, Lucy, tell me exactly what happened.'

With her voice shaking, she explained that Greg had turned up at her house around eight the night before. She'd assumed that he'd been drinking and wanted to try and talk her into getting back together. She hadn't wanted to let him into the house but relented as soon as he said that her career was on the line. He'd recounted, in a calm but arrogant manner, the events of the evening when Matthew Dunford took his own life. He'd then asked, with a smirk, what she thought her bosses at the prison would think if they knew where she was that night. Lucy had tried to convince him that Dunford had taken his life after her shift had ended. Greg only laughed at her.

'He told me I'd lose my job either way, because if the prison governor didn't believe him, the papers certainly would. I'm screwed, Gilly; we're screwed,' she sobbed.

'It's his word against yours, Lucy.'

'No, he said that the tart he was with that night would back him up, and it gets worse.'

After a gulp of wine, she continued.

'The wanker filmed me on his phone whacking that slag and the footage is time and date stamped. He's got me every which way.'

'Jesus Lucy, that's bad shit. So, what's he want? To get back with you?'

'God, no. He said he wouldn't touch me with a bargepole. He's up to eyes in debt and wants money.'

'Fuck. How much?'

'Ten grand, and he wants it this week. I'm going to have to give it to him.'

'You know that if you pay him he'll be back for more.'

# SCREWED

'Yeah I know that, and the worse thing is, the bastard knows exactly how much I've got,' she sniffed.

Razor knew that Lucy had received an inheritance a few years back, but she'd never told him how much. But she'd obviously told Greg, and now it looked like he intended to help her spend the lot. A plan began to form in Razor's mind, but he had to see someone first.

'Listen, Lucy; I think we sort this out.'

'How can we possibly sort this shit out, Gilly?'

'I've got to see someone first.'

'Who?'

'Just a man I know who can sort things out,' replied Razor with a wink.

Lucy calmed down, so Razor took the opportunity to go the bar and get another round of drinks. When he returned, Lucy seemed to be almost back to her usual self.

'So how you finding the new job, Luce?'

'I must admit it's a cushy number. I get to have my phone with me all day. I can even go to the pub for lunch and, the best thing of all, no fucking cons.'

'What exactly do you do all day then?' he asked cheekily.

'Not a lot, just updating prisoners' records and shit like that,' she laughed.

# SCREWED

It was the 'shit like that' that Razor liked the sound of, and he gave an involuntary smile.

'What you grinning at?' she asked.

'Nothing. I just can't imagine you sat at a computer all day. I'm so used to seeing you dragging prisoners around the wing.'

They finished their drinks and agreed to meet back at the pub at around six. Lucy went back to work feeling a lot happier but wondering how Gilly could sort her problem out.

# SCREWED

## CHAPTER FORTY-ONE

Techno let the dog off the lead, picked it up and hopped over the stile. The light was beginning to fade and there was a chill in the air. He made the trek to the top of the hill and unpacked the drone from his rucksack. Since Bonzo's move to wing 3C sales had nearly doubled, and Techno was very pleased with the amount of money they were making every week.

Ten minutes later, Techno was watching the tiny screen on his handset as the drone hovered outside the prison wall. Normally at this point the image would jerk, as Bonzo unloaded the cargo, however the image stayed perfectly stable. Techno waited another five minutes, the image still didn't move. Reluctantly he hit the 'home' button and waited for the drone to return. This was the first time in over thirty runs that Bonzo hadn't unloaded the cargo. Something didn't feel right. Techno packed up the drone and headed for home.

Sleep was difficult for Techno, as he couldn't understand what had prevented Bonzo from collecting the package. It wasn't as if he could have nipped out or anything like that, so something must be wrong.

## SCREWED

The next morning, still feeling concerned, Techno called HMP Doncaster and, feigning to be a concerned relative, asked about Bonzo. After being transferred four times, Techno was passed to a prison liaison officer who began to explain about Bonzo's death. Before the officer had finished his first sentence Techno cut the connection and collapsed sobbing.

Once Techno had finally composed himself, he did an online search to see what had apparently happened to his friend. The details were sketchy and, whilst the police had stated that they were still investigating the crime, it was confirmed that Bonzo's death was murder.

Techno found it difficult to comprehend the fact that his friend and business partner had been murdered. Bonzo was far too streetwise not to realise something was wrong and would have no doubt mentioned to Techno if he had had concerns regarding any other prisoners. Techno gave the matter a lot of thought. On the one hand he was convinced that the murder had to be in some way connected to their drugs business, but then on other, it didn't really make sense. It was too extreme to murder someone without some sort of warning or indication first.

# SCREWED

Either way, Techno vowed that he would put every effort into finding out who was responsible and why. Then he was going to somehow make them pay and pay dearly.

## SCREWED

# CHAPTER FORTY-TWO

Razor had to decide on the best way to deal with Lucy's situation. He didn't want to ask Johnny for help until he'd got Johnny's mate the cushy job in the prison kitchen. Maybe Ishmael was an option. No doubt he'd know someone who could sort out Lucy's ex. He found a call box and dialled Ishmael's number. The call went straight to voicemail, which was odd, as it was gone two in the afternoon. Maybe Ish was on another call. He waited a couple of minutes and dialled again. Again the call went straight to voicemail. Razor kept trying Ishmael's number for the rest of the afternoon. By five he decided something must be wrong, and he'd have no choice but to turn to Johnny. After a few minutes dwelling on the subject, he decided he could turn the situation to his advantage. He'd tell Lucy that he could sort out her problem in return for her speeding up security clearance on Johnny's mate. At six on the dot, he was sat at the bar waiting for Lucy. Ten minutes later Lucy joined him and ordered a large white wine. They then returned to the table that they'd occupied earlier that day.

'Sorry about earlier, Gilly. I'm more angry than upset now.'

'It's fine, Luce. In fact, I've given it some thought and had a chat with a mate of mine.'

# SCREWED

'What mate? Someone you know from the force?'

'It's not important, and maybe it's best that you don't know, but we both agree that the worst thing you could do is give Greg any money. He'll just keep coming back for more.'

'I know that, Gilly. So what does this mate of yours think I should do?'

'I'm getting to that, Luce. This friend of mine is very well connected and knows a lot of influential people. He can get all this sorted out for you, but he wants a favour in return.'

'What type of favour?' she asked tentatively.

'Well, remember that VAT fraudster on 1A?'

'Yeah. A pretty decent chap for a change. Not like the usual shit we get on the wing.'

'Well, my friend is also his friend, and he wants a decent job in the staff kitchen.'

'That job needs security clearance and there's nothing I can do about that. Sorry, Gilly.'

'He's not asking for you to mess with security clearance, just put his name at the top of the list to be cleared. Then if security turn them down, then so be it.'

'And I still get my problem sorted out?'

'Yeah, course you do.'

# SCREWED

'These mates of yours, are you sure you can trust them?' she asked with concern in her voice.

'Yeah, they're fine. Relax.'

'Then consider it done. It's not like I'm doing anything wrong, is it?'

Razor hadn't expected her to agree quite so quickly and was now looking forward to telling Johnny the good news. They had another drink, before heading home and agreeing to meet again on Friday for an update. Razor remembered that he didn't have a phone number for Johnny, so he sent Deborah a text message asking for it and to see if she fancied a takeaway at his place later. A couple of minutes afterwards his phone rang.

'Razor old boy, were you after me?' asked the gruff voice.

'That was quick, Johnny. Are you local? I could do with a chat,' said Razor a little surprised that Johnny had called him.

'I'm at the restaurant for the next hour or so, then I'm off home.'

'Great, I'll be there in ten.'

Razor cut the connection and noticed a text had come in during the phone call. It read:

*Forget the takeout, tightwad. You can take me out for a Chinese. D x.*

Razor tapped out a reply as he made the short walk to Pascal's.

*You're on. Meet me at Oscar's at 8. x.*

# SCREWED

Oscar's was a small wine bar near Johnny's restaurant. Razor had never been before, but it seemed as good a place as any to meet Deborah. It also had the bonus of only being a ten-minute walk to the Golden Dragon Chinese restaurant. When Razor arrived at Pascal's the door was locked, so he gave it a couple of bangs. The maître d' quickly unlocked the door and ushered Razor inside. Razor made his way to the back of the restaurant and through the door marked 'Private'. He passed the door marked office and headed to the unmarked door at the end of the corridor. He gave a slight tap and walked in. Johnny sat behind his desk, pulling on a large Cuban cigar.

'Razor old boy, take a seat. You fancy a drink?'

Razor sank into the same high-backed chair that he'd occupied the night before.

'I'll have one if you are, Johnny.'

Johnny eased his large frame from his chair and opened the top of the large globe that housed his drinks. He poured two large measures of brandy from a crystal decanter then, using his hands, added a couple of ice cubes. He gave Razor a glass before returning to his chair and fixing his gaze firmly on Razor.

'So Razor, what can you do for me?'

# SCREWED

Johnny's remark threw Razor slightly off balance, but quickly regaining his composure said, 'I've got your mate sorted; he'll have that cushy number by the end of the week.'

A smile began to form on Johnny's lips.

'You don't fuck about do you?'

Razor took a long pull on his drink. As the burning liquid hit his stomach he began to feel a little more relaxed. He paused, looking down at his glass, wondering how to ask Johnny for the favour.

As if reading his thoughts, Johnny prompted, 'Was there something else?'

'Er well, yeah. Er.'

'Just spit it out man,' said Johnny leaning forward and resting his elbows on the desk.

Razor downed the rest of his drink in one and began. 'I've this friend who's got a problem that needs dealing with sooner rather than later.'

Johnny leant back in his chair and listened closely as Razor recounted the whole story about Lucy and her ex's demands. When Razor had finished talking, Johnny topped up their glasses.

'Consider it sorted. I've got just the man for the job. It'll be his pleasure. Favours for favours.'

'Yeah favours, Johnny,' said Razor feeling pleased.

Johnny smiled but didn't reply, he simply gulped his brandy and banged the empty glass

# SCREWED

down on his desk, signalling the meeting was over. Razor followed suit, drained his glass and stood to leave.

Just as his hand touched the door handle, Johnny spoke again. 'I nearly forgot.'

Razor turned to face him again.

'Have you heard about your mate, Ish?' continued Johnny.

'Ish? No, what?'

'Police busted him this morning. Shut the door on your way out.'

Razor hurried out, his mind in a spin.

Today was getting better and better for Johnny. He'd got rid of that snake Ish, for daring to do business behind his back, Beef would soon be on the receiving end of a good beating, for assisting Ish, and his mates inside would be sitting pretty working in the officers' mess by the weekend. On top of that, it looked as though he was about to add another prison officer to his collection and she was office based. Johnny was looking forward to having some fun with DS Tony Price and gently persuading him to join his organisation.

Razor had half an hour to spare before he was due to meet Deborah and was glad of the time for a quick drink on his own to gather his thoughts. The news about Ish had come as a shock to Razor and the tone of Johnny's voice, when he'd told him, had unsettled him, but he didn't quite know why. He entered Oscar's and ordered a large brandy from an effeminate man who was serving behind the bar. He finished the drink in two gulps, pushed the glass towards the barman and nodded. As Razor sipped the second brandy a wave of hunger washed over him, reminding him that he hadn't eaten all day. The wine bar was far too posh to sell bags of salted nuts, but for three pounds a small dish of cashew nuts could be purchased. When Razor ordered three, the barman seemed to take pity on him and refilled the first dish that Razor had quickly emptied. At nearly twenty past eight Deborah finally arrived and insisted on having a glass of wine before leaving for the Chinese. She was equally shocked when Razor told her about Ishmael getting arrested that morning, or so it seemed.

# SCREWED

# CHAPTER FORTY-THREE

The safe specialist didn't arrive at Ishmael's house until nearly 5.00 p.m., much to the annoyance of Tony. Forensics had failed to find a single print on the outside of the safe which didn't help Tony's mood. However, this changed significantly when an hour and a half later the safe door swung open. Inside was a block of white powder weighing at least a kilo. Accompanying this were ten smaller plastic bags holding at least a couple of grams of powder and eight grand in cash. Not a bad result. The money and drugs were photographed and put into evidence bags. It was nearly 7.00 p.m. when Tony finished up at the house, and he'd already been at work for twelve hours. He knew that if he didn't charge Ishmael Robson that evening, he would be released first thing the next morning. To save time, Tony called ahead to the station to inform the custody sergeant that he was planning on interviewing Ishmael. He also told him to notify Ishmael's solicitor.

Tony arrived in the custody suite to be advised by the sergeant that Ishmael was in interview room one and had already been joined by his solicitor. He grabbed a WPC to sit in on the interview, she wasn't his first choice, but the

# SCREWED

station was quiet at that time of night and he didn't want to waste any more valuable time.

He stuck his head into the interview room and said in the direction of the solicitor, 'You ready for us?'

'We're ready, Detective. But in future do not enter a room where I may be in conference with my client without knocking first,' replied the solicitor in a clipped tone.

Ish grinned at his solicitor's reprimand of the detective sergeant. Disgruntled, Tony stomped into the room, followed by the WPC, and took a seat directly opposite Ishmael. The WPC unwrapped two identical tapes and placed them into the boxy, double tape deck. She pressed the record button, and the two tapes began to turn in unison. After approximately five seconds the machine beeped once, indicating that the recording had commenced. Tony went through the usual routine of stating the time, date and location of the interview, followed by his name and rank. He then invited the others in the room to do the same. He then asked Ishmael if he had been read and understood his rights, to which he answered in the affirmative. Tony then proceeded to ask Ishmael the questions that he'd drafted out earlier that day while waiting for the safe cracker. As usual, Tony knew most of the answers before he'd even asked the questions.

# SCREWED

'Mr Robson, or can I call you Ishmael?'

'Mr Robson to you, innit.' Ish stared into Tony's eyes, he knew this man from somewhere, but he just couldn't place him.

'OK then. Mr Robson, do you currently live at 16 Mansfield Terrace, Doncaster?'

'That's where you found me, wasn't it?'

'For the benefit of the tape, do I take that as a yes?'

'Yeah.'

'Do you own or rent the property?'

'Own it.'

'Mortgaged?'

'Yeah.'

Tony asked a few questions about the lender, monthly repayments, how much he paid for the house and how much he'd borrowed. Ish answered all the questions as accurately as he could. Tony scribbled a few notes and moved on.

'OK, Mr Robson, how about the contents of the house; do you own everything in the property?'

'I'll stop you there, Detective. Unless you rephrase that question, I'll advise my client not to answer,' interjected the solicitor.

'OK, Mr Robson, do you own the furnishings within the property, including the flat-screen TV located in the living room?'

'Yeah.'

# SCREWED

'Are you aware of the safe located behind the TV?'

'Yeah.'

'What is the purpose of the safe?'

'Ain't got no purpose; it was there when I bought the place. I ain't even got a key to it.'

Tony produced four A4 photos from a file and laid them on the table in front of Ish. The first photo showed the safe with the door open, revealing the contents. The other three pictures were close-ups of the cash and drugs.

'Do you recognise any of these items, Mr Robson?'

'No man, never seen 'em before.'

'How do you explain the presence of these articles found locked in a safe located behind your TV in your house?'

'I think, Detective, that my client has already explained that the safe was an existing fixture, he has no key and, as my client is not a safe cracker, he has no means to access it. So we must presume that anything found in the safe was already there when my client purchased the property,' explained the solicitor.

Ish shot Tony a smug grin.

'I put it to you, Mr Robson, that it is your safe and therefore your drugs and your cash. I also believe that you do have the key to it.'

# SCREWED

'I trust, Detective, that you have forensic evidence to substantiate these ludicrous claims,' said the solicitor calmly.

Tony didn't like the way the interview was heading. He knew that without the key, forensics, or a witness willing to make a statement against Ishmael the CPS would not be willing to proceed with a prosecution. His only hope was that forensics would find a print on the drugs or the cash. Just as Tony was about to reply, the door to the interview room opened to reveal Chief Superintendant Paul Johnson. The chief super signalled to Tony to join him in the corridor.

Tony checked his watch and stated, 'Interview suspended nineteen fifty.' He then left the room.

'Are you going to charge him, Tony?' the chief asked as soon as the door had closed.

Tony was surprised to see the chief superintendant still at the station at this time of night, but the question caught him off guard. It struck Tony as rather unusual for a chief super to show any interest in a case like this, and he had to wonder how he even knew about it.

'I don't think I'll be able to charge him yet, Guv. The CPS would throw it out without any forensics, and we're still waiting for them.'

'Look, Tone, you know about my recent statements to the press about cleaning up the streets. This is a prime example of zero tolerance. I want him off the streets. So just charge him, the forensics will come. OK?'

'But with no forensics, his solicitor won't wear it.'

Paul paused for thought; he knew that Tony had a valid point.

'OK, Tony, call it evidence received from a witness or informant.'

'But we haven't got either Guv.'

'Of course there's an informant. Who the fuck do you think called me last night to tip me the wink?' snapped Paul, before realising he'd perhaps said a little too much.

'As far as I was aware, this morning's raid was the result of an anonymous tip-off, but if you want him charged it's your call.'

Paul placed his hand on Tony's shoulder, gave a slight nod and left. Tony stood alone in the corridor wondering what exactly was going on. He'd known Paul for years, and he'd never interfered like this before. At times like this, Tony was glad that he wasn't involved in the politics of management. He went back into the interview room and restarted the tape. In annoyance, he went through the time, date and introduction procedure again.

# SCREWED

'Mr Robson, we have a witness who is prepared to testify about your involvement in the supply of class A drugs.'

'That's bollocks, man. You ain't got no witness.'

'Detective, may I enquire as to the identification and credibility of this alleged witness?' asked the solicitor raising an eyebrow.

'You know full well I can't reveal any details about a witness. Mr Robson, would you like to say anything at this point?'

'Yeah... fuck you pig. This is a fit-up,' he spat.

'OK, interview terminated at twenty seventeen.'

Tony explained that Ishmael was going to get formally charged. A bail hearing would take place the following day at Doncaster Magistrates' Court. The police would submit an application to deny bail on the grounds of witness intimidation.

Ishmael Robson appeared before Doncaster Magistrates' Court the following day at two twenty, charged with possession with intent to supply a class A drug and the laundering of the proceeds. As expected, bail got denied and the judge ordered that Ishmael get remanded in custody until his trial date which would be roughly three months away. At a few minutes

## SCREWED

after six that day, Ishmael Robson sat in a prison transport van as it rolled through the gates of Doncatraz.

# SCREWED

# CHAPTER FORTY-FOUR

Tony had sat in the magistrates' court and watched as the judge denied bail to Ishmael. As instructed, he'd sent a text message to the chief super reading:

*Bail denied. Robson en route to Doncatraz.*

Tony left the court, eager to get back to the station so he could chase up forensics to see if they had found any prints inside the safe. As he walked into the car park and towards his vehicle, he noticed something wedged under his windscreen wiper. He glanced around to see if anyone was watching before carefully lifting the wiper and retrieving the A4 brown envelope. There wasn't another soul in the car park, so he ripped open the envelope. Inside were six large, glossy pictures. One by one he slid them out. When Tony saw his face staring back at him, his knees went weak. He quickly unlocked the car and slumped into the driver's seat. He sat motionless for a few minutes before he could pluck up the courage to take a closer look. The pictures showed him sprawled on a hotel bed wearing nothing except a silly grin. Next to him, and wearing just a pair of stilettos, lay the tart from the Living Room. Her right arm was outstretched where she was apparently holding the phone that took the picture. What had he been thinking? It was bad enough that he'd gone back to her hotel, but then to pose for a naked selfie was just madness. With a profound sense of dread, he turned to the next picture. He couldn't imagine how they could get any more damning. By the time he got to the last picture, which was a still from a video camera complete with time and date stamp, he felt sick to the pit of his stomach. The still showed the surgically enhanced brunette straddling him like she was riding the winner of the 1.45 at Chepstow. His mind began to whirl, and the questions piled up. Why would this girl do this to him? What did she want? Had anyone else seen the pictures? What had he been thinking to do this to the only woman he'd ever loved, the woman he'd married? His thoughts lingered on his wife, his darling, loving Ruth. She'd be devastated if she ever found out. Ruth was loyal and trusting, she'd even been OK when he'd rolled in on the Sunday morning after staying out for the entire night. She'd told him that just because they were married didn't mean he had to stop seeing his mates. At the time this had just intensified his guilt, and it had been playing on his mind ever since. He'd been having trouble sleeping too, so much so that he'd visited the doctors. He had been prescribed some tablets to help him relax.

A sharp rap on the passenger side window jolted Tony from his thoughts.

# SCREWED

When he looked up the first thing he saw was a set of gleaming gold teeth. Johnny opened the car door and coolly climbed in.

'Afternoon, Detective Sergeant. A good result in court today.'

Before Johnny had finished his sentence, the reality hit Tony like a sledgehammer.

'This is your doing you sneaky, fucking bastard,' snarled Tony throwing the pictures on to the dashboard.

'Calm down, Tone. You don't mind if I call you Tone do you? After all, we're all friends together.' Johnny didn't wait for a response and continued, 'It's not like there's any harm done. It's not like that lovely wife of yours has seen them, is it?'

'Leave my fucking wife out of this. Just tell me what the fuck you want. If it's cash you've come to the wrong man.' Tony paused trying to regain his composure before saying, 'I could arrest you for this shit. You do realise that blackmail is a fucking crime?'

Johnny remained very quiet, and with a toothy grin he replied, 'Tone old boy, firstly I neither need nor want any cash. In fact, I'm going to give you some money. I was only saying to a friend of mine the other night how underpaid you guys are. This talk of blackmail, Tone, is very

## SCREWED

hurtful to a businessman like me. After all, blackmail is such an ugly word.'

Tony sat in silence trying to comprehend the mess that was quickly unfolding in front of him. Had this whole thing been a set-up? And if so, was it possible that Gilly was involved in it somehow? The thoughts were making his head spin.

'So why don't you tell me what the fuck you do want?' snapped Tony.

'I just need a favour, Tony, that's all. And I don't expect you to do it for nothing. It's only fair that I at least cover your expenses.'

'Look, cut the shit. We both know you've got me by the bollocks. Just tell me what this favour is.'

Johnny grinned to himself. He knew Tony would co-operate but hadn't expected him to roll over quite so quickly. Johnny then explained that he had a friend called Lucy and how her ex-boyfriend was attempting to blackmail her. He kept the details to a minimum and didn't mention where she worked or with whom.

Johnny concluded by saying, 'So all's I need you to do, Tone, is have a quiet word with the guy and explain it would be in his best interests to keep away from his ex and forget the whole thing.'

'Why can't you have word? I'm sure he'd listen to you,' replied Tony.

# SCREWED

'As I've said, I'm a businessman, I can't go around threatening people.'

'But surely you must know people who could have a word?'

'That's not the point, Tone. The point is I'm asking you.'

Johnny pulled an envelope and a folded sheet of paper from his jacket pocket and thrust them at Tony.

'Here's all the information you need and a little something for you.'

Tony opened the envelope and looked inside to see three banded bundles of twenty-pound notes. Each bundle contained one thousand pounds.

'And what about my pictures?' asked Tony.

'You're welcome to keep those copies, but I'll be holding on to the originals. Let's call them insurance.'

'Insurance,' snorted Tony. 'You mean until you want another favour.'

'If you like, yes. There may come a time when I need another favour. Speaking of favours, if you'd ever like to see Crystal again, you only have to ask. You seem to get on extremely well.' Johnny grinned, nodding towards the pictures on the dashboard.

'Are you having a laugh?'

# SCREWED

'Whatever you say, Tone. Just make sure you take care of that favour by the weekend. OK?'

Before Tony could respond Johnny was out of the car and climbing in the back seat of a waiting Range Rover, complete with a personalised number plate.

Tony considered calling Gilly and asking him outright if he was involved in any of this shit. But then, on reflection, decided it couldn't be possible. He'd known Gilly for years. He'd be seeing him soon anyway. Maybe he could do a little subtle fishing about Deborah and Crystal, and try and piece a few things together that way. Tony's head was starting to spin again. He reached into his jacket pocket and retrieved his pills; he popped a few and took some deeps breaths.

After a minute or two Tony felt himself begin to relax, and his thoughts shifted back to the Robson case. He needed to get back to the station to see if any good news had come in from forensics. He started his engine and sped out of the car park.

When Tony arrived home from work later that day, he'd been distant and distracted. His wife asked him, on more than one occasion, if everything was OK. Tony used to be one of the lucky coppers who was able to leave his work at work and had never let it interfere with their home life. He tried to reassure her by saying that he was just tired. Tony hated lying to his wife, but he could hardly tell her the truth.

His encounter with Johnny had got to him, and those pictures kept flashing through his mind. If only he'd have listened to Gilly and had gone home to his wife, he wouldn't be in this mess. How could he have even doubted Gilly? Maybe he was just looking for someone to blame when the fault was his own.

It struck him that Johnny was an opportunist. Once he'd learnt that Tony was a detective sergeant he'd seized the moment and arranged for that girl to turn up with Gilly's missus. Maybe it was Deborah who was somehow involved with Johnny. As for Crystal, he'd believed that they'd had a connection. Even though he hated to admit it to himself, his time with her in the hotel room had been mind-blowing. He'd found it difficult to get her out of his thoughts. He'd never had sex like that with his wife, or any other woman for that matter. He was now conflicted and confused. His mind was telling him that Crystal was just a pawn in a game directed by a man with gold teeth, but his male ego would then kick in. This side of him was saying that Crystal had felt the same and enjoyed the night as much as he had. Or maybe she was just a bloody good actress. In the big scheme of things it was all irrelevant anyway, he was a married man, in fact, a happily married man. This brought him back to his immediate problem. He had no doubt that Johnny would send the pictures to his wife if he didn't play ball. There was no way back now. The second he'd put the cash-filled envelope into his pocket he was Johnny's. He realised that Johnny would keep asking for favours. He knew he was in this for the long haul. This would take a lot of time and thought to get out of, but for now, that would have to wait. His mind drifted back to Gilly; he seemed to be a different man now to the one he'd known back when they were on the force together. Back then he was just an average sort of guy, one that was happy to have a few pints in the local wearing jeans and a T-shirt. Now he was drinking in trendy wine bars, dressed in designer labels and dating a stripper. Tony hadn't given this much thought before and had just been happy that they were hanging out again, but on a prison officer's wages, he had to wonder how he was affording this new lifestyle. Could Gilly be in Johnny's pocket and, if so, was it such a bad place to be?

Tony was out of the house at 7.00 a.m. the next morning. He lay awake in bed until the early hours, trying to work out the best way of carrying out Johnny's request. He'd retrieved the sheet of paper that Johnny had handed to him. It contained everything about Johnny's 'friend's' ex-boyfriend. His full name, address, car make, model and registration number, and place of work. There was even a small, passport-sized picture stapled to the top of the sheet. It appeared that Greg Huston worked as a manager at a local gym. A photocopy attached to the back of the sheet detailed the gym's rota and showed that Greg was not due to work until midday this week.

On his way to the station, Tony pulled up outside a twenty-four-hour supermarket and purchased half a kilo of sugar, some cling film and a roll of duck tape. He spread the cling film on to the back seat and emptied the sugar on to it. Tony then formed a block and bound it with duck tape. When he'd finished he admired his handiwork, the package looked exactly like the block of cocaine that he'd found in Ishmael's safe. Tony tucked the packet under his seat and continued on to the station. He had a few hours to kill before he planned to visit Greg at his home address. The DS then located a young PC and instructed him to come and collect him at 11.00 a.m., as he needed a lift to visit a potential witness in an ongoing case. Tony had decided that Greg would be more convinced by his plan if he saw a police car when

# SCREWED

he opened the front door. Tony fired up his desktop computer and began to type up his notes from the Ishmael Robson arrest. Forensics had failed to find any prints inside the safe, so Tony was now relying on something turning up on the cash, or on the bags of cocaine. Although, in all honesty, he wasn't pinning any hopes on finding anything. At a few minutes before eleven the young PC approached Tony's desk.

'Ready when you are, Guv.'

Tony grabbed his jacket from the back of the door and followed the PC out to the car park.

'I'll be with you in a minute. Take the car out front, I'll meet you there,' instructed Tony, as he made his way to his vehicle to retrieve the package he'd made up earlier.

Using a handkerchief, he put the package into his pocket, walked to the front of the station and got into the waiting squad car. He climbed into the back seat and gave the address to the PC. A few minutes later the patrol car pulled up in front of a semi-detached house on a sixties-style housing estate. A garage adjoined the side of the property, and through the open door Tony could make out Greg's car.

'Pull into the drive,' instructed Tony. 'Then just wait in the car. I won't be too long.'

'Yes, Guv.'

# SCREWED

The PC pulled the car into the driveway of the house and killed the engine. Tony noticed that the lawn, unlike the other houses in the street, was overgrown and unkempt. The building was a little untidy too, the windows were wooden with flaking paint, and some of the sills appeared rotten. This gave Tony an insight into the type of man he was about to deal with. He gave the front door a sharp rap and waited. The door opened almost instantly, indicating that Greg must have heard the car pull into his drive. Greg was a tall, well-built man, who seemed to fill the entire doorway. He was wearing a navy-coloured tracksuit with the logo of the gym where he worked on his left breast pocket. Tony was the first to speak.

'Good morning, sir. Are you Greg Huston?'

Greg was focused over Tony's shoulder at the police car in his driveway. The PC behind the wheel gave him a courteous nod.

'Yeah, that's me.'

Tony removed his wallet, containing his ID, and opened it as he began to speak.

'I'm Detective Sergeant Price. May I come in please?'

Greg stepped back, allowing Tony to enter the house. Tony waited for Greg to close the front door, and then followed him into the sitting room just off the hallway. He noticed that the inside of

## SCREWED

the house was much like the outside, seriously in need of a little TLC. Greg slumped down on a battered settee and nodded at a mismatched chair opposite. Tony remained standing.

'So, Mr Huston, or do you prefer Greg?'

'Greg's fine with me.'

'Well, Greg, I'm here to discuss Lucy Jackson, your ex-girlfriend.'

Greg was straight on to the offensive.

'What's she said? Whatever it is, is a lie. There are a few things I could tell you about that bitch.'

Tony knew that Greg wouldn't be silenced by just talking.

'Calm down, Greg. Did I say she'd said anything? I just want a quiet word with you about her.'

At this, Greg seemed to relax. Using the handkerchief, Tony pulled the package from his pocket.

'Take a look at this,' said Tony, as he tossed the package at Greg who instinctively caught it.

A look of confusion spread over Greg's face.

'What's this? What the fuck's going on?'

'That, Greg, is half a kilo of Columbia's finest cocaine, and that is also a ticket to a minimum of five years inside.'

# SCREWED

Greg dropped the package like a hot potato, and Tony bent to pick it up with a smile on his face.

'What the fuck are you on about?' sputtered Greg.

'Well, what I'm wondering, Greg, is how you're going to explain the fact that your fingerprints are all over enough cocaine to get half of Doncaster high for a month.'

'You bent bastard; this is a fit-up.'

Tony remained deadly calm and began to explain.

'Maybe so, Greg, and maybe a good barrister could get you off on some technicality. In the meantime, you would be arrested, charged, and you'd be all over the papers so would, no doubt, lose your job. The cherry on the cake is you'd spend at least six months on remand in Doncatraz until your trial date came up.'

Greg's shoulders slumped. He'd suddenly run out of steam.

'What is it you want?'

'I thought I'd made myself clear. Just a chat about your ex, Lucy. The thing is she's a little worried about some of the things you've been saying or shall we say, threatening to say, if she doesn't cough up ten grand.'

'I was just messing about,' said Greg sheepishly.

# SCREWED

'Messing about or not, if you open your mouth to anyone, or even contact her again, I will become your worst nightmare,' began Tony, then tapping the package and getting right into Greg's face he continued. 'I'll be keeping this as insurance. We clear now, Greg?'

'Yeah.'

'Good. I'll see myself out. Be good and be quiet.'

Tony left Greg slumped on the settee wondering what had just happened.

The PC let Tony get out at the front of the station then continued to park the car. Tony breathed a sigh of relief, tossed the package into a nearby waste bin and entered the station. Tony didn't see Chief Superintendent Paul Johnson observing him from an upstairs window.

# SCREWED

# CHAPTER FORTY-FIVE

When Razor walked into work he was greeted with the news about the murder of Bonzo. His stomach lurched. Was Ish responsible for doing this? Razor was expecting Bonzo to get a bit of a beating, not end up dead. Wing 3C was now on full lockdown, and the prisoners were getting interviewed by the police. Due to the fact that the murder had happened in the showers there was no CCTV, which made things difficult for the investigating officers.

Razor spent the entire shift trying to rationalise what had happened without much success. Things were spiralling out of control. This was the now the second death that he was somehow linked to. He'd never signed up for any of this. A quick line would sort him out.

Razor finished work and headed to a pub near the prison to meet Lucy. The night before he'd met with Johnny, who'd informed him that his friend in Doncatraz was enjoying his kitchen job and that Lucy wouldn't be having any more problems with her ex. Johnny had then tossed him an envelope containing another two and a half grand. Razor was grateful for the cash, as now that Ish was banged up he was seven hundred pounds a week worse off. Although, he had to admit to

# SCREWED

himself that he preferred this way of working. Just a favour for the right person and he was five grand better off with virtually no risk. Razor had drunk half his pint by the time Lucy entered the bar. Upon seeing him, a smile spread across her face.

'How did you do it, Gilly? I'm so happy! Look at this text I got from Greg last night.'

Razor glanced down at her phone and read the text message.

*Lucy, really sorry for the things I've said. I didn't mean any of it. I was just angry. You won't hear from me again. Take care. Greg.*

'It was down to you, Luce. By doing that little favour with the security check, the favour got returned.'

'Look, Gilly, I hope you know what you're doing.'

'It's all good, Luce. Let's have a drink, we've got things to celebrate. How about we make a night of it?'

'Well I've got no plans, so why not.'

He ordered another pint for himself and a large white wine for Lucy, before moving away from the bar. There were a few other officers from the prison drifting into the bar, and the atmosphere in the pub was getting jovial. While Lucy was at the bar getting the next round, Razor checked his phone. There were two text messages.

# SCREWED

The first was from Deborah seeing if he was free for lunch the next day, the other from Tony that read:

*Early doors Sat?*

He replied to Deborah first, telling her that he'd pick her up around one. Then sent a text to Tony.

*Just early doors then. Remember you're a married man.*

A message came back immediately.

*Ruth is fine with it. Need to catch up.*

Razor hadn't seen or spoken to Tony since the previous Saturday and was curious as to what had happened. He was also looking forward to all the details. He sent a quick text back.

*OK. Same time, same place.*

He'd just finished typing the text when Lucy returned with the drinks. He hit send and slipped the phone back into his pocket.

'Girlfriend checking up on you?' asked Lucy with a smile, but her tone conveyed something more.

'Nah, just a mate.'

'Whatever you say, Gilly.' There was an awkward silence which Lucy broke after a couple of seconds. 'Oh, almost forgot. You know that dickhead who was on our wing?'

'Narrow it down, Luce, the list is endless.'

# SCREWED

'Red dressing gown, Ridgley, or Beef I think his mates call him.'

'Oh yeah, I remember him.' He wanted to add 'better than you might think' but thought better of it.

'Anyway, some idiot approved him for tagging. He gets out in the morning, it was on the computer system, but don't tell anyone I told you.'

Razor had an idea about someone who may be interested to know that Beef was getting released early, and with any luck it may result in another brown envelope. On a visit to the gents, he tapped out a quick text message to Johnny telling him that Beef was going to be released from Doncatraz the next morning.

Lucy suggested that they head into town. Razor didn't know if it was the alcohol, or the fact that they weren't working together any more, but he felt an attraction toward her that hadn't been there before. He had to check himself several times, as he found his eyes drawn to her shapely behind when she'd walked towards the bar. The few drinks they'd intended having turned into a few too many, and they were both feeling pretty drunk.

'Why have you never asked me out, Gilly?' slurred Lucy over the pumping music.

# SCREWED

It was nearly midnight; the bar was heaving. Lucy had been quite flirtatious all night, although Razor had done his best to play it down. Now she was getting a little more direct.

'Well, ever since I've known you you've had a boyfriend.'

'I don't have one now though,' Lucy purred, as she sucked seductively on the straw of the cocktail she was drinking.

'Yeah I know, but I'm seeing someone now.'

'That's not stopped me in the past,' she said with a devilish grin.

Lucy then grabbed him by the hand and dragged him toward a door marked disabled. Razor paused before she managed to open it. He wasn't prudish by any stretch of the imagination, but getting it on in a bar toilet wasn't his thing. His opinion of Lucy suddenly nosedived, knowing that she was willing to do it. He'd always thought Lucy was more of a relationship sort of person, not someone who was into one-night stands.

'Hang on, Luce. You know I'm seeing someone. I think it's time we left.'

She detected a hint of disgust in his voice and suddenly tried to backtrack.

'As if I'd try to shag you in the bogs, Gilly. You know I'm not really like that. Let's call it a night?'

# SCREWED

Lucy passed out in the back of the taxi, so Razor decided it was probably best to dump her on his settee and drive her home in the morning.

Next morning, when Razor took a cup of strong coffee into the living room, Lucy was still fast asleep under the duvet that he'd placed over her the night before. He set the mug down next to the sofa where she lay then left the room to grab a shower. When he returned, Lucy was awake and sipping the hot coffee.

'Morning, Luce. Sleep well?'

'Yeah, I did and thanks for... you know, not taking advantage. I didn't realise how much I'd had to drink.'

'It's fine; we did have things to celebrate. I think we both overdid it a bit.'

'I'm still buzzing that the thing with Greg got sorted, you must have some good mates.'

# SCREWED

# CHAPTER FORTY-SIX

The black Range Rover Sport with tinted windows and gleaming, oversized alloy wheels cruised down Park Lane, Barnsley. The driver was Terry, a white guy in his early thirties. Terry was what most people would call a 'meathead'. He was six foot six and twenty-five stone of pure muscle. Terry's spent every spare hour of his life in Kinetix Gym, where he pumped iron and injected steroids. Terry glanced at the dashboard – 10:36 a.m.

*Plenty of time*, thought Terry. The person he was looking for wouldn't be out of his scummy, little bed until at least midday. His eyes shifted left and right, looking for the street that should lead off Park Lane. His left hand slid subconsciously over his shaven head as it always did when Terry was concentrating.

'Keep a look out for Brook Street, Will.'

'Why don't you just use the satnav?'

'Because, dickhead, we type that address into the satnav on my car and what's it do?'

'Gets us to the place?'

'No, it puts us, or namely me, at the scene, you fucking retard.'

'Good point, Tez,' said Willie feeling a bit stupid for not realising this himself.

# SCREWED

Willie was Terry's business partner. Willie was also white with a shaven head. He stood a little under six feet and was quite well built, but was by no means as obsessive as Terry and he never touched steroids. He was always making jokes about steroids making your balls shrink. He was probably the only person who could get away with this. Terry was a nasty piece of work, and it didn't take much for him to lose his temper.

'Tez, there on the left. Brook Street.'

Terry checked his rear-view mirror, clicked his indicator and manoeuvred the Range Rover left into Brook Street. Terry was a conscientious driver and hated anyone, with a passion, who didn't abide by the rules of the road or exercise common decency behind the wheel. The other reason for his careful driving was he didn't want to attract any unwanted attention from the Old Bill. At any given time, Terry had a butcher's meat cleaver in the pocket of the driver's door, a twenty-four-inch, wooden baseball bat in the boot and, for special occasions, a 22-calibre Glock pistol, with thirteen rounds in the magazine, housed in a secret compartment in the dashboard. Beside his mini arsenal of weapons, he'd have ten to twenty thousand pounds worth of steroids in his boot. This was where Willie and Terry made their main living, selling steroids wholesale to gyms up and down the country. As a sideline, they collected in the odd debt and carried out contract beatings. For Terry the beatings weren't about the money, although this was always a bonus, he just enjoyed dishing out a good hiding to someone and found it very therapeutic. Plus, in Terry's opinion, ninety-nine per cent of the people he was contracted to beat deserved it.

'Who's the geezer we're after, Tez?'

'He goes by the name of Beef, and he's a member of the Brook Street Crew, hence here we are driving down Brook Street.'

'Makes sense. Who's he upset?' enquired Willie.

Terry shot Willie a sideward glance.

'Johnny.'

'And what's the poor fucker done? Nothing major, no doubt. Johnny seems to...'

Willie stopped mid sentence, as Terry shot him another menacing glare. Willie also noticed the vein in Terry's temple starting to pulse, which was never a good thing.

'I mean, yeah. No doubt he deserves it,' said Willie quickly.

Willie saw Terry's grip on the steering wheel slacken slightly as he relaxed. Terry's mood could be up and down like a hooker's knickers. Willie knew, of course, this was mostly down to the steroids. Unlike himself, Terry was a great fan

## SCREWED

of Johnny's and wouldn't have a word said against him.

Johnny had called Terry into his office, at the Living Room, two days previously and explained that one of his dealers had been taking liberties and needed 'a bit of a talking to'. Terry was only too happy to help. He glanced at the street he was driving down. He'd slowed to around 15 mph; he didn't know exactly where the guy called Beef lived, or what he looked like, but as this was Brook Street and Beef was a member of the Brook Street Crew, Terry was pretty sure he wouldn't be too difficult to locate. Brook Street was typical of so many streets in some of Britain's poorest areas. It reminded Terry of a street he had seen on a Channel 4 documentary, *Benefits Street*, where ninety per cent of the people living on the street were on the dole. He gave an involuntary shudder as he thought about the so-called stars of *Benefits Street*. A fat Brummy woman with two mixed-race kids. She was now making a fortune as a minor celebrity, and for what? For being a big, lazy lump of shit with a gob the size of the Channel Tunnel. No wonder the country was on its arse. Terry drove around an abandoned settee that lay in the gutter. Sat on it were two scrawny lads in their late teens, passing a can of cheap supermarket cider between themselves.

# SCREWED

*Fucking losers*, Terry thought.

Spray-painted on virtually every wall were the initials B.S.C.

*What sort of person graffitis the street he lives on?* thought Terry.

Up ahead was a car sat on bricks where the wheels used to be. There was a small army of kids, ranging from about six to eleven, hanging about near it. Terry slowed to a stop alongside the car. Willie buzzed down the passenger window. A kid, of no more than ten years old wearing a hooded top, approached.

'Nice car, bro. Shame if it got scratched, innit,' the boy sneered.

Willie twisted in his seat and grabbed the boy with both hands and dragged him halfway into the Range Rover in one swift movement. The lad's feet were dangling down the side of the vehicle. Willie got his face an inch from his. He could smell stale alcohol on the young lad's breath.

'What colour are you?' Willie snarled. The youngster looked confused. 'I said, what fucking colour are you?' This time Willie's voice had raised an octave, and he was shaking the kid.

'You'd better answer him,' Terry grinned.

'Am white, innit,' the lad managed to say.

'So why you talking like a fucking black then, you little twat?' Willie had nothing at all

# SCREWED

against black men, in fact, despite looking like a member of the National Front, he wasn't the slightest bit racist. He even had a couple of Indian mates and loved it when he got invited round for real Indian food at their homes. Proper Indian food, not the Bangladeshi shit that was served up in Indian Restaurants. No, he had no problem with any race. What he did have an issue with was white kids talking like they were black kids from the ghetto – tossers.

'We're looking for Beef,' Terry interjected.

'Dunno no Beef, innit,' the lad replied.

Willie moved his right hand on to the youngster's throat and squeezed. The boy spluttered, struggling to breathe, whilst trying to get his words out.

'I think, Willie, your little friend is trying to tell us something.'

Willie relaxed his grip a little.

'Beef's still chilling in his crib, innit.'

Willie wanted to snap his neck.

'Which house?' he snarled.

'Numba eighteen. He chills at the playground with his homies from bout one o'clock, innit.'

Willie let go of the lad and pushed him away from the Range Rover. He hit the floor in a crumpled heap. Willie buzzed up the window, and

# SCREWED

Terry eased his foot on to the accelerator, and the Range Rover slowly pulled away.

'You were a bit rough on the little twat, Will. He can't have been any more than eleven.'

'If he can drink booze like a man, then he can be treated like one.'

By this time the lad was back on his feet shouting something at the back of the Range Rover. Then he picked something up from the gutter and hurled it at the back window of Terry's Range Rover. It connected, but luckily for him, with very little force.

'The little twat,' Terry growled, slamming the Range Rover into reverse.

At the exact second the lad saw the reverse lights come on, he turned and ran down the street, disappearing down a small entry between two houses.

'Little bastard better not still be about when we get back, Tel.'

Terry slipped the automatic transmission back into drive and continued down the street. He noted the even numbers were on his side. They'd just driven past eighty-six and eighty-four and as the numbers decreased so did the quality of the houses. After house number sixty the houses came to an end, and there was a gap of about fifty metres. Rusty railings filled the gap, behind which, was what looked like an old playground.

# SCREWED

There was a slide covered in graffiti, a sad-looking frame that once would have had swings hanging from it, a roundabout and a couple of benches. Terry stopped the car parallel to the rusty fence and looked over the playground. There was a knot of lads hanging around near the roundabout. It was hard for Terry to judge their ages as they were all dressed in the typical gang uniform of baggy jeans, which hung halfway down their arses, hooded tops and white trainers sporting either the Nike or Reebok logos. He glanced down at the clock on the dashboard; 11.02 a.m. Still a little too early for Beef according to the young lad at the top of the street.

'What do ya reckon, Tez? We check out that lot then head to the house?'

'Think the house would be the best bet. Apparently, it's just him and some skanky crack whore who lives there, but yeah, maybe best to check out these dickheads first, just in case he's shit the bed and decided to get out of it before lunch.'

Terry turned off the ignition and got out of the Range Rover, sliding the meat cleaver under his jacket. Willie jumped out the other side. Terry pushed the button on the fob to lock the car. The locks clicked, and the hazard lights gave a single blink to indicate that the alarm had activated.

# SCREWED

The two men walked casually over to the group of lads. As they got closer, it was evident to see that the lads were late teens, early twenties.

'Are any of you lot Beef?' Willie asked to no one in particular.

'Who are you? Da po-lice?' laughed one of the lads. The others joined in laughing and bumping fists. Terry grabbed the youth, spun him around and, in one fluid movement, had the meat cleaver to his throat.

'I suggest you answer my colleague's question,' snarled Willie. The rest of the crowd stood motionless, looking down at their trainers.

'Beef ain't ere mate, honest. He'll still be in his crib wit his be'atch,' stuttered the hoody. There were mumbles of agreement from the others in the group.

'Yeah, his be'atch.'

'If you're lying, I'll be back, and I'll castrate every last one of you. Understand?' Terry calmly said, waving his meat cleaver for maximum effect. There were nods all round from the small group.

'Right, you are coming with us,' said Willie, putting his hand on the shoulder of the lad who had just had the pleasure of Terry's meat cleaver at his throat.

'Where we goin'?' asked the lad in a whimper.

# SCREWED

'We're off to see our mate, Beef,' replied Terry with a smile. 'Now the rest of you little twats, fuck off home. Now!' he bellowed.

Terry didn't need to tell them again, within ten seconds the old playground was empty.

'I'll just go and turn the motor round, then I'll see you, and your new mate, outside number eighteen.'

Terry hit the button on the fob unlocking the Range Rover's doors. He noticed that the group standing around the car on bricks had grown considerably.

*Perfect*, Terry thought, as he jumped into the driver's seat and started the engine.

As he slowly pulled off, Willie was starting to walk down the street to number eighteen with the lad from the playground at his side. Willie had a firm grip on the youth's arm. Terry did a three-point turn at the bottom of the street then stopped the Range Rover outside number twelve. He didn't want to stop directly outside Beef's house in case he looked out of the window and guessed something was wrong. Terry couldn't imagine many people on this street having the cash to buy a Rangy Sport. He turned off the engine and hit the button on the dash that popped the boot. Terry had brought some extra goodies with him for the job today. He grabbed the canvas bag from the

# SCREWED

boot and slammed it shut, pushing the button on the fob as he walked to where Willie was standing.

'Now listen and listen good. You knock on that door and get Beef to open it, OK?' snarled Willie, his face inches away from the young lad's.

'How do I get him to do that? He's paranoid, innit. He only just got out of Doncatraz.'

'I don't give a fuck how. Just get that fucking door open, or you'll be going home with your dick in your mouth,' said Terry patting his meat cleaver.

The lad nodded. Terry moved to the right of the door and Willie to the left. The youth was standing in front of the tatty front door, which, by the look of it, hadn't seen a coat of paint in years. He just stood staring, not quite knowing what to do.

'Get on with it,' Terry growled.

The lad gave a timid knock on the door. Nothing happened, so the guy turned his head to look at Terry.

'Knock louder. Don't look at me again if you want your dick to stay attached to your body.'

The lad visibly tensed and gave a hard rap on the door that would put most rent collectors to shame. Again he waited, but only for about five seconds before knocking again. This yielded a result. There was movement inside the house, a door slammed along with a few more bangs and thuds, then the letter box, that was located at waist height, popped open.

'Who'd dare.'

The lad bent over, so his face was level with the letter box. 'It's me, innit.'

'What da fuck da ya want? It's da middle of da fooking night.'

'Me and da homies need some puff, innit. We goin' into town ta do some robbin', innit.'

Willie could feel his blood boiling; he wanted to rip the little twat's tongue out.

'Fook off and come back afta one.' With that the letter box snapped shut.

'Knock again,' hissed Terry.

The young lad hesitated then banged on the door again. The flap on the letter box snapped open again.

'I told ya ta fook off.'

'*No* listen, bro. We take an oz, innit.'

Terry smiled to himself, knowing that any reputable dealer wouldn't turn down the chance of selling an ounce of cannabis. There was a silent pause, then they heard a multitude of locks clicking and bolts sliding back. The door opened a crack. This was all Terry and Willie needed. Terry barged the door with his shoulder, sending it crashing back against the interior wall of the house. Beef, who was in the process of opening the door, was sent flying backwards and landed in a crumpled heap on the floor in the middle of the room. His head had hit the corner of a tatty-looking sofa as he fell and blood was trickling down his face. Terry was first through the door, closely followed by Willie, who had already punched the young lad in the side of the head and told him, in no uncertain terms, to leave. Terry strolled over to where Beef lay on the floor. Willie closed the front door and observed the room. It was a shithole; ashtrays littered every spare surface, all overflowing with ash and cigarette butts. Empty takeaway cartons covered the floor. Willie's gaze shifted to where Beef lay on the ground. Terry had his right foot on Beef's chest. Terry stared down at the guy under his foot; he was a white man in his early twenties, about five foot eight and stockily built. His hair was cropped short. Terry was amazed to see that Beef was wearing a red dressing gown. From what he'd heard, during all Beef's time in Doncatraz the only thing he'd worn was his red dressing gown. Beef had a confused look on his face and was trying to get his breath. He'd been winded when he'd hit the floor, and the fact that Terry's foot was on his chest didn't help matters.

'Who da fook are you two?' Beef managed to say in a raspy voice.

# SCREWED

'Let's just say we're the ghosts of Doncatraz past and we are here to cleanse you of your many sins,' Terry grinned.

Beef let out a loud groan.

'Dat's jail, you ave to do shit.'

'Maybe you do,' replied Terry, 'but two things you don't do are deal without the boss knowing and then take the piss out of one of his employees.'

'Dat screw worked for Johnny?' stammered Beef in disbelief.

'You got it, and you don't deal shit without Johnny's say so,' said Terry, as he gave him a swift kick in the ribs. Beef let out a high-pitched squeal.

# SCREWED

# CHAPTER FORTY-SEVEN

While Razor was standing in the shower, he wondered if he'd done the right thing by involving Johnny in Lucy's problem, as now one favour had been done there would, no doubt, be more to follow. Things were getting messy, two deaths, directly or indirectly, on his hands, and then who knew what would happen to Greg.

Razor planned to drop Lucy off at home then pick Deborah up for lunch, but she'd texted him saying she'd pick him up, so he dropped Lucy off and returned home. As he sat waiting, it occurred to him that he'd never actually been to Deborah's house. Whenever he suggested picking her up, she'd always insist on collecting him or meeting him out. He was sure he was overthinking things.

Deborah arrived at 1.00 p.m. in the Evoque, interrupting his thoughts. He drove, and this reminded him of how much he wanted a fancy car of his own. If Johnny kept needing favours then maybe it was possible. They drove for twenty minutes, passing through narrows lanes, until they arrived at a country pub on the outskirts of the city. As they waited for lunch to arrive, the conversation turned to the night before.

# SCREWED

'It was mayhem in Tens last night. A twenty-strong stag do were in, all pissed as parrots. The stag got thrown out in the end, but it was a very lucrative evening; it will pay for a half decent holiday.'

'I haven't been away for over two years; a holiday would be great.'

Deborah quickly changed the subject.

'What did you end up doing?'

'Oh, nothing much. I just met up with Lucy from work for a couple of drinks, but it turned into a proper session.'

'A session, eh? Lucky Lucy,' said Deborah raising an eyebrow.

'It was just a drinking session. Then Lucy ended up crashing on the sofa,' he replied defensively.

'Razor, relax. It wouldn't be a problem if you had slept with her. It's not like we're married or even living together,' she said laughing.

He was about to reply when a waitress arrived at their table with lunch. There was an awkward silence as the plates were set down, until Deborah finally spoke.

'Have you heard anything from your mate, Tony, since last weekend? I do like him; he's a funny guy.' Her eyes danced as she spoke.

The question about Tony unsettled him a little, but he was glad to be off the subject of Lucy.

# SCREWED

'He wants to meet up tonight, actually.'

'Are you still coming up to Leeds after?'

'Yes of course,' said Razor relaxing.

'Will Tony be coming?'

'Not sure. We're meeting up early doors, so I'm guessing not.'

'Well, it's not a problem if he does, although I can't say for sure if Crystal is about. I don't know if she's working tonight.'

'Would probably be better for his marriage if she wasn't.'

'You're so conservative, Razor,' giggled Deborah.

The rest of the afternoon was spent in Razor's bedroom. Deborah then dropped him off at the pub to meet Tony.

'Let me know if Tony is coming up to Leeds, and I'll be sure to bring a friend,' were Deborah's parting words.

# CHAPTER FORTY-EIGHT

'Unpack the bag, Will. Time to go to work on this piece of shit.'

Willie picked up the canvas bag from the floor, placed it on the sofa and began unpacking it. Beef tried lifting his head, straining, trying to see what was coming out of the bag.

'Keep your head down,' said Terry, pushing his foot harder into Beef's chest.

Willie was looking for somewhere to place the items from the bag. This was the part he enjoyed, the theatre of it all, the buzz he got when they were contracted to teach someone a lesson. Willie saw a coffee table in the corner of the room. Beer cans and overfilled ashtrays littered the surface.

*Perfect*, Willie thought, moving to the corner of the room and tipping the table over so the beer cans and ashtrays clattered to the floor.

He picked up the cheap, flimsy coffee table and placed it near Beef's bare feet.

'Don't think our man here is very comfy. So how about you get a cushion for under his head?' said Terry, who couldn't care less about how comfortable Beef was.

He did, however, want his head lifted up enough so that he could see the surface of the coffee table. Willie snatched a dirty-looking

# SCREWED

cushion, covered in cigarette burns, off the sofa. He then grabbed Beef's nose between his thumb and forefinger and pulled his head up from the floor. Tears welled in Beef's eyes, and he let out a piercing scream. Willie jammed the cushion under his head and let go of his nose.

'What the fuck is going on?'

Both Willie and Terry turned to look at the door leading from the kitchen into the living room. Standing there in a filthy, pink dressing gown was a skinny woman who looked about forty, but was probably only in her twenties. She had bleached, blond hair with at least five inches of black roots showing. The front of the dressing gown was gaping open. Unable to help himself, Willie had to have a sneaky peek, but all he got a glimpse of was the top half of a bad tattoo and a few fag burns. He cursed himself for even trying to get a look at the skanky whore's tits. In her right hand, she clutched a mobile phone.

'You two betta let him go, or I'm going to call the coppers,' she spat.

'Fook off upstairs, bitch,' hissed Beef.

'You'd be wise to listen to your man. Just leave the phone with us,' instructed Terry.

'And what the fuck are you gonna do if I don't, big man?' she retorted.

Terry pulled the meat cleaver out of his belt.

# SCREWED

'I'll cut your fucking tits off or what there is of 'em.'

She froze, her gaze on the meat cleaver. Willie took this opportunity to grab the phone from her hand. He threw it against the wall, and the phone smashed into four or five pieces.

'Now get upstairs and keep your skanky beak shut.'

She wisely followed Willie's instructions and backed out of the room. They heard her slow footsteps heading up the stairs and into the room above. Willie looked down at Beef and grinned.

'Right, after your small reprieve it's back to business.'

Willie placed the canvas bag next to the coffee table and slowly unzipped it. The room was deadly silent, and Beef's eyes were bulging as he tried to see what was going on. The sound of the teeth separating on the zip sounded quite sinister in the quiet room. First Willie removed a roll of two-inch wide, grey gaffer tape and placed it on the coffee table. Next, he took out a ten-inch, flat blade screwdriver and put that next to the gaffer tape. Beef was watching intensely, a sheen of sweat forming on his brow.

'What da fuck is dis? I've got some green stashed upstairs, we can work dis shit out.' Beef's voice faltered as he spoke.

# SCREWED

Willie ignored him and continued unpacking the bag, while Terry just gave him a wink. A two-point-five-litre tin of black gloss paint was next on the table. Then a black marker pen, a few sheets of white paper and finally, a claw hammer. For additional theatre, Willie spent a few seconds making sure all the items were parallel to each other on the table. Beef was now sweating profusely despite the room having a damp chill to it.

'I think our man here is a bit hot, Will. What do ya think?'

'Guess you're right, Tez. What can we do about it?'

Both Willie and Terry pretended to think for a moment.

'Think that silly, red dressing gown needs to go, Tez.'

'You a pair of fucking homos?' spat Beef.

Terry gave a little swing of the meat cleaver, that he still had in his hand, and removed his foot from Beef's chest. Beef wriggled out of the dressing gown, leaving him lying on the floor wearing only a pair of greyish boxer shorts that looked as if they were once white.

'OK, get on your hands and knees,' Terry instructed.

Beef simply stared at him; Terry gave him a sharp kick in the kidneys.

# SCREWED

'Now,' he shouted.

Beef complied reluctantly, his head now facing the table.

'Pass us the hammer, Will.'

Willie picked up the hammer and gave it to Terry with his right hand, while taking the metal meat cleaver with his left and carefully placing it on the coffee table. Beef had his eyes fixed on the hammer, wondering what these two nutballs had in mind.

'Now, Beef,' started Terry, in a very calm tone, 'because I'm not a total twat, I'm gonna give you a choice. Pretty decent of me, eh?'

Beef gave a slight nod, so Terry continued.

'Because you're a little scrotum who does deals behind his boss's back and can't keep his mouth shut, I'm compelled to punish you. Do you think it's wise to try and compromise one of Johnny's people?'

Terry enjoyed this part immensely, speaking down to scumbags like Beef as if they were retarded children. He loved the slow build up to the inevitable beating, as much as Willie enjoyed his theatre with the tools from the bag.

Beef remained silent. Terry lifted his chin using the handle of the claw hammer.

'When someone asks you a question, especially when the person asking that question is holding a twenty-ounce claw hammer, then it would seem prudent, and let's not forget polite, to have the decency to answer them.

'So,' continued Terry, his voice slow and calm, 'I will ask my question again. Do you believe...

'No,' Beef almost screamed.

This insane talking was driving Beef nuts. He'd had the occasional beating in the past, but they had been straight to point, someone would either just jump you from behind or simply try and punch you in the face. But all this talking and then not knowing what this mental case standing before him was going to do was scaring the shit out of him.

Terry jabbed the handle of the hammer into Beef's throat.

'Did your mother teach you no fucking manners? Don't you know it's rude to interrupt when someone else is talking? Don't answer that it was rhetorical.' Terry loved rhetorical questions, a chance to fuck a little bit more with the undereducated scum he dealt with. And judging by the vacant look on Beef's face, he too fitted perfectly into that bracket.

'So with that cleared up, I will repeat my original question... Do you agree that big-mouthed, lowlife scum, such as yourself, should be punished? You may answer now.'

'Yeah,' grunted Beef.

## SCREWED

'Now that wasn't too difficult was it?'

'No,' Beef spat.

'So as a said I'm going to punish you, and your punishment is going to take the form of me smashing one of your hands with my hammer.'

This was too much for Beef, he felt his bladder go involuntarily weak, and he pissed all over the floor. The urine soaked into the cheap carpet then spread, wetting his knees. Willie roared with laughter. Beef wasn't the big man any more. Terry ignored Willie's laughter, and the stink of piss, and continued.

'Now, as I'm a decent sort of guy I'm going to give you the choice of which hand I'm going to smash, and here's how it's going to play.'

Terry explained to Beef that he was going to count backwards from five, and by the time he hit zero Beef needed to have pushed one of his hands forward, and if he didn't Terry would bury the hammer in his head. Beef was in no doubt that this mad bastard would be true to his word. Terry was slowly starting to count backwards.

'Five, four, three...'

Beef was trying to think of a way out; it only took him until Terry reached three to realise he had none. He was right-handed so thought the only option was to push forward his left hand and hope it would be quick. The word 'one' seemed to leave Terry's mouth in slow motion. Beef pushed

# SCREWED

forward his left hand, Terry smiled. Easier than he thought. He crouched beside Beef, lifted the claw hammer and smashed it into the knuckles of Beef's left hand. There was a splintering sound as the hammer crushed into Beef's hand. Beef seemed to suffer a delayed reaction because his hand stayed where it was. It took Terry a split second to realise this, lift the hammer and smash it down again on to Beef's shattered hand. This time there was a reaction; Beef screamed in pain, vomited and fell forward, so he was lying flat on the floor in his own urine. His left hand looked like a lifeless object, battered and oozing blood.

'Double hit, nice one, Tez,' Willie commented.

'Yeah, I'm pleased with that. Right, get this job wrapped up.'

Beef didn't seem to be moving or making any noises, so Terry gave him a little kick, provoking a grunt. Good thought Terry, still conscious.

Terry roughly grabbed Beef's right arm and moved it behind his back then did the same with his left, causing Beef to cry out in pain. Willie passed the roll of gaffer tape over to Terry. Terry fiddled with the tape, until he found the end, then proceeded to wrap the tape around Beef's wrists.

'Give us a lift with this sack of shit, Will.'

# SCREWED

Together Terry and Willie lifted Beef to his feet; he stood swaying slightly. The colour drained from his face. Terry pushed Beef's knees together and then taped them, resulting in Beef only being able to take tiny steps.

*Perfect*, thought Terry.

Beef's eyes widened, and Terry thought he was going to pass out. He was staring at Willie who had picked up the screwdriver from the coffee table. Willie was spinning the screwdriver between his fingers while keeping his gaze firmly on Beef. He continued this for about twenty seconds, although to Beef it felt ten times longer. Willie then stopped spinning the screwdriver and used it to take the lid off the tin of black gloss paint. Beef exhaled deeply.

'Talk like a black man and act like a black man, we'll help you look like a black man.' Willie said this as he poured the entire tin of black gloss paint over Beef's head. The black paint oozed down Beef's face and on to his chest. Willie picked up two sheets of white paper, then with the marker pen, he wrote 'twat' in bold letters on each sheet. He then stuck the paper to Beef's back and chest.

'What do ya think, Tez?' said Willie pleased with his handiwork.

'Very nice, William. Your spelling is impeccable. Now take a couple of snaps for the boss,' Terry said. 'Right, Will. I'll get the motor; you pack up then get this twat outside.'

Willie took a couple of snaps of Beef on his mobile phone while Terry left the house, hit the button on the fob and jumped into the Ranger Rover. He started the engine and manoeuvred the car to a standstill outside number eighteen. Willie picked up the hammer, tape and screwdriver, and packed them into the bag. He tucked Terry's meat cleaver into the back of his trousers. He left the empty paint tin lying on the floor. He knew there was no need to take it. People like Beef didn't believe in going to the police. Beef just stood in the middle of the room, not quite knowing what was going to happen next. His hand was in agony. His boxer shorts were soaked with his own piss, and the paint had run down his leg and was pooling at his feet. Willie picked up the canvas bag and opened the front door, Beef's spirits lifted, they were finished with him. His elation was short-lived.

Willie with a nod of his head said, 'OK, big man, out the door.'

Beef didn't move. He just stood there trying to comprehend what had just been said.

'Has that paint made you fucking deaf? I said outside,' Willie said, pulling the meat cleaver from his trousers.

# SCREWED

Beef tried to walk, but the tape binding his knees together made moving difficult, and he nearly fell forward on to the coffee table. He managed to regain his balance and shuffled towards the door.

'Now my scrotie, little friend, I'm going to get into that nice, shiny Range Rover there and you,' Willie jabbed him in the back with the meat cleaver, 'you are going to walk in front of that beautiful, shiny Ranger Rover all the way up this fucking street. Do anything silly and my mate there, behind the wheel, will mow you down like the rabid dog you are. Understand?'

Beef nodded his understanding. Willie pulled the door closed behind them, walked over to the Ranger Rover and put the canvas bag into the boot. Beef started to shuffle up the pavement.

'Not the pavement, dickhead. Middle of the street,' boomed Willie's voice from behind the Range Rover.

Beef shuffled to the centre of the road, his eyes not leaving his paint-covered feet. Willie opened the passenger door and jumped in. Terry eased the Range Rover forward, so the bumper was inches from Beef's legs, then he gave five long blasts on the horn. The noise from the horn caused quite a stir from behind the doors and curtains of many of the houses up and down the street. Those residents who weren't already outside their front doors were looking out of their windows to see what the commotion was. They were all greeted by the sight of Beef, the lowlife drug pusher who thought he owned the street. They witnessed him stripped to his boxer shorts, hands taped behind his back, covered in black paint, with the word 'Twat' on his back and front. As Beef slowly shuffled up the street, the Range Rover was inches behind him. Terry and Willie were watching the residents of the street staring, pointing and laughing at this once swinging dick of a bully shuffling away in his piss-soaked underwear.

'Good result eh, Tez? Think everyone's happy.'

'Fucking perfect. I think our work here is done.'

Terry pulled the Range Rover around Beef and drove on up the street. He gave a quick glance in his rear-view mirror to see the kids in the street had surrounded Beef and were taking it in turns hitting him. Terry grinned, flicked on the indicator, checked left and right, and manoeuvred on to Park Lane.

SCREWED

## CHAPTER FORTY-NINE

When Razor entered the pub, he spotted Tony stood at the bar draining the last of a pint. His empty glass hit the bar just as Razor joined him.

'Two pints, barman. Alright, Gilly mate? Don't think I can get used to calling you Razor.'

It was evident that Tony had consumed more than one pint already.

'How's it going, Tone? Didn't think you'd get a pass after last week. Did you get into any shit with the wife?'

'She's cool, mate. She doesn't want me to lose touch with my friends. Just so happens that she's in Manchester this weekend visiting her sister,' he said with a grin before taking a gulp of his pint. 'It's been one hell of a week, buddy. You sure mix with some interesting people,' continued Tony suddenly looking serious.

He then recounted his week, everything from Crystal and the photos, to meeting Johnny outside the courthouse, and his encounter with Greg and the fake drugs.

'To be honest, Gilly, I thought that you'd had a part in setting me...'

Razor, who had been listening in stunned silence, began to try and speak, but Tony ploughed on.

# SCREWED

'Relax, mate; I'm a detective, it was just a fleeting thought. I soon disregarded you. But I bet I'd be right in guessing that you know the girl who Greg Huston was trying to blackmail. My guess is you asked your gold-toothed friend to help her out. Am I close?'

'You're spot on, mate, and, to be honest, I feel shitty about it.' Razor focused on his pint glass as he spoke, not wanting to make eye contact with Tony.

'Not your fault, Gilly. If I'd have kept my pants on, I wouldn't be in this situation. I think it was just a case of wrong place, wrong time for me and your mate Johnny boy just seized an opportunity.'

Tony had decided to omit the detail about Johnny giving him a fat, brown envelope as a down payment.

'All that aside, not a bad week,' said Razor trying to lighten the mood. He didn't feel comfortable knowing that Johnny was blackmailing his friend.

Tony gave a loud laugh; his mind kept flipping to the second brown envelope that he was due to collect from Johnny, now that he'd performed his little task. He decided to change the subject.

# SCREWED

'To be honest, that was the easy part of my week. Did you read about that young, black lad who got busted on Monday?'

Razor instantly knew that Tony was referring to Ishmael and wondered where this was heading. He gave a slight nod of his head and then took a long pull on his pint. So Tony carried on his narrative.

'Anyway, we got this tip-off; or rather someone tipped off the chief super. It was a good tip. Told us exactly where the drugs were. They were in a safe behind a flat-screen TV, if you can believe that! We would never have looked there.'

Tony went through the whole story from start to finish. He knew he probably shouldn't be discussing an ongoing case, but he needed to vent and, after all, Gilly was ex-job. When Tony got to the part about the chief superintendent wanting to charge Ishmael without any proper evidence, Razor's stomach did a summersault.

'Then, to really fuck my weekend up, I got the forensics report back this morning. Not a single print anywhere. Robson's barrister will laugh us out of court. Paul wasn't best pleased.'

This made Razor's ears prick up again.

'The chief super was in work on a Saturday morning? I'd have put him on the golf course at the weekends, not work.'

Tony let out a loud laugh.

# SCREWED

'That was the good bit. He was on the golf course but insisted I keep him updated the second the forensics came back. I ruined his game apparently.'

'Why is Paul so interested in a low-level drugs case?' asked Razor trying to sound casual.

Tony realised that he'd perhaps said a bit too much so thought he better change the subject.

'Beats me. We having another one in here or moving on?'

'Tell you what, Tone, let's have a swift one then head up to Leeds and check out a few bars. Then we'll head to the Living Room. No doubt there'll be some champagne on the house.'

Tony headed off to the gents, while Razor ordered another round. He was replaying everything that Tony told him and trying to make sense of it all. Why was Paul so interested in Ish, and could it connect somehow to Johnny? But then how did Johnny benefit from Ishmael getting busted? It was ultimately Johnny's cocaine and Johnny's cash that was sitting in an evidence locker at the local nick. If Paul was connected to Johnny, surely he would do his best to get Ishmael off the charge. Razor concluded that Paul couldn't be working for Johnny. Maybe it wasn't him who he'd seen at Johnny's mansion that evening. Tony returned from the gents, breaking Razor's train of thought. He seemed to be on a mission; he'd finished his pint before Razor had even taken the head off his. Tony then reached into his pocket and pulled out a foil packet containing yellow, torpedo-shaped tablets. He cracked the plastic, releasing two tablets, and popped them into his mouth.

'What's with the pills, Tone?' asked Razor suspiciously.

'Just something the doctor gave me. Nothing major, they just help me relax. Now drink up, Leeds is calling.'

Razor thought this was out of character and was a little concerned but decided now was not the time to ask any more about the pills, so he took a couple of gulps of his pint then placed the half-full glass on the bar. They hailed a taxi and headed to Leeds city centre. Tony insisted on paying the cab fare. He peeled off a couple of twenties from a think wad of cash. Razor noted the bundle but again said nothing.

On entering the first bar, a trendy place full of people who made Razor and Tony feel quite old, Razor let Tony fight to the bar while he went to the gents. He went directly to the cubicle and tapped out a small pile of party powder on to the back of his hand. With a quick snort, all the powder disappeared up his left nostril. There was no way he could match Tony's drinking without it.

# SCREWED

Razor was pretty impressed with himself for keeping his drug use to the weekends. He had lapsed a bit at first by having the odd snort as a pick-me-up in the morning, but he'd managed to knock that on the head, more or less. He was now officially a social user only, though he would need a top-up tonight courtesy of Claudio. The drinking slowed down as they moved from bar to bar, although it wasn't intentional, more down to how busy the bars were getting.

'I'm getting pissed off with all the queuing for drinks, Gilly. How about we go to the Living Room for a bit of table service?'

'Not a bad idea. Let's go.'

'I take it Deborah will be meeting you there later?'

'Yeah, why?'

'Well, I was wondering if she'd be on her own or not?'

'Fuck Tony, you're a married man. Look what happened last Saturday.'

'Look, Johnny's already got his blackmail material, so whatever I do this week won't change anything, will it?'

Razor just stared at his mate.

'Anyway, I just want some cute female to chat to. What's wrong with that?'

'You're so full of shit, Tony.'

# SCREWED

'Come on. You going to ask for me or not?' said Tony draping an arm around Razor's shoulder.

'OK stud, leave it with me.'

Razor fired off a quick text to Deborah letting her know that Tony would be with him later that evening and that he wanted some company.

SCREWED

# CHAPTER FIFTY

The usual pleasantries were exchanged as Tony and Razor passed through the main entrance of the Living Room and then on into the VIP area. Stood at the bar chatting animatedly was Claudio and Johnny. Johnny's gold teeth gleamed in the dim light. The more Razor saw Johnny the more he reminded him of an evil character in a Bond movie. As soon as he clapped eyes on them, Johnny strutted over. He moved between them and laid a heavy arm over each of their shoulders.

'How are my two favourite gentlemen tonight? I guess you'll be a lot better once you've consumed some of my champagne.' He then snapped his thick fingers at a waitress. 'Champagne for my guests, sweet cheeks, and don't let me see them with empty glasses tonight,' he barked.

The server quickly prepared an ice bucket, three flutes and a bottle of Bollinger. Once all three glasses were full, Johnny turned to Razor.

'If you won't mind excusing us for a minute, Razor old boy, Tone and I need a little chat.'

As Johnny lead Tony off into the back office, Razor took the opportunity to have a quick word with Claudio about topping up his silver vial.

# SCREWED

'I hear your little assignment went well, Tone old chap.' Johnny opened a desk drawer and handed Tony an envelope similar to the one he'd given him outside the courthouse. Tony stuffed the envelope into his pocket not wanting to insult Johnny by looking inside it.

'Enlighten me as to how you persuaded him to back off.'

'Come on, Johnny, a man's got to have some secrets,' said Tony with a grin.

Tony wasn't sure if it was the drink or the pills he'd been popping, but tonight Johnny didn't intimidate him. All of his anger toward the man had evaporated, perhaps the cash helped too.

Johnny nodded his stubbly head and let a slight smile dance across his lips.

'Fair enough. Now tell me about that black kid you arrested on Monday. How's your forensics evidence mounting up?'

Johnny knew already that there were no forensics to link Ishmael to the drugs. Johnny had underestimated Ish on that score. Tony wasn't sure why Johnny was interested in the case, but he decided to hold back a little.

'Still waiting for forensics to confirm a few things. Should know something soon.'

Johnny hadn't expected Tony to lie, but he didn't want to tip his hand by letting on that he'd already read the forensics report. That could compromise Paul, and he didn't want that.

'Suppose you must be confident you'll find his prints, as you've charged him, right?'

Tony didn't answer; instead he drained his champagne flute.

'Look, Tone, I'll be frank with you. It's pretty important to me that the kid goes down, and I'm sure it's as important to you that he doesn't walk free from court, so I'm going to help you along,' Johnny said, moving from behind the desk to a flat-screen TV on the wall.

He swung it to one side to reveal a safe. Tony instantly thought of the one in Ishmael Robson's front room but said nothing. Unlike Ishmael's safe this one had a keypad, not a keyhole. Johnny quickly tapped in a five-digit code, and the door swung open. Johnny removed a clear plastic bag that looked very much like a police evidence bag. He passed the bag to Tony who held it up to examine the contents. Inside the evidence bag, was a smaller bag containing white powder. It was identical to ones taken from Ishmael's safe.

'That little bag holds the key to you getting a conviction. That bag has Robson's prints all over it.'

Tony felt a chill creep over his body. He couldn't start tampering with evidence.

# SCREWED

'Johnny, this is serious shit. Having a little chat with some scumbag blackmailer is one thing, but planting evidence, fuck, that's a whole different ball game.'

'Tone, Tone,' said Johnny, placing a hand on his shoulder and squeezing just enough to make Tony feel uncomfortable. 'You're looking at this all wrong.' His voice was jovial, but his grip remained. 'The fact is the black kid is guilty. The drugs in that safe are his. You know, I know it, he knows it. Now without a little assistance, he's going to be back on the streets selling drugs to schoolkids.'

Tony stayed silent. Johnny's grip on his shoulder tightened, and his demeanour changed.

'If you don't get a conviction then your little wife gets some pictures in the post. Understand?' Johnny's low, gravelly voice was now very menacing.

Tony managed a slight nod.

'Good man, now let's get a refill. I hear a particular lap dancer is coming here when she finishes work.' The friendliness had returned to Johnny's voice, and he was all smiles again. They left the back office and joined Razor at the bar, who was chatting away to Claudio. Johnny rattled off a story about some top Tory MP who used to visit one of his strip clubs and ended up getting photographed by a tabloid journalist in a hotel with three strippers and enough cocaine to keep the Columbian army marching for a week.

'At the time he was championing family fucking values,' boomed Johnny.

Tony had downed two glasses of champagne during the story. He had contemplated leaving after the experience in the office, but Johnny's story and the champagne had relaxed him somewhat. He now only had one thing on his mind, large, surgically enhanced, dress-stretching breasts. He would be staying, exactly where he was. Johnny stayed and chatted, telling more stories, until the second bottle of champagne was empty. With a snap of his fingers the empty was replaced, and Johnny returned to the back office. Razor and Tony moved to the booth to wait for the girls and to watch some of the other attractive women moving on the dance floor. It wasn't long before Deborah and Crystal entered the VIP area. Razor and Tony watched as other men mentally undressed the pair as they glided across the dance floor to the booth, this still gave Razor a slight twinge of jealously. The girls were in high spirits and appeared to be in a mischievous mood. Razor guessed that they'd already been on the party powder. Instead of sitting next to Razor, Deborah slid down next to Tony and gave him a long, lingering kiss as way of a greeting. Crystal was next to Razor, but his

# SCREWED

attention was fixed on Tony and Deborah opposite. Deborah finally released her lips from Tony's, glanced over at Razor and gave him a wink.

'Come on, lover. I want to dance,' she purred.

They left Tony with Crystal and moved on to the packed dance floor.

'What are you playing at, Deborah?'

'Hey, chill out. We're just having fun, that's all.'

Tony and Crystal soon joined them. Tony had completely put the conversation with Johnny out of his mind, and he was having a ball. Nothing was going to stop him making the most of the evening. After the week he'd had he felt he deserved to wind down.

Deborah drove Razor and Tony back to Doncaster the next day. As soon as Tony walked into his house, the guilt hit him like a train. He gazed at the pictures of his wedding day, which were hung in the hallway, and felt awful. As he stood under the hot jets in the shower, he tried to sort out his thoughts. What he'd done last night had been wrong on every level, but he'd loved every minute. He had a beautiful wife who he loved dearly with all his heart. In seven short days, he cheated on her twice. He knew it had to stop before it got out

## SCREWED

of control. He made up his mind to spend the next few weekends with his wife. Maybe a nice restaurant or a hotel somewhere, screw the cost, he was really going to spoil her. For now though, he had a more pressing problem, what to do about the little plastic bag that Johnny had given to him. It did make sense what Johnny had said. The kid was guilty, so should he go free just because of some technicality? No matter what though, he had to plant the evidence or Johnny would send the pictures to his wife. He couldn't work out why he wasn't pissed off with Crystal, after all, it was her who had taken the pictures and given them to Johnny. If it wasn't for her, he wouldn't be in this mess.

His wife wasn't due back until early evening, so he popped some pills, poured a large whisky and then spent the afternoon dozing in front of the TV. Sleep had been non-existent the night before. He was awakened by the front door slamming. His wife, Ruth, came into the front room with an enormous smile on her face.

'I'm pregnant. We're going to have a baby,' she gushed.

Tony jumped up from the sofa and embraced his wife.

'Ruth, that's fantastic. My God, I'm going to be a dad. It's incredible.' Tony was genuinely pleased and decided, there and then, that he wouldn't be making any more trips to the Living Room. He had some serious making up to do and Ruth's pregnancy had only served to fuel his guilt further.

The news about Ruth's pregnancy had elated Tony. He couldn't think of anything else. He'd even taken the day off work on Monday to spend some quality time with his wife; it was just what Tony needed to take his mind off recent events. The other thing the pregnancy had taken Tony's mind off was the little plastic bag that Johnny had given to him on Saturday night. He hadn't wanted it in the house so had stashed it in the glovebox of his car on Sunday morning and not thought about it since.

Tony opened his desk drawer and retrieved the packet of tablets; he popped some then swung his feet up on to the desk and started daydreaming about becoming a father. Tony had always wanted to be a father, and he still couldn't quite believe it was happening. The phone on his desk suddenly buzzed, indicating an internal call. He picked up the phone, cradling the handset on his shoulder.
    'DS Price.'

# SCREWED

'Tony, Paul here. Listen, we've had Ishmael Robson's solicitor on demanding to know the results of the forensics report.'

'I thought I told you on Saturday, sir.' Tony paused, wondering why Paul was asking a question to which he already knew the answer. His mind then suddenly flashed to the contents of his glovebox.

'Well, I was wondering if anything had changed, or maybe something may have been missed.'

A thought exploded into Tony's mind.

*Was it possible that Paul and Johnny were trading information? They had to be.*

It all began to make sense to Tony. Johnny must have known that the forensics report had turned up nothing, that's why he gave him the plastic bag with Robson's prints on it. It was also obvious that Paul knew that there was now some evidence that could convict Robson. He was merely giving Tony a nudge. He certainly hadn't bargained for this.

'Tony, you still there?'

Tony, so lost in thought, had forgotten about the chief super on the end of the phone.

'Yes, sir. Still here. Look, just an idea, but it may be worth sending those bags of cocaine back to the lab for a second look. You never know, maybe something was missed.'

## SCREWED

'Splendid idea, Tony. I'm sure you're right. I'll tell Robson's solicitor that we're still waiting on the report. Let me know the second they find the prints. If there are any, of course.'

'Certainly, sir,' replied Tony, feeling a little better about the situation now he knew that he wasn't in this mess on his own.

He now had to work out how to come up with a good enough reason to get forensics to retest the bags of cocaine. He left his desk and headed to the car park to retrieve the bag of cocaine from his glovebox and slipped it into his jacket pocket. Once back in the station, Tony made his way to the evidence room. He signed and dated the logbook then located the box that contained all the items taken from Ishmael's house. In the box were a number of evidence bags. He was relieved to find that the bag containing the ten smaller packets of cocaine had been returned after the forensics testing. He pulled out a fresh evidence bag, filled in the paper label and emptied the ten small packets into it. He then snapped on some latex gloves and dropped the bag that Johnny had given to him into the evidence bag along with the others. Tony was sweating as he resealed the bag. He then stuffed the original evidence bag and latex gloves into his jacket pocket. Picking up the new evidence bag containing the cocaine, he left the evidence room and breathed a deep sigh of relief. Tony walked up one flight of stairs to the forensics department. He pushed through the double doors and into a large, open space filled with various equipment and six technicians busily working away. He spotted Jennifer, the supervisor, on the phone in the small office located in the corner of the room. Jennifer had the stereotypical look of a lab technician. She was mid forties, wore steel-framed glasses, no make-up, and her dark brown hair was always tied up in a tight bun on the top of her head. The long, white lab coat finished the look perfectly. Tony imagined that with her hair down and a touch of make-up she could be quite attractive. Jennifer was always efficient and professional.

As Tony entered her small domain she told the caller to hold on for a moment, then covering the mouthpiece said, 'DS Price, what brings you to the third floor?'

'I need a favour, but it's a bit of a rush job. I've got the super on my case for a result on this little lot,' said Tony holding up the evidence bag.

Jennifer looked at the bag, and its contents, and scowled.

'There's a day's work in there, Tony. You know how long drugs testing takes.'

# SCREWED

'Hear me out, Jennifer. Look, I don't need full tests, just fingerprints. You just get me the prints, and I'll even run the matches.'

'OK, give me till the morning, and you owe me big time.'

'You're a star, Jen. Anything you ever need, just ask.'

Tony left feeling pleased with how that had just gone. Jennifer finished her phone call and took the evidence bag into the lab. Fingerprinting was relatively straightforward, so she gave the task to one of the junior technicians.

'Give this priority, Geoff, please. Just fingerprints, OK?'

Geoff took the bag and looked at the contents. He thought to himself that the drug squad was certainly busy at the moment, as this was his second bag of narcotics in two days. Geoff grabbed the lab's logbook and noted down the details from the paper label on the bag. As he entered the subject's name, something seemed familiar. Robson, he was sure that he'd already checked some bags from this case on Friday. He scanned back up the list in the logbook. He was right, the name Robson was written next to Friday's date. Geoff concluded that it must be a big case, as he broke the seal on the evidence bag and removed the first plastic packet. By lunchtime, Geoff had tested three bags without

# SCREWED

finding a single print. If Friday's results were anything to go by he wasn't expecting to find any prints either. Mr Robson was obviously a careful man. After a quick sandwich in the canteen, Geoff returned to his mundane task. Bags four and five both turned up negative, but the trend ended on bag number six. Geoff found a perfect thumbprint on one side of the packet and a partial fingerprint on the other side.

'Bingo!' he cried out.

He took the bag to a machine that resembled a large photocopier. Placing the bag on the machine, he made a paper and electronic copy of the prints to run through the police database. Once the print was transferred, Geoff took the paper copy through to Jennifer's office.

'Got a result, Boss. Perfect thumb and partial fingerprint on bag six. I've uploaded the image and here's the hard copy,' explained Geoff as he handed over the paper.

'Good work, Geoff. You'll have made DS Price a very happy man. How many have you got left to test?'

'Should be four more. Must be a big case he's working on.'

'What makes you say that?'

'Well I tested ten bags of drugs from this case on Friday, then ten more bags today, that's a lot of coke, Boss.'

# SCREWED

'It is, Geoff, yes. Give me a shout if you find anything else. I'll give the DS the good news.'

Jennifer considered what Geoff had just told her. Generally, when evidence was sent to them, it all came in together not in dribs and drabs. She'd have to see what Tony had to say on the matter. She picked up the phone and dialled.

'DS Price.'

'Tony, we've got a hit on those items that you dropped off earlier. We've uploaded the prints, so they're all yours.'

'Jennifer, you're a diamond.'

'Just one thing, Tony. Why didn't you send all the samples on Friday?'

Jennifer's question threw Tony off balance; she apparently thought that the bag contained different samples from the same raid. This could cause problems in a court case. On the other hand, she wouldn't be happy if he told her they were the same samples and he'd duped her into retesting them. He decided an earbashing from Jennifer was preferable to one off some fancy barrister in court.

'Oh sorry, Jennifer, didn't I make it clear? The samples I dropped off were Fridays, the chief super insisted on a retest.' Before she could respond he quickly added, 'And by the look of it, it's a good job he did. One of your people apparently missed something first time round.'

# SCREWED

'I'm not happy, Tony. I'm going to take this up with the chief super personally. We are stretched enough up here without testing things twice, and I find it incomprehensible that my man missed a print last week.' Jennifer slammed down the phone.

She was angry with Tony for trying to pull a fast one on her. But then she was equally annoyed with Geoff. She knew that fingerprinting was a tedious job, but it still had to be done correctly. If Tony hadn't resent the bags for testing, then Geoff's mistake would have gone unnoticed, and a criminal could have walked free. She decided to have a word with Geoff at the end of the shift.

Tony loosened his tie, he knew Jennifer was not a happy, but he'd got the result that everyone wanted. At this rate, he'd be able to buy a new car by the end of the month. If Johnny had paid him five grand for a simple chat with Greg Huston, then the job he'd just pulled off had to be worth at least ten. He hit a few keys on his computer, and two prints appeared on the screen. All Tony needed to do now was run the prints through the database and let the computer come up with the match to Ishmael Robson. He tapped a few more keys, sat back and waited. The computer took

# SCREWED

about thirty seconds before an icon box flashed in the centre of the screen 'MATCH FOUND'.

'Result,' said Tony out loud, before snatching up his desk phone and dialling the fourth floor.

'Chief Superintendant Johnson's office,' announced Paul's secretary.

'DS Price speaking. Could I speak to the chief please?'

Paul was pleased with the news and suggested that Tony and Ruth join him for dinner at the weekend.

# CHAPTER FIFTY-ONE

Ishmael Robson lay on his bunk on the induction wing. The visit with his solicitor had begun well but had rapidly gone downhill. Ish had sat across from his brief in the tiny legal conference room at HMP Doncaster. There were ten of these cubicle-type rooms a row. From one metre up they were all glass, so you could look down the row and see the occupants of all ten small spaces. The table and two chairs had reminded Ish of the ones that he'd sat at in school, metal and plastic but not bolted to the floor. When the immaculately dressed solicitor had entered the room, he'd told Ish that the so-called witness would not be coming forward to make a statement against him. Ish already knew that no one would ever make a statement against him, as there were only two people who knew about the safe and its contents. The speed at which those dumb coppers had found his safe led him to one conclusion, someone had tipped them off. Johnny wouldn't say anything, as it was his cocaine that was in the safe, so it had to be Razor, the treacherous, fucking screw. It was evident to Ish that Razor wanted him out of the equation so he could keep all the money from the Spice selling for himself. An extra £1,000 per week was a good enough reason to stitch someone up. A tip-off would be easy to do, but he knew Razor

# SCREWED

would never have the balls to make a formal statement against him without putting himself in the frame and jeopardising his job. He concluded that Razor would have assumed that the police would find prints in the safe.

*Nah, Razor man, you're wrong on that score*, thought Ish to himself.

The solicitor spoke, jolting Ish from his thoughts, and what he said made Ish want to beat him around the head with one of the plastic chairs.

'Unfortunately, Ishmael, the police have found your fingerprints on one of the bags of cocaine from inside the safe. This, therefore, gives all the credibility they need to prove their version of events, namely the safe and its contents are yours. I strongly suggest that we try cutting a deal with the prosecution in exchange for a guilty plea.'

Ishmael shot to his feet, his voice loud. 'That's bollocks, man. There ain't no prints, it's a set-up. You're all in it together.'

A prison officer had entered the room when he'd heard Ishmael raised voice.

'You can fuck your guilty plea.'

The officer had to restrain Ishmael to stop him hitting the shocked-looking solicitor. He then dragged Ishmael out of the room.

# SCREWED

Minutes later Ishmael was back in his cell trying to work out how he could get out of this situation. He never went near his safe without gloves; he knew this was a set-up. Then it hit him like a freight train; he remembered where he'd seen that detective before. He was Razor's mate; he'd seen them together in the Living Room the night Deborah had arrived with that bitch, Crystal. Ish was on his feet pacing. Fucking Razor, he didn't want to believe it, but it all added up. He felt the rage building up inside, he snatched the TV up from the metal table and flung it against his cell door.

## CHAPTER FIFTY-TWO

Geoff looked at the evidence bag; two small bags remained inside. He counted the bags laid out on his work station; there were nine. That made eleven in total; he double-checked the label on the evidence bag it stated:

*Contents: ten bags – white powder*

Geoff counted again to be one hundred per cent sure, before going to the corner office where Jennifer was tapping away at her computer keyboard.

'Have you got a minute, Boss? I'd like you to take a look at something.'

'Can't it wait, Geoff? I'm a bit busy at the moment.'

'I think you'll want to take a look at this, Boss.'

Jennifer followed Geoff to his work station, where he explained what he'd just discovered. Jennifer studied the label on the evidence bag and then counted the bags. Geoff was right; one extra was present. She told Geoff to carry on fingerprinting, photograph the eleven bags, then call it a day and leave it with her. Jennifer then returned to her office; she had some serious thinking to do. She'd worked with Tony for five years and always thought him to be an outstanding detective. This just didn't feel right,

# SCREWED

but maybe it was just an honest mistake. Hopefully, this was the case, so Tony would have nothing to worry about. She reached for the phone on her desk and dialled an external number.

Early Wednesday morning, two men, wearing dark suits and serious expressions, walked into Doncaster police headquarters. They flipped open identical badges at the front desk and asked to see Chief Superintendent Johnson.

Paul was a little taken aback when his phone buzzed, and his secretary announced that there were two officers from Internal Affairs to see him. Paul greeted the two officers and led them to his desk. They both declined the offer of coffee and insisted on getting straight to business.

'We're investigating one of your detectives,' announced the first suit.

'DS Tony Price on the drug squad and we'd appreciate your full co-operation,' added the second.

'Not as we need it, you understand, but it does make life a lot easier.'

Paul had taken an instant dislike to suit one, but in his position, he couldn't let his feelings show.

## SCREWED

'I'll assist in every way I can, gentlemen. What exactly has DS Price supposed to have done?'

'We're not at liberty to discuss that at the moment, but to start with we'd like to view your CCTV recording from yesterday morning; then we'd like to speak with Jennifer Ross and Geoff Hodgkins from your crime lab. After that, we'd like a chat with DS Price. We'd also like all of this kept as quiet as possible.'

'Of course,' said Paul.

The two suits left for the CCTV control room. Paul reached into his jacket pocket, pulled out his mobile and dialled Tony's number.

Tony was sat at the kitchen table reading the back page of the *Express* when his mobile rang.

'Morning, Paul. What do I owe the pleasure?'

'Where are you, Tony?' Paul's voice had an urgent tone.

'I'm at home, but I'm just about to leave.'

'Listen carefully; Internal Affairs have just left my office, it seems they're looking into you. If you've got anything you should dump it now, and then get to work ASAP.'

He cut the connection. Tony felt the blood drain from his face; he dropped the phone on to the table and went out to his car. He opened the

# SCREWED

glovebox and removed the envelope of cash. Then he remembered he'd still got the other envelope in his coat pocket from his first meeting with Johnny. He dashed back into the house and up the stairs. Ruth was in bed when he burst into the bedroom and snatched open the wardrobe door.

'Is everything OK, Tony?' asked Ruth sleepily.

'Yeah, fine. Something cropped up at work, and I'm running late.'

He located the envelope and rushed back down the stairs. He put both envelopes into an empty evidence bag then stuffed it under a bush in the garden. He then got into his car and headed to the police station. It was when he pulled into the car park that he realised that he'd left his phone on the kitchen table. He figured that he'd probably not need it if he was getting a grilling from Internal Affairs so decided not to return home to fetch it. Tony couldn't think of anything that Internal Affairs could have on him, but a feeling of dread still consumed him. He tried to act normally, as he entered the station and headed to his desk. He popped a handful of pills and tried to busy himself on the computer, but he found it impossible to concentrate.

# SCREWED

Tony checked his watch, it was nearly 2.20 p.m. and still no sign of Internal Affairs. He managed no work at all and had done nothing but think about what the IA people may have on him. The phone on his desk buzzed, when he answered, a voice he didn't recognise asked him to go to the interview suite. Tony removed his jacket from the back of the chair and proceeded to the interview suite. Standing outside interview room one were the two suits from Internal Affairs. They introduced themselves to Tony and showed their ID badges. They then led Tony into the interview room and invited him to sit.

'Do I need a solicitor?' asked Tony.

'There's no need for that at this stage; this is just an informal chat, no notes, no recordings,' suit two explained.

'Although tomorrow it could be a different story, depending on how this goes,' added suit one.

Tony nodded. What neither Tony nor the two suits knew was that Paul had quietly entered the room next to interview room one and was watching and listening to everything that was being said. Suit one spoke first.

'So, DS Price, we've been reviewing your record. Fifteen years on the force, fast track promotion, good arrest record, great conviction rate, not a black mark against your name.'

# SCREWED

'Now we'll cut all the shit and save that for the official taped version tomorrow. We know, for a fact, that you planted an extra bag of cocaine which had a fingerprint on it, in with some existing evidence.'

Tony began to speak, but suit one held up his hand and continued, 'You fucked up, Tony. When you added the bag with the prints you should have removed a clean one.'

'You'll find that in chapter one of how to be a bent copper. Chapter two covers not tampering with evidence when the CCTV is running,' added suit two with as much sarcasm as he could muster.

Tony just sat and stared at them. He knew they had him bang to rights, so why not just arrest him? Suit one then took over; they were like a double act.

'Thing is, Tony, we don't believe that you're a bent copper per se but maybe a misguided one. What we're interested in is who's been misguiding you and why.'

'You help us, we help you, and if you don't help us, you're screwed,' said suit one bluntly.

Paul didn't like what he'd just heard, he slipped out of the observation room and returned to his office. From his desk, he took out a mobile phone

# SCREWED

that held just one number. Paul hit the call button and waited.

'Yes.'

'We've got a problem and it's serious. A couple of chaps from Internal Affairs have got Tony bang to rights and are pushing him for information. Can you sort it out?'

'I've got just the thing. Leave it with me,' came the gruff reply.

'I know that's a lot to take in, Tony, so we're going to let you think about it overnight. We'll be back in the morning, and then you may just need that solicitor,' said suit one. 'In the meantime, if you feel like you need to talk, call me any time,' he continued, placing a business card on the table in the front of Tony.

'We'll see you tomorrow, DS Price,' said suit two as they both stood and left the room.

Tony didn't move; he simply sat staring into space. How had it all gone so wrong? Two weeks ago he was a happy newly-wed with a promising career, now he was an adulterer and about to lose his job if he didn't talk, or lose his wife if he did. Ruth would never forgive him either way. He patted his suit pocket desperately looking for his pills.

'Shit, shit, shit,' he said out loud.

# SCREWED

## CHAPTER FIFTY-THREE

Ruth was preparing dinner when Tony's phone pinged. She'd already answered four calls, informing the callers that Tony had left his mobile at home but was reachable at the station. She looked at the screen and saw that Tony had received a video message. She'd never known Tony to receive a video message before and, thinking that it could be important, she touched the screen to play the video. The small screen filled with three words: *Silence buys silence.*

Feeling confused, she continued to watch as her husband's naked body came into focus. Ruth watched in horror, as she witnessed her husband's antics with some unknown woman. The first thought that shot through her mind was that this must be some old video and this was some sort of sick prank. She then noticed the time and date stamp on the top of the screen; the reality struck her and tears began to run down her face. This was the man with whom she thought she would be spending the rest of her life, the man whose child she was carrying. She had trusted him implicitly. How could he? The video clip abruptly ended, and Ruth couldn't help replaying it for a second time. As she focused on the date stamp a stabbing pain shot through her stomach and she felt her legs go weak; she fell to the floor

# SCREWED

cracking her head on the marble worktop as she went down.

Tony finally eased himself from the chair, his body was so numb and he was starting to feel nauseous. He picked up the business card and stuffed it into his pocket, then remembered he had a packet of pills in his desk drawer. He rushed off in search of his nerve-calming, yellow tablets that were fast becoming his new best friend.

Tony left the station in a daze; he'd taken six tablets in an unsuccessful attempt to calm himself down. He jumped into his car, drove to a nearby corner shop and purchased a litre bottle of vodka. Tonight he planned to get well and truly wasted. Tony opened the bottle and gulped down the fiery liquid. By the time he pulled into his drive, a quarter of the bottle was gone along with the remaining six pills from the packet.

'Ruth, I'm home,' Tony slurred, as he pushed open the front door. There was no reply. He assumed she was out so went straight to the living room and slumped into one of the armchairs. At least he could get slowly wasted on his own. He took another long pull on the bottle. Tony suddenly decided he wanted a glass and ice for his vodka, so he headed to the kitchen. As he entered the kitchen, he saw Ruth in a crumpled heap on the floor. He stared down in disbelief at her unmoving body. There was a pool of blood surrounding her head where she lay on the tiled floor. Tony rushed towards her, falling to his knees and checking her pulse. She was cold to the touch. He let out a high-pitched scream and held the body of his dead wife. It was then he noticed the blood seeping through her skirt. The realisation then hit him that his baby was also dead. Tony's body was shaking uncontrollably, and he suddenly vomited. He lay down next to his wife and rested his arm across her lifeless body. He then felt something dig into his side. Instinctively, he felt to see what it was. His hand found his mobile phone. The screen was frozen with the image of him and Crystal in a pose straight out of the *Kama Sutra*. That would have been the last image Ruth saw before she died.

    He held her tightly, rocking her back and to, whispering over and over, 'I'm so sorry, Ruth. I love you.'

    Tony didn't know how long he'd been lying on the floor, but the blood was beginning to congeal and stick to his hair and skin. He pulled himself into a sitting position and reached for the vodka. Tony gulped the clear liquid until the bottle was empty. He was still clutching the phone, and as he touched the screen the clip restarted from the beginning.

# SCREWED

*Silence buys silence.*

Despite being intoxicated, Tony understood the message. Say nothing to Internal Affairs and his wife need never know. She was never meant to see the clip, he was. If only he'd come back and collected his phone, his wife and unborn child would still be alive. In a trance, Tony pulled open the door of the range cooker that Ruth had loved so much and flipped on the gas. While he waited for the room to fill with gas, he pulled out the business card that suit one had given to him. He tapped out a long message and pressed send. He then hit the ignition button on the range. Those were to be his last actions before the explosion shook the whole street.

# SCREWED

# CHAPTER FIFTY-FOUR

Johnny had decided it may be best to spend a few weeks out of the country. Paul had sounded pretty rattled about the Internal Affairs visit, so it wouldn't hurt to keep a low profile for a week or two. He knew he wouldn't be able to contact Razor as mobiles weren't permitted inside the prison, so he'd have to wait until he'd finished his shift before he could reach him. He decided it would be quicker to wait in the staff car park for Razor to come out.

Razor signed the log and made his way off the wing. Another day over and another pittance earned. How he wished he could be like Johnny and not be a wage slave. His thoughts were still on Johnny's empire; all built on criminal enterprises. Now Ish was out of the picture, his earnings had taken a significant dip. As he walked out of Doncatraz and into the car park, Razor spotted Johnny's black Range Rover with its engine running. The back window buzzed down, and Johnny beckoned Razor over. As he got close, the door opened.

'Jump in, Razor. We need a chat.'

Razor climbed in next to Johnny and pulled the door shut.

'So what can I do for you, Johnny?'

# SCREWED

Razor thought he may as well ask, as he knew Johnny well enough by now to know he wanted a favour.

'Well it's not really what you can for me, my good man, but what you can do for my mate in there.' Johnny nodded his head toward the prison. 'Speaking of which, he was very grateful for that thing you did for him, so add this to your collection.' Johnny handed him a fat envelope, which Razor put into his pocket, and waited for Johnny to continue. 'Anyway, my friend has just received the bad news that they want to send him to a cat C prison and that doesn't fit with his plans, so he wants his category changing from C to D.'

'Could a difficult one that, Johnny.'

'I know it's a big ask, but he is willing to pay accordingly.'

'How much we talking?'

'Twenty grand. You get paid as soon as he's moved.'

'I'm making no promises, Johnny, but for 20K I'll do everything possible to make it happen.'

'Good man, Razor. I'll leave it in your capable hands.'

Johnny then spoke to the driver, indicating that the meeting was over. Razor took the hint, got out of the Range Rover and made his way back to his car. He couldn't take his mind off the

## SCREWED

money, an extra twenty grand and he could buy a house within the next two years and maintain his lifestyle. The only problem now was how to convince Lucy to do this much bigger 'favour'.

Razor got home, flicked on the TV and headed off for a shower. His thoughts drifted to Lucy and how he could convince her. She wasn't exactly short of money and she wasn't the type to be easily corrupted by material things and, if he was candid, he wanted to keep all of the twenty grand for himself. While Razor was in the shower, he missed the early evening news, which led with the story of the tragic death of newly-weds, Tony and Ruth Price. A suspected faulty gas appliance had apparently caused the explosion at the couple's house, although fire service investigators were unable to confirm any details.

Razor got out of the shower in time to catch the weather forecast. He'd made up his mind to call Lucy and see if she fancied a drink. He'd got the perfect tactic to try on her. When he picked up his mobile to call Lucy, he noticed two missed calls from Deborah. He was in no rush to call her at the moment, as he needed to keep his mind focused on Lucy and earning the twenty from Johnny. Deborah would keep until the weekend when, hopefully, he'd be in a very comfortable financial position and they could really make the most it.

# SCREWED

He dialled Lucy's number; it rang and eventually went to voicemail. He left a brief message and disconnected. No sooner had he put the phone down and it rang.

'Lucy, thought you were ignoring me.'

She giggled and said, 'Why would I want to do that? I was just in the shower as it happens.'

'Off out are you?'

'No, I've got a bottle of wine in the fridge and was about to have a sad bastard meal for one. But if you aren't doing anything, how about we order a Chinky? My shout.'

'Well, as you're offering, why not. About eight OK?'

On his way to Lucy's place, Razor called by an off-licence and picked up an extra bottle of wine. He figured it may help convince her. When Lucy answered the door, Razor noticed that she was wearing make-up and a quite sexy outfit. He also thought that maybe she'd already started on the wine. She invited him in and they spoke about nothing in particular as they drank the first bottle of wine. It was getting toward nine when Razor suggested they order the food. He insisted that Lucy chose the food and he'd pay.

'About thirty minutes,' she informed him as she hung up the phone.

# SCREWED

'Lucy, I've got to confess, I've got an ulterior motive for coming here tonight.'

She joined him on the sofa, sitting extremely close.

'And what's that then, Gilly?' she said blushing, as a smile danced across her face, and she moved in to kiss him. He instantly pulled back.

'Lucy, no. Sorry, it's not that.'

Her face fell, and her eyes dropped to the floor.

'What then? Am I that unattractive?'

'No, it's not that, Luce. I've got a problem, or should I say, we've got a problem,' he said, emphasising the 'we'.

'A problem? What are you talking about, Gilly? I thought everything was sorted.'

'Well, remember the issue with Greg that got sorted out?'

'Course I do and I'm very grateful. Really I am.'

'Well the security clearance was a down payment. Now they want the balance.' Razor continued to explain that to repay the favour for dealing with Greg entirely, she was now expected to change the category of someone in Doncatraz. If it didn't happen, he could end up in serious trouble.

# SCREWED

'These people are heavy hitters, Lucy. They can get to you anywhere.'

It was true they were heavy hitters, however, Razor felt a little guilty for trying to manipulate Lucy the way he was doing.

'But it's nothing to do with you, Gilly, they helped me out. So if they've got a problem then wouldn't they come to me?'

'It's not that simple, Luce. I asked them to do the favour for you, so they'll hold me responsible if it's not repaid and remember, they also now know what Greg knows.'

Razor had only just thought about that last part and was quite pleased with himself.

'Gilly, I can't do it, it's just too risky. I'm sure they're just trying to scare you. This isn't Chicago; you don't get gangsters running around Doncaster doing bad things to prison officers.'

The doorbell chimed, and Lucy looked relieved by the interruption. As she got up to answer the door, Razor put his hand on her leg.

'Just promise me you'll think it over. I'm scared, Lucy, I really am.' He tried to sound as timid as he possibly could.

'Look, Gilly, it's not only my job, but I could get locked up for something like that. I'll think about it, but I'm making no promises.'

Razor wasn't too concerned, as he knew that he could wear Lucy down over the next few

# SCREWED

days. While Lucy was getting plates for the food, Razor sent a text to Deborah apologising for missing her calls and asking her to call or text him back when she could.

By the time they'd eaten the food, the second bottle of wine had been consumed. Lucy had also found a bottle of brandy in the kitchen cupboard, and they'd proceeded to work on that. Razor was feeling quite fuzzy-headed and judging by the way Lucy was giggling, the drink had affected her too. He'd checked his phone a few times and there was no response from Deborah. Razor was beginning to get a little annoyed, as she was obviously getting him back for ignoring her earlier. He hated games.

'I don't think I should be driving tonight. I better call a taxi.'

'You can stay over if you want.' She was looking straight into his eyes as she spoke. This time it was Razor who moved in for the kiss, and she didn't resist.

Surprisingly, Razor didn't feel awkward the next morning. Deborah still hadn't texted him back.

Lucy prepared a light breakfast before Razor headed off for his last shift of the week at the prison. Lucy left her house an hour later, the

## SCREWED

joys of office hours. It didn't go unnoticed in the office that Lucy was in high spirits.

'Someone's chirpy today. Have a good night did you?' said Tom Cooper, as he dumped a thick pile of files on to her desk.

Tom was Lucy's manager; he liked to throw new staff in at the deep end and was heavy-handed with the work he issued. He wasn't very popular with many of the admin staff, but Lucy found him OK if you towed the line. She'd sussed out from day one that the odd flirty comment also went a long way with Tom.

'You'd never believe me, and it might even make you blush,' she replied with a wink.

'Maybe you should try me,' he said raising an eyebrow.

Then he was back to business.

'Categorisation files. This little lot needs transferring to the prisoners' permanent records. I know this is new to you, but I'm sure you'll get the hang of it. Give me a shout if you get stuck.' Then with a wink, he added, 'I'd always be happy to help you out.' He then turned and left her to plough through the files.

Lucy booted up her computer and opened the first file. The work was straightforward enough, just a little monotonous. It involved transferring information on handwritten forms on to the computer system so that any other prison in the country could access it. In the past, a physical file would follow a prisoner from prison to prison, but often files would go missing. The computer system made information sharing a lot easier. She worked through the first nine files then, looking at the time at the bottom of her screen, decided she had time for one more before lunch. Lucy froze when she opened the file and saw the name at the top, *Thomas Jenkins*. That was the man she'd put at the top of the list for security clearance, the very man whose category Gilly's friends wanted changing from C to D. Lucy thought back to what Gilly had said, surely he was overreacting. Then she wondered if he'd slept with her just to get her to do the 'favour' for him. He'd never bothered with her in that way before.

*Would he stoop that low?* she wondered.

Her mind skipped back to the times Gilly had turned her down in the past. The only difference this time was that he wanted a favour. She concluded that he had used her and her mood dipped dramatically. She sat staring at the file, her mind in turmoil. She didn't know what to do for the best.

She was debating whether to just put the file to the bottom of the pile so she could think it over some more, when a voice behind her said, 'Everything OK, Lucy?'

# SCREWED

Tom was standing behind her, looking at the screen.

'Sorry, Tom, I was miles away. Yeah, everything's fine. I'm motoring through this lot.'

She started tapping away at the keyboard, entering the various details exactly as they were written. Then she came to the category section. All she had to do was select a single letter from a drop-down menu. She hesitated, and then thinking back to how Gilly had used her last night, decided she wouldn't do it. She picked 'C', closed the file on Thomas Jenkins and went for lunch.

# SCREWED

# CHAPTER FIFTY-FIVE

Razor was sat at the officers' desk drinking his third coffee of the day, chatting to Dave and Martin. The prisoners were locked away until teatime at half four. The wing had been surprisingly quiet since Mr 'Beef' Ridgley had been released on tag. It was incredible how one prisoner could have such an adverse impact on an entire wing of ninety-four people. The unit manager entered the wing and approached the desk.

'Afternoon, gents. I need a small favour. Any volunteers?'

'Depends on what it is,' ventured Dave.

'1B needs some cover in the morning until about one.'

'I'd love to, but I'm fishing in the morning,' shot back Dave.

Martian came up with some excuse about his mother-in-law.

Razor debated with himself for a few moments, he certainly didn't need the money, but maybe it would earn him a few brownie points with management, so he said, 'I can manage a few hours in the morning. I've not got a lot planned for tomorrow.'

'Cheers, Gilly. I owe you one.' The unit manager left as quickly as he'd arrived.

# SCREWED

Next morning, Razor walked on to 1B just before the morning unlock. He assisted one of the other officers in opening all the cells and supervising the prisoners as they had breakfast. By nine thirty breakfast was over, and all of the prisoners were locked back behind their doors.

A couple of hours with the newspaper, then he'd be on his way home without seeing any more prisoners today. Razor's radio buzzed, disturbing him from an article on drugs in prisons. An officer on the induction wing had a prisoner that needed transferring to wing 1B. He wanted to know if Razor would nip down and escort the prisoner. Razor entered the induction wing, glad of the opportunity of a walk around the prison for half an hour.

'You got one for 1B,' he said, as he approached the wing desk.

'Yeah, Robson. He's in 106. Help yourself,' replied the officer, barely glancing up from his newspaper.

Razor walked over to cell 106 and unlocked the door.

'Come on, Robson...' he stopped mid sentence. Ishmael was stood in the doorway, his eyes blazing with hatred.

'You fucking, grassing bastard,' he snarled, grabbing a ballpoint pen from the desk behind him. With all the strength he could muster, Ishmael plunged the pen into Razor's neck. By the time the other officer had run over to the cell, the pen had punctured Razor's neck three more times. The officer hit the respond button on his radio that sent out an alarm call that would summon backup. He then flung himself at Ishmael, bringing him crashing to the floor. Razor lay in a heap, blooding pooling around his body.

News of the stabbing spread around the prison like wildfire. Lucy was sat at her desk, wading through the categorisation files, when Tom Cooper broke the news of the stabbing to the office. He informed them that Prison Officer Gillmore had been stabbed by a prisoner on the induction wing and was currently in the intensive care unit at Doncaster Infirmary. His condition was critical. Lucy's eyes filled with tears and Razor's words came flooding back to her.

'These are heavy hitters... They can get to you anywhere.'

Was it her fault for not changing the category, or was it just coincidence? Maybe this was a warning. But then how would they find out so quickly that she hadn't changed the category? Maybe there were others involved who she didn't know about. Her mind was in turmoil. She decided she couldn't risk it, if these people could get to

# SCREWED

Gilly then they could also get to her. Lucy made a few clicks on her mouse and found the file that she was looking for. Jenkins, Thomas. She selected amend and changed his categorisation from C to D, she then saved the changes and exited the file. Simple as that, maybe if she'd just done it yesterday Gilly would be OK. The tears started to flow, and she felt a hand on her shoulder.

'I understand if you want to call it a day and shoot off home.'

'Thanks, Tom. I will.'

# SCREWED

# EPILOGUE

The two suits from Internal Affairs entered Doncaster police headquarters and took the lift straight to the fourth floor. They stormed past the chief superintendant's secretary and into his office, where they found Paul polishing the buttons on his dress uniform, in preparation for the funeral of DS Tony Price.

'What do you think you're doing barging in here like this?' demanded Paul.

'Chief Superintendant Paul Johnson, you're under arrest on suspicion of corruption,' said suit one, before reading a speechless Paul his rights. Paul was then led from the police station and into a waiting, unmarked police car.

Lucy sat teary-eyed on the hard, plastic hospital chair. She held Razor's hand feeling numb and becoming hypnotised by the steady beeping sound coming from the heart monitor. The doctors had said that there had been no change in his condition since he was rushed in three days ago. He'd lost so much blood he'd needed three transfusions. Since the stabbing, a single hour hadn't passed without Lucy feeling that she played a big part in what had happened. Added to this was a constant feeling of trepidation about the up-and-coming investigation and what it may uncover.

Lucy jumped as the curtain that surrounded Razor's bed was pulled to one side. She looked up to see a tall, black lad in his late teens starring at Gilly. He wore thick glasses and she couldn't help noticing the braces on his teeth.

'Sorry miss. Wrong room,' he said in a polite, educated tone, before giving Razor one last glance, then turning and walking away.

Thomas Jenkins lay on the top bunk in cell 206. He was watching something mind-numbing on the TV when he heard the familiar sound of the screw's key in the lock of his cell door. As afternoon unlock wasn't due for another three hours, it must mean that the screw wanted to speak to him. He sat up and looked expectantly at the screw stood in the doorway.

'Get your shit together, Jenkins. You're off to cat D.'

Ishmael Robson was escorted, in handcuffs, into courtroom number two at Doncaster Magistrates' Court. After the usual preliminaries, the prosecution barrister stood and addressed the court.

'If it would please the court, the Crown seeks an adjournment of twenty days in order to ascertain whether the charge of attempted murder should be amended to premeditated murder.'

The judge peered at Ishmael over his half-moon glasses before replying.

'The court will be adjourned for twenty-eight days pending an update on the condition of Prison Officer Gillmore. The defendant will remain in custody. Take him down.'

The judge banged his gavel before retreating to his chambers. Ishmael Robson was roughly returned to the holding cells below the courthouse to await his return to Doncatraz.

Veronica's Strip in Tenerife was about half a mile long and packed with bars, clubs and takeaways. Due to the all-year round climate, it was also filled with tourists 365 days of the year. The estate agent fumbled with the keys, then unlocked the door to the only vacant unit on the Strip. He stepped aside to let his two clients enter. The agent felt slightly intimidated by the mere size and persona of the man who accompanied the striking blond. He wasn't convinced that this man, in his Union Jack shorts and tacky gold, was a serious client and was sure that was why his boss had given him the job of showing the unit. He felt as though his boss didn't really like him and only gave him the shit jobs. During his short time at the estate agents he was yet to earn any commission.

'What do you think, Debs? Time we took Perfect Tens international?'

'It's perfect, Johnny.'

Johnny turned to the agent and held out a meaty hand.

'We'll take it,' he grinned, his teeth glinting in the afternoon sun.

Coming soon

# Vodka And Tonic

www.facebook.com/leekautor

www.twitter.com/leekauthor